Professional organizer Maggie McDonald manages to balance a fastidious career with friends, family, and a spunky Golden Retriever. But add a fiery murder mystery to the mix, and Maggie wonders if she's finally found a mess even she can't tidy up . . .

With a devastating wildfire spreading to Silicon Valley, Maggie preps her family for a rapid evacuation. The heat rises when firefighters discover the body of her best friend Tess Olmos's athletic husband—whose untimely death was anything but accidental. And as Tess agonizes over the whereabouts of her spouse's drop-dead gorgeous running mate, she becomes the prime suspect in what's shaping up to become a double murder case. Determined to set the record straight, Maggie sorts through clues in an investigation more dangerous than the flames approaching her home. But when her own loved ones are threatened, can she catch the meticulous killer before everything falls apart?

Visit us at www.kensingtonbooks.com

Books by Mary Feliz

The Maggie McDonald Mystery Series
Address to Die For
Scheduled to Death
Dead Storage
Disorderly Conduct

Published by Kensington Publishing Corporation

DISORDERLY CONDUCT

A Maggie McDonald Mystery

Mary Feliz

LYRICAL PRESS
Kensington Publishing Corp.
www.kensingtonbooks.com

First Electronic Edition: July 2018
eISBN-13: 978-1-5161-0526-7
eISBN-10: 1-5161-0526-5

First Print Edition: July 2018
ISBN-13: 978-1-5161-0529-8
ISBN-10: 1-5161-0529-X

Printed in the United States of America

For the hardworking members of California Fish and Wildlife, who protect our natural resources with their hearts, souls, and lives. May we one day compensate you and outfit you in accordance with the work we ask of you.

Acknowledgments

Thanks, as always, to my editors, Martin Biro and Rebecca Cremonese. And to everyone at Kensington and Lyrical, including those I've not yet met, who have worked to put Maggie's stories into the hands of readers. And to everyone in Sisters in Crime, a fantastic organization of women and men who get it. And to my husband, George, who, among all the many other wonders he brings to my life, holds everything together while I spend time with my imaginary friends in Orchard View.

Chapter 1

A crisis is a terrible time to develop an emergency plan. Be prepared.

From the Notebook of Maggie McDonald
Simplicity Itself Organizing Services

Sunday, August 6, 8:00 a.m.

I told the kids it was a drill. I told myself it was a drill. But I wasn't fooling anyone, especially not the cats.

Late summer in California is fire season, and the potential consequences had never been more apparent, nor closer to home. Air gray and thick with smoke and unburned particulates was so dry it hurt to breathe. My compulsive refreshing of the Cal Fire website throughout the night revealed that the cause was an illegal campfire abandoned on the coastal side of the Santa Cruz Mountains. Thirty-six hours later, it now encompassed miles of state- and county-owned hiking areas and threatened to jump the ridge and barrel down on the South Bay, Orchard View, and our family home.

This morning, a dry wind originating in the Central Valley had driven the firestorm back across land it had already transformed to charred desert. Firefighters hoped it would burn itself out due to lack of fuel, but I knew anything could happen at any time, and I needed my family to be ready.

Like everyone else in flammable California, we work year-round to keep vegetation from growing too close to our house. Wide stone and concrete verandas surround our hundred-year-old Craftsman house on three sides, while our paved driveway and parking area protect the east-facing walls. A plowed firebreak separates our barn and field from the summer-dry creek that borders our land.

"Do you want these in the car, Mom?" Brian, now thirteen, would one day tower over me. For now, I pretended that perfecting my posture and straightening my spine would maximize my five-foot six-inches and preserve my position as the taller one. Brian held an empty cat carrier in each hand.

"Leave them here in the kitchen for now. Leave the crate doors open."

"David," I called to my fifteen-year-old, who was now unquestionably the tallest in the family. To the chagrin of my husband, Max, David had recently gained the few inches he required to realize that Max's luxuriant walnut-colored curls were thinning. "Make sure to leave room on the back seat for the animals and two passengers."

"Two?" David entered the kitchen from the top of the basement stairs.

"Ideally, we'll take both cars. But I want to be prepared for anything." I tilted my head toward the view outside the kitchen windows. A plume of smoke filled the sky on the far side of the ridge to the west. "If that blaze shifts direction and marches this way, we'll need to clear out fast, no matter what. If one of the cars breaks down, I want us all to be able to jump into the other one."

"We could strap Brian to the roof." David's eyes twinkled as he nudged his younger brother.

I rolled my eyes, but a smile escaped when I saw that both of my thrill-seeking boys were intrigued by the idea. I turned my attention back to packing up snacks, water, and our perishable food. Our initial plan, should we be forced to evacuate, was to camp out in the living room of my dearest friend, Tess Olmos, whose son, Teddy, was fourteen and a buddy of both Brian and David.

Tess's house was a great Plan A, but I'm a belt-and-suspenders kind of gal and I needed a backup strategy. We packed as though we might resort to Plan B and end up in a shelter for a day or two. As a professional organizer, it's part of my job to help people anticipate emergencies. It's my superpower and my business. I sighed and pushed my wavy light-brown hair back from my forehead. Using my skills to streamline the lives of friends and strangers was a snap compared to getting my own family in line.

I heard a scuffle on the kitchen tiles, looked up, and burst out laughing. All three of our animals, Belle, our boisterous golden retriever, and Holmes and Watson, our marmalade-colored cats, assisted Max as he loaded their food, travel dishes, water, and kitty litter into a plastic bin. Watson's head was buried in a bag of cat kibble, while Belle nudged Max's arm with her snout. She knocked Max's steady hands out of alignment as he poured dog chow from a ten-pound bag into a one-gallon screw-top container. Dried nuggets skittered across the floor. Belle scrambled to help by gobbling up each morsel as quickly as possible. Holmes, Watson's more reserved brother, batted at a tidbit that had bounced to a stop at his feet.

"When you're done with that, hon, can you help the boys gather up the electronics? It's too soon to put them in the cars, but I'd like them all down here charging up and ready to go."

"Yes, ma'am," Max said, saluting without looking up from his task.

"Too many orders? Too bossy?" Under stress, I tended to bark out instructions without thinking about how they might be received by the folks around me—even the people I loved the most.

My phone rang, saving Max from responding. I pulled it from my pocket and glanced at the screen as I answered. "Hey, Tess," I said. "We're nearly there. Did Patrick show up?"

The day before, Tess had told me that Patrick hadn't responded to her phone calls. She'd wanted to let him know we might be camping out at their house for a few days to get out of the path of the potential firestorm. She'd speculated that he'd gone on an extended run or become caught up in a project at work. A devoted engineer, he often vanished into the thicket of a thorny technical problem and lost track of time, especially on weekends. But Patrick had been out of touch longer than usual, and I knew Tess was worried.

"That's just it." Tess's voice caught, and I could hear her take a deep breath.

"What's wrong? What's happened? Do you want us to make alternative plans? If it's not convenient—"

"No. No. No. It's not that. It's..."

"It's what? You're scaring me. Spill."

"It's Patrick. The police think they've found him."

"The police?" The words I was using and the strained tone of my voice must have worried Max. He looked up and furrowed his brow.

"Does she need help?" he asked. "Take off if you need to. The boys and I can finish up and meet you in half an hour."

I flapped my hand at Max, urging him to stop talking so I could hear Tess, who was, uncharacteristically, having trouble completing a sentence. She sighed.

"Oh, Maggie. The sheriff's office just called. Around dawn this morning, they found a man up off the old Pacific Gas and Electric maintenance road. It looks like he fell. Patrick runs there all the time. They...they think it's Patrick."

"Is he hurt? Where is he now? Do you need a ride to the hospital? Is he conscious? Why don't they just ask him who he is?"

"He's dead." Tess's voice broke with a sob. "I mean, the guy they found is dead. It's not Patrick, but they think it's him."

I couldn't think of a thing to say, and Tess didn't give me time.

"Can you get down here, Maggie? Can Max and the boys stay with Teddy? They want me to identify the body, and..." Tess coughed and soldiered on. "I mean, they want me to confirm that it's not my Patrick so they can figure out who he really is, poor guy." Tess struggled to get her voice, tears, and breathing under control. In her grief, she sounded as if she'd just finished a marathon. Breathless and exhausted.

"Of course. Whatever you need. We'll be right—"

Tess didn't let me finish. "I don't think I can drive safely, Maggie. It's in Santa Clara. The medical examiner's office." She sniffed. "This is so stupid. I keep bursting into tears. But it's ridiculous. Of course it's not Patrick. He's at work. Only he's not answering his phone. The battery is dead, I'm sure. You know how he is."

I did know Patrick. Keeping his phone charged wasn't high on his priority list. But my skin rippled with goose bumps and I shivered. Whatever we discovered at the medical examiner's office, I suspected the lives of Tess and her son, Teddy, would never be the same again.

Chapter 2

Emergency plans should include provisions for your pets and for anyone in the family such as infants, small children, the elderly or those with special needs who might need extra help or individualized supplies.

From the Notebook of Maggie McDonald
Simplicity Itself Organizing Services

Sunday, August 6, Morning

I'd driven as quickly as I could to Tess's house, a typical Northern California ranch-style tract home built in the early 1960s, down the street from the local middle school. I parked in the driveway and took a moment to collect myself. I'd dashed out of the house so fast that I hadn't taken the time to consider my outfit. Were the jeans, T-shirt, and clog sneakers I'd thrown on at dawn appropriate for meeting with a county official? Looking in the rearview mirror, I finger-combed my hair and plucked a cobweb from my shoulder. It would have to do.

I walked through the side gate and into the backyard, where a well-appointed covered deck served as an outdoor entertainment area in all but the worst winter storms. Tess's kitchen door was always open to friends of the Olmos family. I opened the door without knocking, entered the kitchen, and smiled at Teddy, who sat cross-legged on the checkerboard-patterned tile floor, hugging Mozart, a German shepherd with a perpetually puzzled expression.

Mozart looked up and wagged his tail, but stuck close to Teddy. I wasn't sure what to say to a fourteen-year-old who was waiting to learn if his father had perished. I didn't know what Tess had already told him.

"Hey, Teddy," I said.

Tess, with high heels clicking, burst into the room, saving me from finding words appropriate to the situation.

"Is this stupid? This is stupid. No one gets dressed up to visit the medical examiner." She tugged on her black suit jacket and straightened her already perfectly aligned skirt. I had a hunch she'd chosen her outfit to boost her confidence. Her fashion sense had two modes. At home, she was schlumpy Tess in sweats and Uggs. At work, in the rocket-fast, megabucks world of Silicon Valley real estate, she was a fashionista in designer shoes and suits, with her velvet-black hair confined in a neatly pinned French twist.

In her kick-back clothing, Tess was my best pal. Dressed up, she was scary, and I referred to her not-so-secretly as "the dominatrix." The Tess who stood before me now was terrified and had donned the suit as armor to help her face today's horrifying news. I pulled her into a reassuring hug. Whether the gesture was for her comfort or my own, I wasn't certain.

"Don't you dare say anything nice," Tess said. She returned my embrace, then gently pushed me away. "If you do, I'll fall apart."

Teddy cleared his throat and spoke in a voice an octave lower than his normal boyish alto. "I want to go with you." I turned from Tess to Teddy. Teddy still had his arm wrapped around Mozart, who nudged the chin of his boy with his snout. The young teen's eyes filled with tears. I couldn't say whether his wish to accompany Tess was that of a nearly grown man desperate to protect a loved one, or that of a young boy looking for comfort from his mother. I suspected Teddy wasn't sure either.

Tess shook her head, took a deep breath, and knelt by Teddy's side. Instead of the hug I'd expected, she leaned into him, mirroring the posture of the German shepherd on her son's right. It was a portrait of love, made irresistible by the befuddled look on Mozart's face created by the combination of his tilted head and one-up, one-down ears. Nobody spoke. At least not in words.

I heard car doors slamming in front of the house, and assumed that my chaos-inducing family was about to dramatically alter the atmosphere in the Olmos kitchen.

"Teddy—" I began, but stopped as soon as I realized Tess was speaking softly to her son while patting his arm.

"It would be a waste of time," she told him. "You know it's not Dad. He wouldn't have been running up there in the smoke. Not with the fire approaching. Not on the ridge. There were actual flames up there late last night. He's smarter than that. Much smarter." Mother and son looked into each other's eyes, with a big, unspoken "*but what if...*" suspended between them. I interrupted. "Teddy," I began. "Your mom is right. You need to stay here to answer the phone in case your dad calls. Or so you can text your mom to let her know if he turns up here."

What sounded like an entire cleat-shod football team of young men clomped across the redwood deck. It was Brian and David, along with Max and Paolo, a friend of the family and the youngest officer in the Orchard View Police Department.

Brian and David burst through the door as usual, but then stopped quickly and took a step back. Both boys glanced from Teddy to their dad, as if terrified that losing a father was contagious. Max, thankfully, seemed sensitive to all the emotions in the room. He patted each of his boys on the back, then rubbed his hands together, stepped forward, and tossed his keys to Teddy. With an athlete's instincts, Teddy deftly palmed the keys.

"We need your help to unload the car, Teddy," Max said. "Up and at 'em. You wouldn't believe what's packed in there. I've been tasked with taking you all to In-N-Out for lunch. Unless we start shifting the boxes, I'll have no room for an extra passenger."

"Or unless we put Brian on the roof," David added.

Teddy grinned, looking reassured by Max's action-filled agenda. He dangled the keys at the other two boys and said, "Where should we go? Is there a concert at Shoreline?" His teasing words clashed with the heavy dose of anguish in his voice, but my boys played along.

"If we're stealing a car, we're heading to the Boardwalk in Santa Cruz," David said. "Roller coaster here we come."

But Brian was impatient. "Hurry up," he called over his shoulder as he headed out to the deck. "Where do you want the cats? Holmes and Watson will be super ticked off after the car ride. We got to get 'em out of there first."

The rest of the conversation trailed off as the boys moved toward the cars.

Max gave Tess a quick hug, and Paolo held up his keys. "Stephen and Jason will stop by later, but they asked me to drive you to Santa Clara, using full lights and siren if needed. They're thinking that with a police officer in tow, you'll cut through any bureaucratic red tape as quickly as possible. We'll go in, get it done, and get out in a flash. Let's go."

Paolo turned, looking over his shoulder as if he expected us to troop behind him as ordered. His demeanor seemed rushed, impersonal, and not at all like Paolo. But then I realized…He was doing it on purpose—helping

Tess by keeping her moving and preventing her from thinking too much. He'd apparently been thoroughly briefed by Jason Mueller, the current chief of the Orchard View Police Department and Paolo's first partner on the force. A marine veteran with years of law enforcement under his duty belt, Jason knew how to care for the worried and bereaved. Stephen, Jason's husband, had been injured in Afghanistan and now worked with human and canine survivors of America's wars at the Veteran's Administration in Palo Alto.

But Tess looked hesitant to leave her home, where undoubtedly she still felt confident Patrick might walk through the door, apologizing for worrying everyone.

"Come on, Tess." I held her arm and pulled gently. "There won't be room for us in here in a moment anyway. Stephen and Jason will bring Munchkin. With Mozart and Belle here, it'll be like doggy day care. If we get a move on, we'll beat the Sunday traffic as beachgoers get ready for work tomorrow."

Max followed us, blocking Tess from any means of retreat. "We've got our plan. First the car. Then a run for the dogs. And the boys. Then food. I'll keep 'em moving 'til they drop. Your Teddy is in good hands."

Tess lifted her chin without responding, squared her shoulders, and stepped toward the door. I guessed it was the hardest move she'd ever had to make. I stayed glued to her side as we walked to the car.

Chapter 3

Become familiar with the emergencies most likely to threaten your area, especially if you're new to the region. Annually, prior to the danger season, refresh your plans and your emergency supplies.

From the Notebook of Maggie McDonald
Simplicity Itself Organizing Services

Sunday, August 6, Morning

Our journey south on Interstate 280 to the Santa Clara County medical examiner/coroner's office went smoothly. In my efforts to focus on anything other than the matter at hand, I noted the windborne scent of burning vegetation and blinked my stinging eyes. Looking out the car's rear window, I could still see billows of carbon-colored smoke, but I spotted no flames rising from beyond the ridge. I tore my gaze from the scene, forcing myself to concentrate on Tess. I could help her, but the fire was beyond my control.

Tess sat in the front seat of Paolo's Subaru with her hands clenching and unclenching on her thighs. I suspected she'd be bruised tomorrow, with no idea how those bruises had formed.

No one spoke. I groped for conversation topics to distract Tess from her dreadful task. I'd shoved aside piles of athletic equipment to make a spot for myself in the back seat directly behind Paolo: Swim fins and a snorkel, bike helmet and cleats, a basketball, baseball glove, and catcher's mitt were among the items I could identify, but there were many I could not. Though I'd known Paolo now for more than a year, I was still amused and delighted by the ever-changing array of athletic gear that graced the racks atop his car: bicycle, skis, snowboard, kayak, sailboard, and once, a stainless-steel beer-brewing vat that reflected the sun so sharply I'd had to look away.

I had just opened my mouth to ask about what looked like a neon-colored bulletproof vest stuffed under the driver's seat when Paolo took Tess's hand and squeezed it before restoring his two-handed grip on the steering wheel. "I want to tell you what you can expect from the medical examiner."

Tess shifted toward the passenger door, leaning away from Paolo. "I'll be fine. I'm not worried. I got this. It's not Patrick."

Paolo squinted and frowned. Glancing at me in the rearview mirror, he straightened his shoulders and plowed on. I was sure he'd received training and instructions on what to say to grieving families. Paolo had joined the force hoping to use his computer expertise on forensic investigations that involved little contact with the public. But in Orchard View, the police department was small. Specialties were few. Officers and detectives wore many hats.

"Bear with me, Tess," he told her softly, leaning into the sweeping curve that took traffic from Interstate 280 to northbound Highway 17, an old county road that traversed San Jose. "Most people are comforted knowing that it won't be like TV crime shows. We won't take you into the morgue. You'll be in a small conference room. A medical examiner will come out to you with a photograph. It will be a head shot. You'll see blue medical drapes surrounding the head. There's no rush. You can take as long as you want with every stage of the process—"

"Process? What process? Don't they just pull some stranger out of a freezer drawer, I look, and then tell them it's not him?" Tess's voice quavered, as if she was having trouble maintaining her belief that the man in the morgue was no one she knew. She hadn't absorbed a word of Paolo's description of the photo-identification process.

"To preserve evidence, we no longer ask families to come into the"— Paolo swallowed hard and appeared to be searching for an appropriate word—"doctor's work area. Identification happens with a Polaroid photograph, or more likely these days, a digital image on a tablet." He glanced at Tess to see if she was processing his explanation. She nodded, which he apparently took as a signal to continue. "But if you find it takes a while to gain the courage to look at the photo, that's fine. If you have questions, it's reasonable to ask. No one will rush you. You'll have all the privacy you want. Maggie and I can be with you the whole time. If you want to see a grief counselor or a chaplain—"

"That won't be necessary," Tess snapped. Her response surprised me, because she was typically so kind to Paolo.

I interrupted the conversation to give Tess a chance to collect herself. "Is that normal?" I asked Paolo. "Identifying a body from a photograph? On TV—"

"It's routine," Paolo said. "Most of the time, we don't even need the photo identification. We know who the deceased is because they carried identification or because loved ones, neighbors, or coworkers are already on scene."

"But if Tess can't be certain from the photo?" I asked.

"I'm sure that won't be a problem," Paolo said firmly, cutting off any further speculation I'd been tempted to indulge in. He pulled his Subaru into a parking space directly across from the entrance to what resembled a suburban office building. It was stucco with clean modern lines and lots of glass. Outside, a pocket-sized flower bed defied the hot, dry summer weather. Inside was a small lobby with tasteful artwork and fresh flowers. Two separate clusters of chairs were backed by a counter concealing a receptionist who stepped out to greet us as we entered.

"Officer Bianchi," she said, shaking his hand. "I'm Claire. Thanks for coming. How was the drive?" She turned to me and to Tess, awaiting introductions, but adapted quickly when Tess stepped back.

"I'll take you right in. Dr. Linda Mindar will join you in a moment."

Claire led us to a conference room and invited us to make ourselves comfortable on a sofa and chairs. French doors opened onto a small patio with a garden, bench, and trickling waterfall. Soft new age music played as if we were awaiting spa treatments. I shuddered at my incongruous comparison. While I was sure the environment was meant to be soothing, it heightened my discomfort. I tamped down my urge to run and sat on the sofa close to Tess, taking her hand. She shook off my attempt at providing comfort and I let her. Whatever she needed.

Dr. Mindar joined us and introduced herself. After glancing at me and Paolo, the medical examiner turned her attention to Tess. She pulled up a utilitarian straight chair, sat, and then scooted it forward so her knees were close to touching Tess's. As if she were giving Tess time to digest everything that was happening, she took a few seconds to fuss over the tablet, folders, and clipboard on her lap. Leaning forward, she spoke softly, but clearly and slowly, giving us all time to absorb words no one wanted to hear.

"First, I'll go over a few procedures and let you know what to expect. I have some information you can take with you. I'll give that to your friend here when we're finished. If you have any questions, now, next week, or next year, I'm happy to answer them. All my contact information is in the folder.

"I'm going to show you a photograph on my tablet. I'll ask if you recognize the person. The image shows a man in his mid-40s. He has thick, dark wavy hair and tanned skin. On the left side of his face, immediately above his jawline, there is a half-inch scar that appears to be decades old."

Tess's hands covered her ears. Her brow furrowed, and she shook her head slowly. I vaguely remembered an old story Max and Patrick told about Max chasing his friend straight into a shrub during a cutthroat game of tag in grade school. When Patrick emerged from the bush covered in blood, Max had been sure he'd killed his buddy and had run screaming from the scene. Patrick limped home alone and left bloody footprints between the back door and the bathroom that had terrified his mother. The incident had left a scar on the left side of Patrick's face. Max urged him to cover it up by growing a beard. Patrick said he never would.

Dr. Mindar continued, tugging me from the memory of friends telling ancient stories from their childhood. I licked my dry lips and smoothed wrinkles from my T-shirt, hoping that one move or the other would settle the storm in my stomach. And then I turned to Tess's ghostly face and hard jaw. If I was suffering, what on earth could Tess be going through? I grabbed her hand for my own comfort.

"We've completed our examination and will be able to release your husband to a mortuary shortly. I have some papers—"

"It's not Patrick. Not my husband."

"Of course. I'm sorry." Dr. Mindar tapped the back of the tablet. "Our investigation suggests this man did not suffer. While portions of his body are badly burned, all of the fire damage happened postmortem. After his death."

"What happened?" I asked, forgetting that I'd told myself to keep silent and let the doctor and Tess control the information flow. "When did he die? When was he found?"

"We're still working on our report for the police, but my own observations are that he had a skull fracture. He may have fallen—"

Tess interrupted. "Then it's definitely not Patrick. He was a mountain goat. Never faltered. Never stumbled."

Dr. Mindar turned to Paolo, lifting her chin and her eyebrows. "That's important for the police to know. Thank you."

She turned back to Tess. "Are you ready?"

Tess pulled her hand from mine, inching it toward Dr. Mindar's lap, which held the tablet.

The doctor held it out with the screen facedown. "When it's time, you can turn it over. When you don't want to look anymore, flip the tablet over again. The screen is locked."

Tess opened her hands to take the tablet. I noted that it was protected by a thick rubber protective case, and I wondered how many times a family member had dropped it in their first moments of shock and despair.

We all held our breath as Tess took the device firmly in both hands, bit her lip, and turned it over. She stared at the screen and let out a soft moan.

"Oh, Patrick," she said, touching the screen with an index finger as her shoulders curled forward and her head drooped, her long hair concealing her anguished face.

"Is this your husband?" Dr. Mindar asked. "Patrick Teodoro Olmos?" Tess stared at the photo without speaking. She nodded, gripped her upper arms, and rocked gently. Then she flipped the tablet and let it rest in her lap facedown.

Dr. Mindar turned to Paolo, and he said quietly, "Yes." I guessed his role was to witness Tess's identification.

Dr. Mindar handed a folder to me. "If any of you have questions..."

I shook my head. "Not right now."

"I understand that Mr. and Mrs. Olmos have a son," the doctor said.

I put my arm around Tess, and she crumpled into me, her palm flat on the tablet.

"Yes. Teddy. He's fourteen. He wanted to come." I answered the question for Tess, who seemed temporarily incapable of speech.

"It may be important to him to see his dad. To verify what's happened. Everyone is different. You might want to discuss that with his doctor or one of the other resources..."

"Would that happen here?"

"At the mortuary. As soon as we know which one you'd like to use. There are several in Orchard View. They're all good."

"Can that wait until tomorrow? And these papers?" I tilted my head toward the folder Dr. Mindar still held on her lap.

Tess sat up straighter, gently shaking off my comfort. "Silverstone's," she said. "My family has always used Silverstone's. For my grandparents." She looked fragile, as if a puff of wind could blow her over, or a soft touch might shatter her.

Dr. Mindar made a note on a yellow pad. "Everything official can wait, and the papers can be faxed, mailed, or given to the police." She pushed back her chair, making sure she no longer blocked Tess's path to an escape.

"I'll handle that," Paolo said, standing and offering the doctor his business card.

Tess raised her head, brushed her hair from her face, and stood, slowly, with her hand locked on my shoulder. She returned the tablet to Dr. Mindar, glancing at her, then looking away. "Thank you, Doctor. Linda. Thank you for your compassion. I need to get home to my son."

Tess walked to the door, fumbled to open it, and strode into the hall without looking back. Paolo and I scurried to follow. As soon as we were outside the building, Paolo clicked his key fob, unlocking the Subaru just in time for Tess to fling open the car door, collapse into the front seat, and curl herself into a ball without making a sound. I fastened her seat belt around her as best I could. On the way home, Paolo took five minutes to fill us in on everything else that various law enforcement operations had learned about what might have happened to Patrick, starting with the fact that a county parks ranger had found him around dawn on Sunday morning, though he'd died earlier. The details were sketchy. For the remainder of the forty-five-minute drive, I considered how I could help Tess and Teddy, how the reality of facing Patrick's death would impact my children, and whether our house would escape the fire's relentless hunger for more fuel.

Chapter 4

Crisis planning for pets is easy to do ahead of time, because their food is often nonperishable. You'll need food, water, and any medications. Bring necessary leashes, crates, and comfort toys. Include documentation such as registration, vaccinations, and a photograph of you and your pet together in case you become separated. If your pet is microchipped, verify that your emergency contact information is up-to-date. If you have "Pets Inside" stickers on your doors or windows, remove them when you evacuate with your animals.

From the Notebook of Maggie McDonald
Simplicity Itself Organizing Services

Sunday, August 6, Afternoon

Though the sun wouldn't set until close to eight, you wouldn't have known it from looking at the sky. Plumes of smoke had thrown a dismal pall over the neighborhood. It matched our mood.

But Tess had no time to notice atmospheric conditions. She approached her house slowly. I followed behind, as though she was performing a complicated gymnastics routine and I was in charge of her safety. I had her back, that was for sure, but I couldn't fathom the reserves of strength she'd need to march inside and tell her only child that his father was dead.

We walked through the side gate as usual, but Tess stopped before rounding the corner at the back of the house. "Would you wait here for a moment?" she asked, with her back toward me. "Give me a moment to find Teddy and take him somewhere quiet. Then you can come in and tell everyone else. You and Paolo."

"If you're sure—"

"I don't know if I'll be certain of anything ever again."

I gave Tess the moment she asked for and then walked into a kitchen that was silent save for the breathing of three large dogs, three enormous men, and two teenaged boys. I'd anticipated the cacophony and confusion inherent when such a group gets together. The near silence shocked me. They turned, pulling their attention away from the hallway that led to Teddy's bedroom, where I assumed Tess was delivering the achingly dreadful news.

Max strode forward to hug me, and we expanded our embrace immediately to include Brian and David. Their faces reflected the pain they felt for their friend, but their grief was for more than that. They'd lost the security that children feel when they believe no harm will ever befall their father. Anything that had happened to Teddy's dad could happen to theirs. Belle used her nose as a wedge to ease her way into the center of our huddle.

"He didn't suffer." I voiced the only comforting crumb of information to be found in the situation.

"What happened?"

"How did it happen?"

"What was he doing up there?"

"Why was he alone?"

"Who found him?"

"Where was he?"

Everyone fired questions so quickly that I wasn't sure who was asking what nor where I should begin. I sank into a chair at the kitchen table. Belle thrust her head into my lap under my hands, insisting that I comfort myself and her by rubbing her ears. "Can everyone take a moment to sit down?" I said.

I looked at our friends Stephen and Jason, both of whom were experienced first responders with the skills and compassion required to deliver bad news to grieving families and friends. Paolo hung back, exhausted from driving in traffic, looking after both Tess and me, and making sure all the official requirements had been observed. He wasn't a multitasker. Though he kept a cool head in the direst of circumstances, emotional situations drained him. Whether or not the late afternoon activities would have typically been wearisome for him, Paolo was spent. He leaned against the wall and closed his eyes, but experience told me he would remember every word of the conversation. "Correct me if I get any of this wrong, Paolo," I told him. He nodded once, opened his eyes, and closed them again. It was like communicating with a cat.

Stephen had turned on the teakettle and grabbed Tess's cobalt-blue mugs from a nearby cupboard. David sat on my right, but Brian moved to help Stephen.

Jason sat at the other end of the table, flanked by Stephen's mastiff, Munchkin, and Tess and Teddy's Mozart. Max sat on my left and took my hand, which was met by a heavy sigh from Belle.

"So it was Patrick?" Jason asked. "No question?"

"None."

"Who found him? When?" Stephen asked.

I parroted the information Paolo had provided during our drive from the medical examiner's office. "A man named Kon Sokolov, the night ranger in the county park. He found..." My throat tightened, and Stephen passed me a glass of water. I took a sip and continued. "The ranger found Patrick at about five this morning. Kon had been keeping an eye on the fire. After the wind shifted, he went up on the ridge trail to look for hot spots. The Cal Fire team was busy elsewhere, but I guess all rangers have some fire-control training."

Before I could elaborate, Teddy burst from the back of the house, rubbing his eyes and scowling. "It's not my dad. It can't be. He would never go running alone." He glanced at Brian and David for confirmation. They were all on the cross-country team and had been training together throughout the summer, often accompanied by Patrick.

"He's right, Mom," David said. "Patrick told us over and over not to run alone, especially in the hills, where anything could happen." He shuddered. "He had all these gross stories about rattlesnakes and mountain lions and dislocated knees and broken ankles."

"And even if it was my dad, there's no way he fell. He claimed he was half mountain goat. You guys know that. Dad was always on my case, telling me to pick up my feet and scan the trail for obstacles. He stayed focused on the path ahead. Said watching your footing was a sure way to overbalance and stumble, especially on the steep downhill parts of the trails."

Tess came into the kitchen, wiping her face with a washcloth. She'd changed from her dominatrix-tough black suit and heels into sweatpants and a faded Stanford T-shirt that I suspected had belonged to Patrick. She sat between Teddy and Jason while the dogs rearranged themselves to be closer to their people.

"Teddy's not sure that the body you identified was Patrick's," Jason said, bringing Tess up-to-date.

Tess brushed her hair back from her forehead.

"It can't be." Teddy's voice had a pleading tone.

"Aw, sweetheart..." Tess's face was etched with her own pain and her aching need to soothe her son's agony. "I agree. It can't be. It makes no sense." Her voice broke. "Your dad should be walking through that door right now saying how sorry he is to have given anyone such a terrible scare. The only good thing is that he didn't suffer."

The phrase was losing its comfort value, at least for me. Tess spoke slowly and precisely, much like someone who'd had a little too much to drink and was being careful not to slur her words.

Teddy leaned forward with his hands flat on the table. "That's another thing. I mean, I'm glad this guy, whoever he is, didn't die in agony. But what was he doing on the hillside below the path with a fire coming up the ridge? Dad would have known that was a dangerous place to be. Any idiot would have known that. If he'd gone down there deliberately, he could have climbed out, right? So, something must have happened. Has the coroner checked for other injuries or did he just look at the guy and say, 'Oh, crispy critter. Died of wildfire burns.'"

I winced at the insensitivity and harshness of Teddy's words. David and Brian appeared shocked, then seemed to be battling the kind of hysterical laughter that often emerges in the face of death. I signaled to them to head outside, where they had less chance of offending or distracting anyone while they got their emotions under control.

Tess shook her head and bit her lip. "You're right, Teddy. He did have additional injuries. A skull fracture, the medical examiner said. Consistent with a fall and a collision with a rock."

"But if he fell, *why* did he fall? Let's say this guy truly is Dad. It's not, but look at what happened. Dad must have been *attacked* to have fallen and been unable to climb back up. Someone else might have fallen and hit their head, but Dad—he always won the chicken fights in the pool because no one could knock him off balance."

I felt a palpable shift in the emotional tenor of the group. Moments ago, I'd felt pity for Teddy and his denial of his father's mortality, let alone his actual death. But the boy's arguments were convincing. I was still certain that the dead man found on the ridge was Patrick, but my vision of what could have happened up there had suddenly shifted. This was no accident. Patrick had been murdered.

Chapter 5

Satellites and early warning systems give us time to prepare for many natural disasters. Other crises, like earthquakes or terrorist attacks, might occur at any moment. Your safety may hinge on the planning you do ahead of time. For example, you may have a great emergency kit at home, but what about in your car? You'll need emergency supplies there too. Some of the most important things to include are clothing and shoes that will protect you from the weather if you need to walk an extended distance for help.

From the Notebook of Maggie McDonald
Simplicity Itself Organizing Services

Sunday, August 6, Afternoon

Teddy continued, "Did the guy have any other problems, like a busted ankle or a messed-up knee? Some reason to have fallen on his own?" Teddy pressed his case without giving anyone a chance to answer. "Have you ever known Dad not to suffer? I mean, complaining was kind of his thing. If he was hurt—really hurt—like, from something that could disable or kill him, he would have moaned so loudly we'd have heard it from here, right?"

Teddy was exaggerating, but it was possible we could have heard an injured Patrick from our house, especially last night, when we'd all been on edge, awake, and watchful, eyeing the fire's progress.

Max coughed and then laughed. "I mean no disrespect, but Teddy's right. Patrick wasn't one to underplay an injury. Remember the landscaping day?"

One by one, the rest of us smiled, then snickered, then laughed until tears rolled down our faces. As soon as one of us began to get our emotions under control, someone else would set us off again. After what seemed hours but was probably only minutes, I was able to speak. "Max is right. Patrick dropped that landscaping rock on his foot, and I'm sure it hurt, but he bellowed until every parent who was a nurse, paramedic, or physician had weighed in on the injury. He spent the rest of the day with it propped up, 'supervising,' while everyone else worked."

As memories went, it was one we'd treasure from our time with Patrick and with our children. All the parents and kids at the middle school had been asked to provide the manual labor required over two spring weekends to revamp the school's landscaping, which had come to resemble a moonscape during California's prolonged drought. Now, drought-tolerant native plants tough enough to withstand incursions from middle schoolers had created a welcoming, eco-friendly campus. Both weekends had been laughter-filled family events.

Teddy interrupted with a sound of protest, but Max forestalled his comment. "You're right, Teddy. Your dad was one of those guys who was an asset to a team. He kept us all laughing with his goofy stories, and we had a blast. Could barely move the next day, but we had a great time."

No one spoke while we all took a moment to accept that none of us would work with Patrick again. While we'd all continue to feel his absence, Tess and Teddy were bereft and on their own. Teddy might not be ready to accept it, but he would have to, soon enough. For the first time, I realized how hard it must be for a grieving spouse to summon the energy to deal with all the practical concerns surrounding a death, cope with their own pain, and pick up the pieces when their children fell apart. The last thing that Tess needed right now was to have us camped out on her floor, along with our cats and boisterous golden retriever. The Olmos cats were nowhere to be found. I suspected they were relishing the solitude of a bedroom closet and wondered whether Tess and Teddy would soon be looking for similar comforting hidey-holes.

I tried to capture Max's attention. We needed to come up with a new plan to wait out the firestorm. Surely we knew someplace else close enough to allow us quick access after the blaze burned itself out, but far enough away to be safe. We could find a hotel. One that would take Belle and the cats.

Jason's voice jolted me back to the matter at hand. "Teddy, would it help if you could see the body the ranger found?" I noted that he avoided referring to Patrick by name. "To confirm your mom's observation, or to let us know we need to look in another direction to find your dad and figure out who this guy is?"

Teddy's gaze moved from Jason to his mom, and then to the tabletop, where he pulled at a loose thread in the fringe of a woven place mat. "When you put it that way..." Teddy's voice faded, but he didn't look up. He cleared his throat and started again. "It sounds as though I don't trust my mom to identify my dad. I know there are, like, fingerprints and DNA and stuff to be sure. But pieces of this story don't add up. I mean, my dad? He was just an engineer who liked to run. He wasn't the kind of guy who gets killed and burnt up. Not even by accident."

Teddy's voice broke. He lowered his head, swallowed hard, wiped his eyes, and started over. "I guess I have to see for myself. You know?" He raised his head, confident and with a touch of bravado, as though he expected someone to argue with him. But then his expression quavered, and doubt snuck in. "I mean...he's not gross or scary, is he?"

Tess let out a short, quiet noise I couldn't characterize, probably because she, like the rest of us, couldn't believe we were sitting at her kitchen table overlooking her idyllic and serene backyard, discussing the condition of her husband's dead body. There were no words for the horror we felt.

Jason broke in before anyone else could speak. "In my experience, Teddy, a body at the morgue looks more like a wax figure or a statue than it looks like the person you knew when he or she was alive. The outward appearance is similar, but everything that once animated the statue, everything that made it the person you loved, is no longer there. But it's not scary." Jason watched Teddy closely, and he must have noted that he still appeared wary and confused. "Look, have you ever walked past a neighbor's house and been certain the family was on vacation? From the outside, the house looks the same. They've got lights and sprinklers on timers, and someone is taking care of their garbage and mail—but the life of the house is gone."

Teddy nodded.

"It's like that, I think," Jason said. "Just the shell, with no one home. It's no more the person you loved than, say, an eggshell is a chick after it hatches."

I smiled despite my grief, admiring Jason's turn of phrase, his gentle, soothing voice, and his patience with Teddy.

"I can understand that you'd want to see for yourself," Jason said.

Teddy stopped stroking Mozart and raised his head. "Do I need to set that up? Call the medical examiner or the funeral home?"

"There's no rush." Jason said. "You or your mom can set it up."

Tess's eyes widened, and her lip quivered. Jason held out his hand. "I'm familiar with the forms. Would you like me to go over them with you when you're ready?"

"Sure," Tess said, but then excused herself from the table and escaped to the back of the house.

The doorbell rang. Stephen moved the curtain over the kitchen sink and peered out. "It's Elaine," he said. "With a hot dish and cookies, it looks like. If Tess and Teddy aren't up to visitors, we should pull all the drapes on the front of the house. Or I can answer the door and tell people to come by in a few days."

The seldom-used landline attached to the kitchen wall rang loudly, followed quickly by the cell Tess had left on the table and the phone in Teddy's pocket. Word of Patrick's death, apparently, was out.

Chapter 6

Documents to pack for an emergency:
Medical records, insurance cards, prescriptions;
property deeds and insurance policies;
passport, license, birth certificates, wills, powers of attorney.
Include a written list of phone numbers you may need (even if this information is also on your phone). Consider putting copies of all documents on a thumb drive. Digital versions of these files may speed claims processing.

From the Notebook of Maggie McDonald
Simplicity Itself Organizing Services

Sunday, August 6, Early evening

Elaine Cumberfield lived a few houses down the street from Tess, directly across from the middle school. We'd met while I was investigating the murder of the former principal. As soon as I'd stopped suspecting Elaine, we'd become friends.

She came through to the kitchen carrying a plate of her locally famous gingerbread men. "I rang the bell instead of coming through the back, in case you weren't up for visitors and wanted to pretend no one was home. Am I the first caller? Let me help get things set up. It will be a madhouse before you know it. How on earth does word get out so quickly?" I peeped under the aluminum foil at the cookies. Elaine was known for creating artful cookies, sometimes meant to send a message. Today I wanted to be sure Elaine hadn't been too flippant and created images Tess and Teddy might find disrespectful.

Elaine smiled and I blushed, knowing she'd read my mind. As a retired middle school principal, she was adept at reading tiny clues to a person's innermost thoughts. A few hundred years ago, she'd have been burned as a witch. "Just your garden-variety gingerbread men today," she said. "What did you expect? Angels? Corpses with little x's for eyes? Chalk outlines of dead bodies? Give me some credit, Maggie. I wouldn't hurt Tess or Teddy for the world. How are they holding up?"

I shrugged. "I'm not sure yet how *I'm* holding up. It's early. I think they're both still in shock."

"I don't know who started this dreadful custom of intruding on a family in their grief, but Orchard View will turn out in droves. They all adore Tess—and an unsolved mystery." Elaine handed me a cloth grocery bag that was heavier than I'd anticipated. "I stopped by Safeway and picked up some decaf and juice. Can you brew the mocha java and mix up the lemonade? Make sure she's got plenty of ice."

I dropped the bag on the floor next to the fridge and helped Elaine move the table to create a buffet. She rummaged in a cabinet for a tablecloth while I marshaled the troops.

"Teddy, pull out whatever soda, beer, and bottled water you have in the kitchen or the garage." Action was supposed to be effective for dealing with grief. We'd have to see. "Do you have a tub or a cooler your mom uses for parties? David and Brian, help him get soft drinks on ice on the patio. Beer stays inside so the teens don't help themselves."

David and Brian sighed in an overly dramatic manner and rolled their eyes.

"*Other* teens," I said. "Not you or Teddy or any of your friends. Other teens. Teens I don't know and you don't know. Keeping an eye on the intoxicating beverages is the responsible thing to do. Providing underage people with alcohol is a crime. Do you want your mom to get arrested?" My kids weren't the only drama queens in the family. They rolled their eyes again and got to work. If eye rolling was an aerobic activity, no high school on the planet would need to worry about physical education credits.

I continued issuing orders. "Max and Stephen, find serving utensils and get the buffet set up. Locate whatever pitchers or thermal carafes, cups, and glasses you can find for lemonade and coffee. Pull those dining chairs into the living room. If you see anything that needs to be tidied up or thrown in the wash, do Tess a favor and take care of it without asking. She'll be overloaded with decisions for the next few days, and we don't want to add to her burden. Paolo, you're on fridge and freezer duty. See what you can consolidate or toss. Be ruthless. Clear out as much as you can. Casseroles and dinner salads will start piling up before you know it. I'll track down masking tape and a marker, so we can label any non-disposable dishes with the owners' names."

Max and Stephen stared at me like students who hadn't expected a pop quiz. I said what I thought they were thinking. "Is this kind of heavy-handed? Moving Tess's furniture and taking over her kitchen?"

"Trust your instincts," said Elaine. "I'm a widow. My husband died years ago, but I still remember the pain and the fog. I couldn't have made an extra decision to save my life. Tess probably won't notice or care what we do. And if she does, she'll be grateful. Where is she? She's become a member of the club no one wants to join—parents without partners, subgroup: young widows." Elaine sighed, and without waiting for an answer regarding Tess's whereabouts, strode confidently down the hall toward the bedrooms.

Elaine was right. I'd no sooner mixed the first batch of lemonade and poured boiling water over coffee grounds than the neighbors descended. The first few rang the doorbell, but after that they poured in, all of them bearing food. Kids gathered in the backyard. I whispered to Brian and David to call an adult if they needed any help, but I recognized most of the kids and knew they'd be supportive.

Paolo moved through the crowd with uncharacteristic ease, refilling chip bowls, making sandwiches, and distributing food to the high school students assembled around Tess's gas fire pit in the back. Max and Stephen helped too. We all kept a close eye on Tess to make sure she wasn't buttonholed by anyone with more hot air than tact. Every time I spotted Jason, he was speaking gravely into his cell phone. I hoped that after the spontaneous gathering wrapped up, he'd pass along any news he'd gleaned about the fire and Patrick's death.

The conversation swirled with rumors, mostly about the fire. I shamelessly eavesdropped as I circulated, refilling lemonade glasses, greeting people, and answering questions. "It's too soon to tell," was my go-to response and it fit nearly every query about the fate of our house, plans for a memorial service for Patrick, the cause of his death, or requests for reports on how well Tess and Teddy were coping.

I overheard pieces of conversations:

"I hear it's already sixty percent contained."

"I don't know why everyone is freaking out."

"Attention seekers, I guess. Drama queens—"

"They found multiple points of origin. Can't figure out what caused it. Might be arson."

"The wind shifted, and the fire service has abandoned the original fire line. Mandatory evacuations in the Hidden Villa area. They've relocated all the campers to some old barracks at Moffett Field—"

"Remember that time Patrick..."

Stories abounded, shared by those who'd known Patrick from his childhood in Orchard View, from those who'd worked with him, coached with him, or gone to school with him. And neighbors who'd benefited from his willingness to chip in on chores whenever anyone was laid up or busy. I hoped someone would collect the stories and write them down to save for Teddy and Tess to read later, when their wounds were not quite so fresh.

And then a sour note pierced the blanket of love that friends were knitting with their fond memories.

"I heard they were separated. Could she have killed him?"

I stopped abruptly when I overheard that last line, nearly sloshing lemonade from the pitcher I was carrying all over myself and the person who'd uttered the impossible words.

"Are you talking about Tess?" I asked Pauline Windsor, a PTA volunteer with a perfect, ultraconservative wardrobe, expensively colored and coifed hair, and an entitlement complex. I'd run afoul of her on more than one occasion and tended to grit my teeth on principle whenever I saw her. "You know better than that," I said, adopting the disappointed expression I typically saved for misbehaving children.

The woman whom Pauline had buttonholed, a short woman with fluffy white hair, pink cheeks, and a voluminous quilted purse, blushed and looked away. Muttering an apology, she disappeared into the garage.

Pauline, on the other hand, sniffed and rolled her eyes. "That's what I heard. You know they always suspect family when there's a murder. Are you denying that Tess and Patrick were separated?"

I clenched my jaw until I feared for my dental work, trying to get a lid on my anger before opening my mouth. Pauline's statement, as usual, was full of traps it would be far too easy to fall into. I was tempted to defend Tess, explaining that though she and Patrick maintained separate permanent residences, they were devoted to one another, to their marriage, and to their son. It was an unusual relationship, but it worked for them. And it was none of Pauline's or anyone else's business. I responded slowly, hoping to avoid triggering any of the scandalmonger's land mines.

"I know you like to verify information before you repeat it," I deliberately lied. "Tess would be the person to ask about her personal life with Patrick. To make sure you get the story right."

Pauline took a deep breath, crossed her arms, and opened her mouth to respond, but I cut her off. "And as far as I know, the Santa Clara County medical examiner, Dr. Linda Mindar, hasn't reported on the cause of Patrick's death or the manner of death. She hasn't yet had time to review the science or the facts. At least she hadn't when we talked to her personally a few hours ago." I glanced at my watch. "Have you heard something from her more recently?"

Pauline dodged the question. "It makes sense that the authorities are talking to Tess," she said so loudly that everyone stopped talking and turned toward us. "It's *always* the closest relative."

I was gratified by the number of people, all friends of Tess or Patrick's, who rolled their eyes or sniffed and returned to their own conversations.

Jason appeared out of nowhere and took Pauline's elbow, guiding her outside. "Is your husband here? Your daughter? I wanted to talk to you about a problem we've been seeing in your neighborhood. I need to make sure none of you are in danger."

Pauline gasped. My guess was that her thoughts had immediately and selfishly turned to her own safety, and she was calculating how to get social mileage out of the drama of being protected by the dashing new police chief.

Behind me, the murmur of voices had risen to a dull roar from the shocked silence that followed Pauline's barbed remarks. Apparently I wasn't the only resident of Orchard View who'd learned to dismiss her gossip. Tess had once told me that many of Pauline's whims were indulged by the community only because she was an avid volunteer and handled positions that were tricky to fill otherwise.

Someone tapped me on the back. I turned, and a broad-shouldered man in a wheelchair wearing a Stanford University ball cap held out his glass for a refill of lemonade. With the glass in one hand and the pitcher in the other, I used my chin to point to his cap. "You knew Patrick from his undergraduate days?"

"And grad school. Then we both took jobs at Hewlett Packard. We still work—worked together at one of the Google spin-offs. I run with—ran with Patrick's club, the Orchard View Road Runners." He snorted and shook his head. "I heard what that woman was saying. She's nuts. Tess wouldn't hurt anyone. Did you say there's a cop here? Can you point him out? There are some things that don't add up. Stuff the cops should know."

Chapter 7

If these organizing steps come naturally to you, consider reaching out to become involved in emergency preparedness programs in your neighborhood, community, school, or workplace, particularly to assist people with disabilities who may need extra help adapting in a crisis.

From the Notebook of Maggie McDonald
Simplicity Itself Organizing Services

Sunday, August 6, Evening

Intrigued by the stranger's suggestion that Patrick's death was more complicated than it appeared on the surface, I pointed him toward Stephen. Stephen wasn't an official member of the Orchard View Police Force, but he'd know how to handle the man's information while Jason was dealing with the dreadful Pauline out on the front lawn.

I quickly lost track of the man, and didn't have a chance to follow up with Stephen. At quarter to ten, as though a gong had gone off, guests started to leave one by one, and then in a flood. A few stayed behind to tidy up the kitchen, take out the garbage, and leave Tess's kitchen and backyard spotless. The dishwasher sloshed and hummed with a first load while other dishes were set, rinsed and stacked, on the counter. Bulkier items had been washed, dried, and put away.

Orchard View people aren't perfect. Some, like Pauline, I could barely stomach. But the town took care of its own. Neighbors looked after neighbors. Those connections of kindness, even between people who didn't otherwise like one another, made Patrick's death exceptionally shocking. It seemed like hours later when Max and I unfolded Tess's sofa and climbed into bed. Tess had insisted we stay, saying that it made her feel safe to have us close by.

"This whole situation is overwhelming," Tess said. "I'm preoccupied and certain I shouldn't be driving. Tomorrow morning I'll need your help with issues that haven't even occurred to me yet." She'd sighed and hugged me. "Please stay. There's that fire too. I can't let you go out there. I need to know you're safe. I can't worry about you and Teddy *and* hang on to my sanity. It's too much."

"Of course. Do you want us to sit up with you, or do you think you can get some sleep? What about Teddy?"

"All three boys are curled up on my bed watching some movie full of car chases and explosions. When it's over, I'll kick them out. Your boys can crash with Teddy if they want. Or...they may want to stick close to you two. They're looking pretty shell-shocked themselves."

In the end, all three boys decided to bunk together in Teddy's room. But it wasn't long before David and Brian dragged their sleeping bags into the living room and plopped them down on the floor near us. Belle launched herself from the sofa bed and somehow managed to land on the midsections of both boys at once. Their joint "*ooof!*" set us into gales of much-needed stress-relieving laughter. As our snorts and giggles trailed off and Max's soft snores began, I heard a shuffling sound at the end of the hallway and imagined Teddy was dragging his own blanket or sleeping bag toward his mother's bedroom. Teenaged boys are mostly grown-up, but when they're hurting, they still need their parents. And there was no question Teddy was hurting.

"Mom?" David whispered.

"Yes?" At first, I thought he was looking for reassurance that I was close by, but David's sleeping bag rustled as he sat up. I leaned over the side of the bed where I could almost make out his expression in the light cast by the streetlights through the sheer curtains. David's hair was already tousled from his brief attempt at sleep. He rubbed the back of his neck and squinted at me.

"Something happened when we were all outside. By the fire, in back."

"Okay," I said, to let him know I was still listening.

"Well, um." David cleared his throat and stared into the distance, avoiding my face. "That Mrs. Windsor. Bratty Rebecca's mom."

"Right."

"She's distributing a petition that says Rancho San Antonio, where Teddy's dad was found, isn't safe. She says his murder proves it, and it should be sold for development. She says she has hundreds of signatures already. Can she do that?"

My blood pressure must have skyrocketed. I could hear my pulse pounding. I took a beat or two to get my temper under control before answering.

"Mom?"

"Draw up a petition? Of course, she can. Close Rancho San Antonio? I doubt it. It's too busy a park. Too cherished by the entire community. Could she develop it? She's wanted to for years. Her daddy owns the biggest home-and-office-building construction company on the Peninsula. I expect it's greed that's driving her, rather than a desire for increased safety. My guess is that if she goes public with her petition, she'll be hit with an enormous backlash from all the folks who value it as a nature preserve and recreational area."

David, biting his lip, still seemed troubled, so I continued to reassure him.

"And those hundreds of signatures she mentioned...she probably doesn't have any yet. Maybe she hasn't even drawn up a petition. I've only worked with her a few times, but she's one of those people who talks a good game, but has trouble completing her vision."

David snuggled closer to my side of the bed, and I patted his back. "It will be okay, hon. I promise."

"But murder? She's saying it was murder. Who would hurt Teddy's dad?"

Unsaid, but as audible as if the words had been spoken aloud, was David's fear that anything that happened to Patrick could just as easily bring harm to Max.

"I can't think of anyone who would want to hurt him, can you?" I said softly. "He was too nice." Earlier in the day, when I'd heard the description of Patrick's injuries and Teddy's protests that his father would never have fallen, my thoughts had shifted immediately to homicide. But now, upon reflection, it seemed impossible. Patrick was beloved in all his circles of influence, including coaching, work, his athletic clubs, and around the neighborhood. If there was a contest for Least Likely to be Violently Attacked, Patrick would have won it, every time.

"But...there's something else, Mom." David scrambled out of his sleeping bag and rummaged through the pile of our belongings that oozed outward from the front wall. He came back with his laptop, stepping over Belle and Brian, who both snorted and rolled over without waking. He fired up the computer and clicked open a website. Holmes peered over David's left shoulder while tickling my son's ear with his tail. David pulled Holmes into his lap and handed me the computer. "There," he said.

I gasped. Someone, with obvious malicious intent, had created a web page that appeared disturbingly official. Titled *"On the Trail of a Murderer"* with an entry that screamed in giant font: *"It's Always the Wife."* Photos followed that must have been lifted from Internet obscurity. They showed bunny-suited CSI teams scouring wooded hillsides. Hiking-boot-clad legs were buried in leaf litter unlike anything you'd see in the Bay Area's dry oak chaparral and grassland. Unflattering and overexposed photographs of Tess, Patrick, and Teddy resembled mug shots, and were missing only the blank stares found in FBI Wanted posters.

The page was fake, but convincing. It would deliver its messages in a blink: Patrick was murdered; Tess had killed him, brutally; and she'd left his body to be consumed by fire on a burning hillside. I dropped the laptop on the bed and scooted away from it, as if that would allow me to escape its malicious message.

I took a deep breath. "Well, I can see why that would upset you, David. It bothers me. We need to let Jason and Paolo know about this right away." I searched the side table for my backpack before giving up. "Do you have your phone?"

David reached under his sleeping bag. I should have known. Both boys had long ago given up their attachment to stuffed animals, but now they slept with their electronic devices close by, ready to check their texts upon waking. We had a charging station at home on the first floor, where phones were supposed to be put to bed for the night. It was a rule most often observed in the breach, and we probably needed to revisit it before school started. But right now I was grateful David had his at hand.

Every member of our family had long ago put Jason, Stephen, and Paolo's numbers into their phones. Following our disastrous introduction to Orchard View nearly a year earlier, all three men had become as close as family. Along with Tess, they served as emergency contacts for both boys on school forms.

While we waited for the line to connect and for Jason to answer, Belle nudged my hand, offering reassurance. Watson and Holmes perched on the back of the couch, tails twitching in response to our growing tension. I reached out a hand and gripped David's.

The call went directly to voice mail, with instructions for reaching an emergency contact. I decided the problem could wait until morning, and left a message. "Jason. It's Maggie. Give me a call as soon as you're awake. David's shown me a web page you should take a look at. It's probably as illegal as it is disturbing. It's called 'On the Trail of a Murderer,' and it's ghastly." I paused, thinking there was surely more I could say to bring home the brutal and scurrilous message. I decided to let the page speak for itself. "I'll text you the link. I'm sure it's breaking all sorts of laws. I'll leave a message for Forrest Doucett too."

I ended the call and glanced at David. I hunted through the phone's contact list for Forrest Doucett's number before remembering that I held David's cell, not mine, and there was no reason for him to have the lawyer's number. David retrieved my phone from where it had fallen between the sofa and the side table and handed it to me. I unlocked the screen and dialed the number.

All of *my* electronic devices had numerous ways to reach Forrest, who'd been Max's college roommate. In addition to our long-standing relationship as close friends, in recent months, we'd consulted him as a lawyer, asking for help unsnarling several dicey situations.

Using some electronic magic, my call had been routed to Forrest's direct line. He answered in a sleepy voice.

"'Lo?"

"It's Maggie. We're in trouble."

"You personally, or a friend? Let me get a pad and pencil." Forrest seldom indulged in chitchat, particularly if there was a legal knot that needed to be untangled.

"It's Tess. And a horrid web page accusing her of murder."

"The URL? Web address?"

I gave it to him and waited while he pulled it up.

"What are you doing answering your phone at this time of night, anyway?" I asked. "I'd planned to leave a message."

"I can hang up now so you can do that, if you'd like."

"No, no. I prefer the real you."

Forrest sucked in a breath, which told me he'd reached the site. "Whoa. This is nasty. Is any of it true? Is Patrick dead?"

"I'm afraid so. But we haven't heard anything from the medical examiner about the cause or manner of death. And Tess is certainly not responsible. Even if anyone seriously suspected her, I'm sure she has an alibi. Can we get that trash taken down? Right away? The last thing Tess or Teddy needs is to see something that hateful right now. It's a personal attack, and they're really vulnerable at the moment."

David batted at my leg with his hand. He frowned and shook his head. "Teddy's already seen it. That's what I was trying to tell you."

"It seems the kids have already shared it widely," I said. "Teddy's seen it."

"Unfortunate," Forrest said with a *tsk*. "But probably unavoidable. I swear kids find this stuff as if they've got an army of bots hunting it down and they had social media feeds hard-wired into their elbows. I'll have to hire middle school students to keep up."

Max rolled over in bed, grunted, then sat bolt upright with questions etched in his sleep-wrinkled skin. "Wha—"

I shifted in bed and mouthed the words, "*Hang on*" to Max. To Forrest, I said, "Look, David knows more about this than I do. He's the one who showed it to me. I'll put him on."

David looked nervous and hesitant, but took the phone, pausing before he lifted it to his face. "What do I say?"

"Tell him what you told me. And answer his questions the best you can. You know Forrest. You can trust him."

David swallowed. "Forrest is cool," he said, mostly to himself.

He walked out into the hall while I woke up my sleeping computer to show Max the website. He grimaced as he scrolled.

"Teddy saw this? Has Tess? Seriously...this is terrible stuff. Poor kid. Can Forrest get rid of it?"

"I don't know. I've heard that Facebook is more responsive to cyberbullying these days, but that's just a rumor, nothing official. And I don't know about other platforms, or whether this site is built on one."

"But this is worse than cyberbullying, isn't it? Doesn't it count as libel or something criminal?"

"I'm not sure. That's why I called Forrest. I didn't expect him to actually answer. Does the man ever sleep?"

"He's like an air fern—or at least he was in college. A quick catnap and he's sharp for hours. He used to take twenty-four credits and have more free time than those of us who struggled with sixteen."

"I hate people like that. I mean, except for Forrest, of course."

"Why is David talking to him? Why are our teenagers handling our legal affairs?"

"David's the one who showed me the site. I figured he could tell Forrest directly how long ago he first saw it, whether it has changed, and if he knows anyone who might have created it. It has to be a kid, right? A kid who has it in for Teddy?"

Max shook his head. "I could probably figure it out, but Paolo needs to know about this."

Paolo had joined the police department almost two years earlier, hoping to specialize in cyberbullying and other offenses, particularly those in which adults victimized minors. He'd wanted to work locally, giving back to the community that had nurtured him as a kid who was outside the mainstream. In choosing Orchard View, however, he'd selected one of the few local police departments in which specialization was seldom possible. Each officer had areas of preference and expertise, but in Orchard View the law enforcement staff was so small that everyone did everything, from patrol to detective work and public relations. Still, Paolo was typically consulted whenever a suspected crime involved online privacy, bullying, software, hardware, or data storage.

David returned, holding the phone out in front of him and passing it to me. He debriefed Max while I listened to Forrest summarize the legal issues.

"Is there anything you can do?" I plugged one ear with my finger to avoid going insane from listening to two conversations at once.

"Yes and no. We can call the web host's legal team, explain the problem, and hope they'll tell us who the page owner is and take the site down. The site violates copyright laws because they don't have permission to use the likenesses of Tess, Teddy, or Patrick. Probably not for the other shots, either, because some still have the protective watermarks."

"Watermarks?"

"Stock photo companies do it to protect the copyrights of their artists. You can use images for design purposes at no charge, but to display them without a blurred logo marring the image, you need to pay the artist and the stock house. Check the onscreen picture of the crime-scene guys in bunny suits. No way they paid for that image. I doubt any of the federal agencies will pursue it, but Orchard View and Santa Clara County will be interested. Both have cyber-safety teams that protect kids online."

"Will that work?"

"Probably. As awful as it is that the web page targets Teddy, it may help us kill it. Web hosting services are responsive to shutting down sites that bully children, but the interpretation of free speech is broad online when it comes to adults. That's changing, but any shift in the law would be too slow to help your friends."

"But you've got a plan, right?" My voice caught, revealing my desperation. Max and David stopped talking and turned toward me, brows furrowed with concern. I smiled and waved my hand, trying to reassure them. Both seemed skeptical.

"We've had success with stern letters on legal letterhead," Forrest said. "I'll alert the law enforcement offices too."

"Thank you. Teddy and Tess don't need this right now. Or ever."

Forrest sighed. "Modern bullying may have moved into the cyber realm, but some things don't change. The best protection against this kind of stuff is friends. You look after Tess and Teddy, and I'll do my best to make this problem go away. Tell Teddy to let me know if any other sites crop up. If he's in charge of calling me, it may give him a greater sense of control."

"When did you become the teen whisperer?"

Forrest laughed. "And tell Tess to call me when she's ready. We can help her with all the paperwork that follows any death. It can be almost as big a nightmare as the death itself, and the pain of it drags on for ages."

I started to thank him, but the sounds coming from the phone changed enough to let me know he'd ended the call. Forrest could be abrupt, but he was one of the good guys.

Little did I know how quickly we'd be calling him for more help.

Chapter 8

Your supplies should include a gallon or more of water per person or pet per day. Remember that you'll need water for drinking, washing, and preparing any dried foods. If your stash includes canned items, don't forget a can opener.

From the Notebook of Maggie McDonald
Simplicity Itself Organizing Services

Monday, August 7, Morning

Max and I dragged ourselves to the kitchen at the first stirrings of life among our critters, hoping to get the dogs outdoors, fed, and watered before they woke the entire household. Afterward, we set out cold breakfast items and brewed what would likely be the first of many pots of strong fresh coffee.

I made a grocery list and put it on the table for others to add to, then created another to-do list outlining questions I needed to ask Tess and projects my own family needed to tackle if we were ever going to return to our own digs.

Max didn't need to read the words on the pad to know what I was doing. After nearly two decades of marriage, he knew my morning routine, every morning, involved a list of one kind or another.

"I'm taking personal days for the rest of this week," Max said, twirling the dial on Tess's kitchen radio. "I want to get up to the house today if I can. Al Johnson put a note up on Nextdoor offering his Bobcat tiller to anyone who needed it to plow firebreaks on their land."

"He has a Bobcat? What for?" Few Orchard View properties were large enough or rurally oriented enough to warrant full-time ownership of a Bobcat. Most people, I thought, rented them if and when they were needed.

"He uses it to keep the weeds down, he says, to prep the soil for his vegetable garden, and to maintain that long gravel driveway. I think he transports it up to his Tahoe property in the winter to use as a snowplow." Max's eyes twinkled. "We need one, don't ya think?"

I gave him a little shove, then handed him a fresh cup of coffee and tilted my head up for a kiss. "No, I don't think we do," I said. "We paved our driveway, remember? But thank him for loaning it to us."

Max turned to his phone, scrolling through messages on what must have been the Nextdoor website. "Al started a trend. Local organizations are offering heavy equipment services to anyone who needs them."

"Like who? I had no idea anyone had equipment like that."

"PONY baseball, the schools, the city. Apparently, those giant ride-on mowers come with other attachments that can be useful. Who knew?"

"Make your calls. Are you taking the kids up with you? The dogs?"

Max bit his lip and pushed his hair back. "Let's wait and see what we can find out about the state of the fire. If they can be safe up there, I'd be happy to have their company and their help. They could hose down the yard, the roof, and each other. But if conditions are uncertain, or if the air quality is bad, I'd like to leave the dogs and kids down here. Those fires can shift on a dime."

"If it's *that* iffy, I don't want *you* up there, either."

"Let me get the information first, then we'll compare notes."

I thought about Max's plan for a moment. "Won't plowing the grass and weeds increase the odds of erosion and mudslides once it starts raining?" I asked. "We don't want to exchange one dire threat for another."

Max shook his head. "Let's deal with today's threat. Once the fire moves on, we can plant something that will keep the soil in place. We've got months before we see any significant rainfall."

I soon realized that rain would be the least of our problems.

Tess and Teddy came to the table and poured juice and cereal they didn't touch. Both had deep circles under their eyes and downcast expressions. Tess stared at the bottom of her mug. "Coffee?" I asked, holding up the pot.

Tess smiled, briefly. "Thanks. I was having the hardest time figuring out how to make that happen. My brain is on strike." She rubbed her eyes, tried to continue smiling, and failed. "Thanks for getting the breakfast

stuff out. I'm a terrible hostess. Someone did the laundry yesterday too..."
She paused, stricken. "What am I going to do with Patrick's clothes? His
sports equipment?" Her rich olive complexion turned gray-green, pale,
and lined with pain.

I hurried to her side and hugged her. "There'll be time enough to figure
that out. And people to help, if you want that. Try to think of one thing at
a time. Do you and Teddy want to visit the funeral home?"

Tess looked blank, so I prompted. "You talked yesterday about letting
Teddy see Patrick. Patrick's body..." I wanted my language to be clear
and precise, because both Tess and Teddy seemed to be having trouble
processing anything. I didn't know how much they remembered about
yesterday. I tried to stay alert to their reactions, in case my terms were
too clinical or caused discomfort. Adding to their burden was the last
thing I wanted to do.

Tess squinted at Teddy, who nodded.

"Do you want to do that first thing?" I asked. "Would you like a
chauffeur? I could drop you right at the door so you don't have to worry
about parking."

"That'd be great, thanks. I don't think I'm safe to drive." She startled
and half-stood, to gain an angle from which she could peer out the front
window. "What's that?"

I heard it too—loud voices from the front yard accompanied by the
sound of enormous trucks with heavy engines. My first thought was that
someone was delivering the construction equipment Max had talked about.

Max and David ran to the window over the sink, jostling for position.
David turned away immediately. "News trucks," he called in a voice loud
enough to reach down the hall to Teddy's bedroom. "Teddy. Brian. Help."

I looked to Max for answers. "Pull down the blinds and close the
curtains. No one's going anywhere," Max said as he lowered the kitchen
mini-blinds with a clatter. Shaking his head, he dashed to the door leading
to the garage. In a moment, I heard the motor of the garage door, and then
his voice from the front yard.

"This is private property. I have to ask you to leave."

Unintelligible shouted questions followed, drowning out anything else
Max had to say.

Belle and Mozart scratched at the front door. A siren blurted briefly,
and I assumed that Jason or Paolo had arrived. After a brief period of
additional shouting, we heard the garage-door motor again. Max entered
the kitchen, followed by Jason, who let the frantic dogs out into the garage,
where their barking added to the din.

"Let them bark," Jason said. "They'll make it difficult to record commentary and will keep any particularly earnest reporters out of the backyard. If the journalists dare to spin a story about vicious dogs, I'll find a station that will do a feel-good follow-up with Belle and a little kid with an ice cream cone." He reached for a coffee mug, and I filled it. "I moved them off the lawn. With rush hour heating up, they're going to make enemies if they snarl up traffic in the street."

Tess lived on a quiet road with a fifteen-mile-an-hour school-speed zone. With the advent of real-time traffic data on cell phones, it had become a congestion-dodging commuter route to the freeways, especially in the summer, when working people didn't have to compete with school traffic.

Jason parted the slats in the mini-blinds and peered out. "It looks like they're moving down the street to the school parking lot. I'll call the district administrators and see if we can't move them along."

Peering over his shoulder, I watched him signal to two motorcycle patrol officers, who then followed the news vans to the school down the street.

I stepped back and turned toward the breakfast table, where Tess, Teddy, Brian, and David stared in varied degrees of horror.

"But, Mom, we were headed to the park to play Ultimate Frisbee." said David.

Brian sighed. "Will we be trapped inside *all* day?"

Tess scrolled through her phone. "I have to cancel my appointments for the rest of the week."

And Teddy's face fell. "Does that mean we can't get to the funeral home? Will they...keep him? Do we have to call?"

I glanced from Max's distraught face to Jason's stern one. Were they going to address Teddy's question, or was I? What were the answers? If Patrick had truly been murdered, was someone out to get him or the entire family? Either way, killing Patrick was an evil, unforgivable act that had devastated his wife and teenaged boy. They might never recover any semblance of what they previously called their "normal" life.

"Look, all of you," I said, making direct eye contact with each boy in turn. "We'll figure this out. We'll not be cowed by an Internet bully, vicious rumors, or gossip mongering talking heads from the television news. We're tougher than that. We're better than that." I stood as straight as I could and squared my shoulders, trying to exude the confidence of a superhero. "Roll up your sleeping bags, take turns with the shower, and get dressed. By the time you're finished, and you've cleaned up the bathroom"—the boys moaned, which told me at least one thing had returned to normal—"we'll have a better sense of how, exactly, we'll beat this thing."

Brian and David took off for the back of the house, with the dogs following. Teddy stayed behind. He gripped my arm and tugged at it, like a small child aching for a grown-up's attention. "Mrs. M., you'll help us find the truth, right? And make that web page stop telling lies about my mom and dad?"

I silently consulted Max. I seemed to have become embroiled in a number of dramatic legal cases recently, and I'd promised Max that I would stay far away from law enforcement, detective work, and especially murder. But this was Tess and Teddy we were talking about. Surely we couldn't leave them in the lurch. With all they had on their plates, and the suffering they had in store as they grieved and tried to define their new normal, there was no way they had time to ferret out the truth. Would those investigating the case see through the nonsense on the web page and identify it as what it was: childish muckraking worthy of the worst of the supermarket tabloids?

Max nodded in answer to my unspoken questions. Before I could reassure Teddy that I'd do what I could to track down the facts, the doorbell rang, startling us as though a firecracker had gone off. Between shock, frazzled nerves, and little sleep, none of us had a firm grip on our emotions.

Max sighed, put down his coffee mug, and walked toward the door, muttering about annoying newspeople who wouldn't allow Tess a moment's peace. I expected him to speak sternly but politely to whoever was ringing the bell. But he said nothing. Nor did whoever was responsible for interrupting our breakfast. I leaned forward to peer around the kitchen counter, but I couldn't see anything. I scooted my chair back and prepared to stand and join Max at the door. But before I could do that, he came through the archway that separated the hallway from the kitchen. A Santa Clara County sheriff, hat in hand, followed closely on his heels.

"Please, sit down," he said. When my husband had taken his seat and grasped my hand under the table, the sheriff spoke. "I'm Sergeant Thanh Nguyen, from the investigative division of the Santa Clara County Sheriff's Office." He stood formally, with his feet shoulder width apart, his back straight. One hand was poised ominously close to his firearm, while the other gripped his olive-green Smokey Bear–style hat. Khaki stripes down the sides of his uniform trousers made Sergeant Nguyen look taller than he probably was.

His voice was soft, but firm, and commanded attention. Rationally, I assumed he was here to update us with news of the investigation into Patrick's death, and possibly to report on firefighting efforts. But my lizard brain was trying desperately to convince me to flee from a danger and tension in the air that I could feel but couldn't see. And I wasn't the only one who felt threatened by Sergeant Nguyen's arrival. Teddy was biting his lip and staring at his mom in panic. Tess's hands clasped each other with white knuckles. Max might have appeared calm to a stranger, but he had a death grip on my hand that was more frightening than it was reassuring. Jason stepped forward to shake the sheriff's hand. "I'm Jason Mueller, chief of police here in Orchard View. What can you tell us?"

Jason's presence and warm greeting seemed to have set Sergeant Nguyen slightly off balance. A bead of sweat appeared on his forehead. What on earth could be making him so nervous? This family and our community had already received the worst possible news. Surely anything he had to say would pale in comparison.

Sergeant Nguyen took a deep breath and let it out slowly. "Mrs. Teresa Olmos," he said slowly, "we have a warrant to arrest you for the murder of your husband, Patrick Teodoro Olmos." He stepped back and waved two young deputy cadets forward. One pulled handcuffs from the back of his duty belt, while the other read Tess her Miranda rights.

Chapter 9

If these preparations sound daunting, consider taking advantage of the emergency kits sold and prepared by many community groups as fundraisers. The kits range in size and price from a personal first aid kit to all the supplies a family of four would need for a week.

From the Notebook of Maggie McDonald
Simplicity Itself Organizing Services

Monday, August 7, Morning

Jason stepped between Tess and the deputies. Teddy grabbed his mother's hand. She put her arm around him and kissed his head. "It'll be okay, buddy," she said. Teddy's expression said he knew that the bottom had fallen out of his world again. With each blow, he was becoming less successful in rebuilding a firm foundation on which to stand—that platform that everyone needs, but that is truly essential to teens trying to discover who they are and how they'll navigate the adult world. I nodded to Tess and Teddy. Max and I would protect Teddy—feed him, nurture him, and protect him to the best of our ability for as long as it was necessary. Because that's what friends did. I reached for my phone to call Forrest Doucett.

Tess lifted her chin and squared her shoulders like a proud French aristocrat on her way to the guillotine.

Jason held his arm out, palm down, toward the nearest cadet. It reminded me of the way I'd approach a dog while trying not to spook it. He shifted his attention to Sergeant Nguyen. "Are you actually arresting her, or just inviting her to come in for questioning?" Jason asked in a gentle but firm voice. "What is the charge? Can you please show us the warrant?" Nguyen reached inside his jacket and pulled out several folded documents, which he then handed to Jason. "Arrest warrant, search warrant, affidavits, and a list of items we're looking for, including handguns." Jason examined them quickly, then handed them to me. "They look in order, but snap a photo of them and send them to Forrest."

"Guns? But why?" I asked.

"It's in the warrant," said Nguyen, stepping forward until he was nearly toe to toe with Jason, as if daring him to do...something. It was a classic display of men squaring off and taking each other's measure. Tension rose, and I feared that the tiniest movement on anyone's part would land us in more trouble than we already faced. I held my breath.

Jason stared at the sergeant, but continued to speak so softly that, had the room not been so deathly quiet, or if I hadn't already had a good idea of what he had to say, his words would have been inaudible to anyone other than Nguyen. "The cuffs won't be necessary. Mrs. Olmos is happy to cooperate. I'd be pleased to bring her to the district attorney's office or wherever it is you intend to question her." He paused. "I know you have the paperwork required to arrest Mrs. Olmos, but I assume you'll want to search the house while she's here and question her to see if her statement proves more reliable than that of any other witnesses you've interviewed."

"Witnesses?" I must have spoken too loudly, because Tess startled and everyone else stared at me with varied degrees of astonishment. "How can there be witnesses? Tess didn't do anything. She couldn't. She wouldn't." I sucked in a deep breath and forced myself to close my mouth and stop talking. As much as I wanted to defend my friend, I was upsetting Tess and Teddy, and that was the last thing I wanted to do.

Nguyen sighed, then nodded, first to Jason and then to his men, each of whom took several steps backward until they stood behind their boss. "Chief, as a courtesy to you, I would be happy to question Mrs. Olmos before we take her to the jail. Is there somewhere we can talk without interruption?"

"I'm sure we can set you up with a room here from which you can conduct your interviews and supervise the search for the items named in the warrant," Jason said. "Mrs. Olmos will want to wait for her lawyer, so that will give us plenty of time to create an interview situation that works for everyone."

I stepped into the living room as I selected Forrest's office number from my contact list. I hoped I'd find him in his Orchard View location—a high-rise upscale business suite he'd recently opened as a satellite to the firm's headquarters near AT&T Park in San Francisco. He'd joked that he needed the new location to be closer to our family and friends, making it easier to respond to my "constant calls" for help. I suspected the real reason was that the bulk of the firm's business was connected in one way or another to Silicon Valley commerce. Forrest had once told me he spent as much or more time arguing cases in San Jose as he did in San Francisco.

The call connected, and I briefly explained to the receptionist that I was a friend and a client of Forrest's, and that I needed help for another friend who was being arrested for murder. The words seemed as foreign as if I'd suddenly begun speaking a language I'd never studied, but they didn't seem to faze the receptionist. "Please tell him there's been a new development," I added.

He transferred me to Forrest's office, where an automated system invited me to leave a message. "Forrest, the Santa Clara County sheriff has a warrant for Tess Olmos's arrest and paperwork to search her home and garage for firearms and a number of other items. Everything is happening quickly, so we need you or one of your colleagues here as soon as possible. It looks like Jason has convinced Sergeant Nguyen to question Tess here at the house and hold off on arresting her. I doubt Jason will let Tess answer any questions until you get here. I took photos of the warrants and the other forms Nguyen gave to Tess. I'll send them to your personal phone." Forrest responded with a quick text before I'd finished sending the documents.

In town. On my way.

I took a minute to breathe deeply and think about what I needed to do when I walked back into the kitchen. The most important thing was to project confidence. The boys needed to know that the adults had the situation in hand and that there was nothing to worry about.

I heard a vehicle pull up outside and peered through a gap in the living room drapes. Forrest hopped out of the cab of a dented pickup truck that sported more primer than paint but appeared to have originally been red. It was old, but not yet vintage, and it had a bit of a coughing fit when Forrest turned off the engine. It was a far cry from the sleek black Tesla he normally drove. His faded jeans, gray sweatshirt, and dusty hair indicated he'd come as soon as I'd called. If he was working from home today, he wasn't catching up on lawyerly paperwork nor meeting clients—not without his tailored suit, silk tie, and crisply starched shirt.

"Excuse my appearance," he said after he'd introduced himself. "I wasn't expecting to conduct any business today. It's Lizzy's birthday, and we're landscaping. I'd just made my first trip to the hardware store when you phoned."

Forrest, exuding more confidence than I'd been able to drum up, met with Tess in a small courtyard seating area off of Tess's bedroom. Jason joined them, but not until after he'd told me that Stephen and Paolo were on their way. Until they arrived, it was my job to make sure Sergeant Nguyen and his men adhered to the limits of the warrants. I nodded my agreement, but I was as out of my depth as I would have been if Jason had handed me a baby manatee and asked me to feed it some lunch.

I smiled bravely at the boys and spoke quickly before toddling off to dog the heels of the sheriff's men. "Forrest knows exactly what to do," I said, adding, for Teddy's sake, "He's a lawyer and an old friend of Max's. He's helped us out on several occasions and I trust him." Teddy relaxed a little, but he seemed more comforted by Max's reassuring hand on his shoulder.

"Jason asked them to be careful and tidy in their search," Max added. I hoped the sheriff's men would comply. There were few feelings creepier than having strangers paw through your personal belongings. The last thing Teddy needed was for them to accidentally break something he treasured as a memento of his father.

"I need to watch them," I said, pointing toward the garage, where the men had launched their search. We could hear the sounds of boxes being moved and drawers being opened and closed a bit more roughly than I thought was necessary.

"Go," said Max. "I'll call Elaine. She wanted to keep an eye on the news vans. If they've left, I think we could use her help. Stephen's too."

"With what?"

"I'm not sure, maybe just to tip the scales—increase the number of people here who are squarely behind Tess and Teddy."

Brian followed me to the garage and bumped into me as I paused to open the connecting door. "Mom?"

I stopped, turned, and put my arm around him. Whereas his normal adolescent instinct might have been to duck out of my reach, today's extreme circumstances made him lean into my embrace. "Is this weird?" he asked. "I mean, Jason's a cop."

"What do you mean?" I had no idea what he was getting at.

"I mean, Jason told you to call Forrest. He convinced Nguyen to talk to Tess here instead of at the station. He's the one who asked you to watch the deputies. But he's a cop. Shouldn't he be on their side?"

It was an easy question for me to answer. "You know Jason. He's on the side of the law. He takes his vow to serve and protect literally. Right now, he's protecting Tess and Teddy. Making sure the sheriff's guys follow the law. Not every cop might see that as part of the job, but Jason isn't any cop, now, is he?"

Brian's shoulders relaxed.

"Your dad and I are going to look after Teddy and Tess as long as necessary," I told him. "This is a tough time for them, but they'll be okay. We'll see to that."

"Mom..." Brian bit his lip, and his gaze dropped to his shoes. "Yesterday I was feeling sorry for us. I was afraid our house would burn down. I worried about the damage the fire was doing. Today, I'm pretty sure that doesn't matter much."

I gave him a hug and kissed the top of his head. I knew exactly how he felt.

Chapter 10

Emergency contact information greatly aids first responders. Many athletes who train outdoors carry copies of their driver's licenses in their shoes or helmets. Other options are downloading an ICE (in case of emergency) app on your cell phone that will provide all relevant information if your phone is unlocked. Another commercially available but inexpensive and durable solution is a Road ID tag that can be worn on your wrist or attached to your clothing.

From the Notebook of Maggie McDonald
Simplicity Itself Organizing Services

Monday, August 7, Lunchtime

The intrusion of Nguyen and the deputies seemed as outrageous as if an entire circus troupe and their elephants, tigers, and trained seals had descended upon us. They combed the house and garage and prepared to leave after bagging their evidence, which included two guns.

"Where did you find them?" Tess asked, eyeing the firearms as though she expected them to explode. "I'll kill that man. He was supposed to have gotten rid of them." Her eyes filled with tears, and she slapped both hands over her mouth when she realized what she'd said.

The younger, thinner sheriff's deputy held the guns and described them, as the second deputy jotted notes on the inventory portion of one of the pages that had come with the search warrant.

Forrest took Tess's hand and held it firmly. She peered up at him. "If you know anything about the firearms, I see no problem in telling the officers."

Tess sat near the end of the kitchen table, where the second deputy was writing. "May I?" she asked. He slid the smaller handgun toward her. Tess picked it up with a rustle of the sealed evidence bag. "This one was Patrick's grandfather's. He liked to target-shoot, and at one time was being considered for the Olympic team. PopPop called it a free pistol. Neither Patrick nor his dad took up the sport, but Patrick wanted to hang on to it in case Teddy was ever interested.

"It takes a .22 round, I think, but I'm sure we don't have any ammunition for it. Patrick was supposed to store it at his parents' house or in our safety deposit box. I guess he hadn't gotten around to moving it." I heard a catch in her throat, but she gamely kept going, reaching for the second gun, a long one that the first deputy shoved toward her when Tess held out her hand. "It's empty," he said. "I checked."

Tess examined the gun. "Does the warrant cover this? It's not a handgun." Nguyen nodded to the cadet, who pulled out the warrant, flipped through pages of small print, and read: "Any handgun or other weapon that could fire or be adapted to fire a .22 round."

"That's a Remington .22-250," Forrest said. "My dad had one. It fits the description."

Jason frowned and turned to the sergeant. "When you told me 'handguns' earlier, did you misspeak or deliberately mislead me?"

Nguyen flushed. "I apologize for my lack of precision," he said mechanically, not sounding at all sorry. I shivered and was glad I'd called Forrest. If Nguyen was going to be playing games and trading semantics, I was way out of my league.

Meanwhile, Tess peered at the long gun through the enormous and unwieldy evidence bag, making more noise than someone sneaking potato chips at midnight. Through the bag she flicked some mechanism and then flicked it again. "Force of habit," she said. "Never take hold of a gun without checking the safety devices. This gun was my grandfather's. Remington .22-250. He used it to keep rats away from his horse feed. We've got no horse, no feed, no rats, and no ammo. Patrick was a local history buff, and he hung on to a lot of mementos from my granddad's ranch."

"More firearms?" asked Nguyen. Tess shook her head. "A branding iron, a sharpening stone. I don't know of any other guns, but then, like I said, I thought Patrick had gotten rid of these years ago. I don't know if they still work, let alone shoot straight. Why are you so interested in them? Are you sure they're included on the warrant?" She looked across the table at Forrest, who had pulled out a chair and sat at the end of the table facing the deputy.

"Go ahead, counselor," said Nguyen.

Forrest put the palms of his hands down on the table, his fingers spread wide. "The warrant allowed them to look for a firearm that took .22 rounds. Both the Olympic free pistol and the Remington fit that description. I understand that the crime scene investigators uncovered some .22 shells near the scene. The medical examiner found a bullet lodged in Patrick's scapula that could have come from either one of these guns."

Teddy held up his hand for Brian to reward him with a high five. "I told you he was murdered," he said. "Dad wouldn't have fallen from that ridge trail on his own." Almost immediately, Teddy's jubilation fled. His shoulders dropped, and his face drooped as he realized what connections the sheriff was trying to make. "But Mom's right. We don't have ammunition for those guns. Dad told me he'd teach me to shoot one day, but like Mom said, guns spooked him. We didn't go. I didn't know they were still here."

"We found the long gun in the rafters of the garage where it abuts the kitchen," said the sergeant. "We could see it from the garage floor, but not easily." Forrest started to protest, but Nguyen held up his hand. "Calm down, counselor. It's a righteous search. We've found other long guns stashed in similar places. Once we knew where to look, we could see it, though it blended into the shadows of the rafters. When it comes to hiding firearms, it's as common a hiding place as a porch flowerpot is for keys."

"And the second one?" Forrest asked.

"Ah, now, that was interesting, seeing as how no one here knows anything about it. We found that one on the workbench."

I gasped at the news and struggled to force my brain to catch up with my need to defend my friend and the rest of us. "That can't be," I said. "We've all been in and out of the garage, both last night and this morning. There was no gun there, I'm sure of it."

I checked the expressions on the faces of my friends and my family members. But everyone seemed as horrified as I felt. "Sergeant Nguyen, both Tess and I are extremely firm about guns and gun safety. No one here would have left a gun out where it could be so casually picked up. No one. Frankly, if I'd known Tess and Patrick had guns stored here, I'm not sure I'd even let my boys hang out here. We'd have had a long discussion about it, anyway. We used to live in Stockton. I grew up there and lost more than one member of my high school and college classes to random violence. In my mind, a gun—any gun, loaded or not—is a murder waiting for the right circumstances. Firearms can't tell the difference between a human, a pet, or a wild animal. Neither can bullets. I've got nothing against hunting, hunters, or target shooters, but I don't want guns anywhere near my kids." Max nodded firmly in agreement, as did Tess. All three boys were shaking their heads. "If that gun had been there yesterday," David said, "we would have seen it. Along with dozens of friends and neighbors who were here last night. I'd have assumed it was an Airsoft replica. I probably would have picked it up and brought it to Teddy, to ask how he'd convinced his mom to let him buy it."

Sergeant Nguyen watched each of us closely as we exchanged looks of confusion. "Do you have a list of who was invited last night?" he asked.

Tess sighed and pushed her hair away from her face, twisting it into a loose bun. "It wasn't like that. It was neighbors coming over to lend support. Bringing casseroles, offering to help, that kind of thing."

"Did you know everyone who was here? Could you put together a list?"

Tess shrugged. "There were people here I didn't recognize, but I assumed they were friends of Patrick or Teddy's. Or that I didn't recognize folks I knew but hadn't seen in a while. I'm not sure I'd have recognized my own face in the mirror yesterday."

Murmurs of agreement moved around the room. Max spoke first. "I'll write down the names of everyone I can remember and give that list to Forrest, if it would help."

"It would." Nguyen turned from Max to Forrest. "If everyone could do that, and get the list to us as soon as possible, it'd be great. We'll check for fingerprints on the weapons, of course, but if they were planted, I doubt we'll find anything unexpected or helpful. You never know."

The second deputy finished completing his paperwork and handed the pages to his boss, who signed them and passed copies to Tess. "I think we're done here," he said. "Unless you have any questions, we'll see ourselves out and be in touch." I wondered when he'd decided he didn't need to arrest Tess and take her in, but there was no way I'd ask the question out loud, just in case he'd forgotten his original plan.

Forrest leaped to his feet. "I'll see you out. I wouldn't be doing my job if I didn't."

I wasn't sure what he meant, but I assumed it had something to do with making sure that they didn't search more extensively than the warrant allowed. Forrest accompanied them to their vehicles and returned quickly.

"Are the news vans still in the neighborhood?" I asked. He shook his head. "The president has a fund-raising event scheduled in Woodside. He's flying into Moffett Field, so television crews have migrated there. We've been granted a bit of a reprieve, but I don't know how long it will last."

Max glanced at his watch and grimaced. "That took up most of the morning. I'm going to check on the fire online. I still want to try to get back up to the house." He took his phone and computer to Tess's shaded deck. The boys were supposed to be taking showers, but I could hear the unmistakable sound of a video game being played. I shrugged. With everything else going on, none of us wanted the boys to go anywhere alone for fear they'd be pounced upon by overzealous journalists. They had to do something. It might as well be video games. None of the adults, including me, had put together a better or more constructive plan. It was nearly one o'clock. I'd made no progress in discovering who'd killed Patrick or created the dreadful website. Max hadn't been up to the house. We were getting nowhere.

The irony of our situation hadn't escaped me, but while paradoxes usually amused me, I found nothing funny about our predicament. While we waited for the signal from Cal Fire and Santa Clara County fire officials that would allow us to move back to our house, the official lifting of restrictions on our neighborhood would come from the sheriff's office. That would be the same sheriff whose suspicions threatened Tess.

Outside, the air was still overly warm, dry, and smoky. Inside, we were all a little hot under the collar from the combination of heat, stress, grief, worry, too much caffeine, and not enough food or sleep.

One of those problems I could solve, so I busied myself making sandwiches. I called the boys to lunch, then went to the doorway of Teddy's room to make sure they'd heard me. The smell of hulking teenaged men was overpowering, so I suggested they get their showers in before lunch. As I passed the thermostat in the hall, I adjusted the fan on Tess's central air-conditioning to "high." Later, when the evening fog came barreling in from the coast to provide our area's natural air-conditioning, it would help dampen down the fire and reduce the smoke. I couldn't wait to open the windows and air out the house. For the first time since Saturday morning, I wanted to be back home instead of camping out in Tess's living room.

Elaine and Stephen joined Max, Jason, Tess, and me for lunch. Tess moved grapes and a half sandwich around her plate, but didn't eat. Elaine poured her some lemonade that she barely sipped. She could not have looked more exhausted had she just finished a triathlon.

No one spoke. I cleared my throat, afraid to speak but determined to give us something positive to think about and to act upon.

"Let's talk about this," I said. "We all know Tess didn't kill Patrick. But we also now know there was at least one person up on the ridge who shot at him, conked him on the head, and left him there, knowing the fire might overtake the trail. We know at least one person left a firearm out on the workbench here, possibly after using it to hurt Patrick. That person had to have some sense of where Patrick had stashed the guns, or at least know what kind of guns the Olmos family had owned at one time. How many people fit that description? It can't be many. Can we put together a list? A timeline? Or think about who might have wanted Patrick..."

I couldn't finish the sentence. Saying that someone wanted Patrick dead was unthinkable. It also seemed harsh to utter those words in the company of Patrick's widow and orphaned child. But I needn't have worried about offending Tess. She finished my thought for me. "Someone obviously wanted him dead, or at least wanted to injure him—but why?"

Teddy, hair wet from a haphazard shower that had left a few bubbles of lather clinging to the back of his head, had disappeared into the garage when I'd started talking. He now returned lugging a stack of poster board sheets covered with cobwebs and dust. The panels turned out to be from old elementary school science projects. He flipped them over, blank side toward the room, and lined them up on the sill of the window between the kitchen and the deck, securing them to the café curtain rod with giant orange clamps. He held a marker in one hand, and labeled each panel with a heading: *Suspects, Motives, Questions.* He left the other cardboard sheets blank.

"Timeline, maybe?" I suggested. Teddy repositioned a fourth board so that it was horizontal instead of vertical, and drew a line across it. "I last saw my dad when he dropped me off at soccer practice around two o'clock on Saturday. Did anyone else see him after that?" Teddy wrote "*Saturday 2:00 p.m.*" at one end of the line.

"Does anyone know when they found him?" Elaine asked.

Tess spoke, her voice hoarse. "The sheriff called me yesterday. I called Maggie right away. What time was that?"

I checked my watch. "Close to eight thirty in the morning, I think."

Max added, "It was more like 8:20. I remember because I was supposed to pack up food for Belle and the cats, and I was trying to decide if there was time to feed them before we left."

"So that's our window," I said. "Someone said he'd been found around five o'clock. Paolo maybe? When we were at the medical examiner's office? I can't remember." I glanced at my watch again, having already forgotten what it said when I'd checked the time just seconds earlier. My short-term memory had gotten lost somewhere in the swirl of dreadful events.

"I think that's right," said Jason. "Write it down, anyway, Teddy. I'll verify it later and change it if we've got it wrong."

"David, can you find anything online that says what time the fire reached the top of the ridge? And what time the wind shifted?" David left the table and headed into the living room, where I'd last seen his laptop. Tess tapped the table with her long fingernails. "Wait. I'm pretty sure Paolo said that the ranger found Patrick sometime around dawn. Why would it take so long for them to contact me? What time is dawn, anyway? Five-ish? Why would it take hours?"

Chapter 11

Our family and our neighbors prepare for wildfire conditions by clearing firebreaks around our property, home, and outbuildings. We put away outdoor cushions, furniture, and flammable materials. Outside of fire season, however, more fires are started from inside a home than outside. Learn the fire risks and dangers most apt to impact your family and prepare accordingly.

From the Notebook of Maggie McDonald
Simplicity Itself Organizing Services

Monday, August 7, Early afternoon

Tess's face threatened to crumple, and Teddy took over. "Mom's right. Dad always ran with a copy of his license pinned inside his T-shirt, and he had a Road ID tag on his running shoes. You gave it to him, Jason, didn't you?" I looked at my feet. Last Christmas, Jason had given each of us Road ID tags for our athletic gear, printed with our emergency contact information. With all the trail running the kids did, their tags were scratched and becoming difficult to read. Mine, however, was nearly pristine. I made a mental note to jump-start my exercise routine as soon as the immediate crisis was over.

I checked my watch and gasped. "We need to wrap this up if we're going to make our two o'clock appointment at the mortuary." I tried to read Teddy's expression. "That is, if you still want to go?" Teddy reached for his phone and stood.

Max pulled his car keys from his pocket. "That's something I can do to help. I'll pull the car around in front of the Baxters' house on the next block. You and Teddy can cut through the back gate into their yard to avoid the press. The news vans have left, but who knows when they'll be back."

Tess spoke then, pressing her hands against the sides of her head as though she feared her brain would explode. "Thanks, Maggie. Unless... Teddy, do you want me to take you? Would you be more comfortable?"

He shook his head. "With or without you, there's no way I'm going to be comfortable in a mortuary, and I don't want to have to worry about you. If you're there, I will."

"Yes, sir," Tess said, lowering her hands. If I hadn't known them both, their conversation might have seemed flippant, dismissive, or even disrespectful. But it wasn't. Teddy was trying to be tough and honest about his feelings. Tess was trying not to fret and attempting to show Teddy that she respected him as the near-adult he was. Both Tess and Teddy, outwardly, were organized and in control. I hoped the hurricane of emotions that had stolen their appetites might somehow become equally well contained.

"I've got a ton of calls to make." Tess stood and grabbed her phone from the table. "Family and friends need to know. I'll transfer my clients to other agents. There's no way I can stay on top of multimillion-dollar negotiations this week, let alone counsel families through traumatic moves."

Stephen put a hand on her arm. "I can help with those calls if you'd like."

Tess's expression softened. "I'll make a list."

Forrest left after preparing paperwork that would make Max and me Teddy's temporary guardians and give us her power of attorney so we could pay her bills and sign on Teddy's behalf if Tess should, after all, be arrested. He promised to bring the completed documents back before the end of the day.

Forrest wanted to be sure that Teddy would not be taken into foster care if the sheriff arrested Tess. Chances were, even the most hard-hearted authorities would allow Teddy to stay with us instead of in foster care, but Tess said she'd worry less if the paperwork was in order.

The wind shifted, and Max returned from moving the car, saying that we had clearance to pack up our temporary refugee camp. The fire service had widened the firebreak, and the fire was now 80 percent contained.

I glanced at Teddy. His skin was gray, and his jaw was clenched. But he led me out the back door and through a gate in the fence separating his backyard from the neighbors.

I was clicking my key fob to open my car door when I heard my name. "Maggie, wait!" I turned. Tess ran toward us. "I don't know what I was thinking. This is a time for family to stick together. I have to go with Teddy."

I nodded. I'd wondered earlier about Tess's decision to delegate this task to me, but I hadn't argued. Everyone grieves in her own way. If what seemed essential to me wasn't important to Tess, who was I to question her decision? I held out the keys to Tess. "Take my—"I began, then stopped. "Would you allow me to drive?"

Tess put her left arm around Teddy and reached for the car door with her right. "Thanks. My attention span is minuscule."

The funeral home wasn't far. As we stepped inside the building, I was struck by its similarity to a chapel—peaceful, cool, with a pleasant scent that prompted thoughts of candles and flowers. The entryway was formal but homey, with chairs upholstered in floral cotton.

"I'm Stone, Roger Silverstone, but everyone calls me Stone to differentiate me from my dad and my granddad, who started the business." We completed the introductions, and while my friends were both wide-eyed and pale, Stone seemed completely at ease. He invited us to sit in a reception area to the right of a center hall. While Tess and Teddy took places on a sofa that put as much distance as possible between themselves and the funeral director, I excused myself and stopped in the ladies' lounge. When I returned to the room, they'd moved on, presumably to take a look at Patrick's body.

While waiting, I examined a display case that held an assortment of urns ranging from a no-frills cardboard box to elaborate carved wood and cast metal. I wondered what I'd pick out if I were in Tess's position, then realized I had no way of knowing. There was no way I could possibly imagine what she was going through. I shuddered. To distract myself from my morbid feelings, I reflected on Stone and how different he was from the stereotypical Hollywood mortician. In a crisp collared shirt, tan chinos, and loafers, he would have been at home at nearly any Silicon Valley firm. "Stone, Roger Silverstone," he'd said. In my head, it sounded much like the introduction of the world's most famous spy as "Bond, James Bond," and I giggled at the incongruity between my thoughts and the situation at hand. I strode to the window and looked out on a meditation garden with a waterfall fountain and hummingbird feeders that had attracted a number of the tiny birds jockeying for the prime positions.

I lost myself in watching them until I slowly became aware of the soft music broadcast over the sound system. The music was designed, I was sure, to blend into the background, provide comfort, and sound familiar, while at the same time, avoid offending or intruding. It was neither religious nor funereal, and I wondered what sort of job title might be assigned to a person responsible for selecting inoffensive arrangements of popular songs to be played in a mortuary. So far, the only pieces I'd been able to identify were Beatles tunes and other songs from the pre-disco era.

I was about to take a seat on the sofa when Tess and Teddy returned with Stone. While their faces remained nearly colorless, they both seemed less on edge. Tess collected some papers from Stone, thanked him, signaled to me, and we exited—to the discordant sound of what sounded eerily like a soft-rock arrangement of Springsteen's "I'm on Fire."

Tess turned to me, eyes wide in recognition of the song's title. "Do you hear that?"

I nodded, horrified, but trying not to lose my self-control.

In the car, Tess exploded in uncontrollable laughter, both hands clutched to her belly. Her laughter was contagious and soul cleansing. For several minutes, we were incapable of responding to Teddy's pleas for us to explain, but as I dried my eyes and started the car, Tess took a deep breath and responded: "Inappropriate song titles for a crematorium soundtrack."

Teddy frowned, then snorted. "What was it? 'Light My Fire'?"

Tess shook her head. "'I'm on Fire'. Springsteen. You know..." She hummed a few notes before giving in to the laughter again.

Teddy and I offered up a few more fire, flame, and heat-related titles, until I slammed on the brakes to avoid a cyclist who'd veered into traffic to dodge a broken shopping cart on the shoulder. It was a wake-up call. I needed to pay more attention or we'd end up joining Patrick sooner rather than later.

"So, Teddy," I said. "Can you tell me about it?"

He composed himself. "It wasn't Dad." He seemed convinced, but his voice held none of the elation I'd expect from a teen who'd discovered in one fell swoop that his father was not, in fact, dead, and that he'd been right while the adults were wrong.

"That's great..." I said, hesitating to elaborate until I knew more about what was going on.

"Oh, no no no," Teddy said. "The body was definitely Dad's." He shook his head as if continuing to deny it. "I didn't want it to be, but it was. But it was just a body. A shell, like Jason said. I mean, they say that beauty is only skin deep and all, but I guess I never realized how little a body matters to who the person is underneath." Teddy swallowed hard and cleared his throat. I thought he was having trouble discussing his dad's dead body, but then he continued. "I didn't want to be disrespectful or anything, but I...um...I had to poke him to make sure he wasn't, like, a mannequin or a doll or something. Like that thing we practiced CPR on in school." Teddy paused again. A glance in the rearview showed that a flush had returned to his pale cheeks. "I guess I wasn't supposed to do that. Stone moved my hand away and covered him up."

"He's your dad," I said. "I'm sure whatever you did was fine."

We stopped at a red light, and I turned to face Teddy with what I hoped was a reassuring expression. Tess put her hand on Teddy's arm. "Of course it was fine. Did you notice that Stone tucked him in, almost like a mom saying good night to a toddler? It was sad and weird, but also gentle, and sweet." She shook her head and stared out the window, growing distant.

"He didn't suffer," Teddy told me, reiterating what the medical examiner had told Tess the day before. "He died before the fire. Stone told us the death certificate will say that Dad died from a blow to the head. I asked him to show me, and he did. I think the medical examiner told Mom that it could have been a fall, but it sure seemed like he'd been hit with something to me... Maybe one of those tools the firefighters use. A Pulaski, I think they call them." Teddy waved his hands, sketching the object in the air. "Like a pick on one side and a sharpened hoe thing on the other. We've got a little one at home in the shed." His voice trailed off, but before I could speak, he began again. "He showed me the bullet wound in Dad's shoulder too. Looked like it must have hurt. A lot. Especially since it hit the bone. Maybe that knocked him over. Why would someone attack him with a pickax if they had a gun? Could there have been *two* people who wanted Dad dead? Who decided to confront him and kill him, both on the same night?" Teddy's voice trailed off as he explored his reaction to what he'd seen. "It's hard enough to believe there was one. But two?" He shook his head. "This is kinda gross. But kinda not, since wherever Dad is now, he's not in that fridge. That body is just, you know, the clues he left behind to help us figure out what's going on." Teddy squirmed in the seat, scooting his bottom back, sitting up straight, and squaring his shoulders. " If he'd fallen and hit his head, he'd have a giant bruise, right? Like when I got hit by the ball in Little League. And since it was bad, it might be all kinda smooshed in, but it wasn't."

It was taking me a few minutes to get used to Teddy talking about his own father's remains in such a clinical fashion. But Tess had told me that Teddy loved his science classes, and that he'd expressed some interest in becoming a surgeon. He'd convinced our local veterinarian, Dr. Calvert Davidson, to let him watch a few surgical procedures. Assuredly, he'd mastered the necessary outlook on bone, blood, and tissue. He spoke of his own father's body as if he was a car mechanic explaining a badly damaged engine. It seemed oddly detached and strange to me, but I reminded myself that I firmly believed there wasn't a right way or a wrong way to grieve.

Death was so overwhelmingly shocking to living human beings that we couldn't be sure how we or anyone else would respond. Crazy laughter, like we'd just indulged in moments before, gushing tears, or stoic silence were equally genuine responses. Teddy's was probably right in there among them. I drew my attention back to Teddy. "I think the bruising would depend upon how quickly after the impact his heart stopped. At least that's what they say on TV."

"And we all know how accurate TV is," Teddy scoffed.

"So, if someone made that wound with something like a hatchet, a super-sharp one that cut into his brain, it might have killed him quickly before it had a chance to bruise. But didn't the medical examiner say she thought he'd hit his head on a rock? That his skull was depressed? I guess I'd been thinking of it as a concave shape...like an indented sphere." I tilted my head and pursed my lips. I wasn't sure it was accurate to assume that, because a dead body wasn't bruised, it hadn't received a blow that would have created a giant hematoma in a living person. When the human heart stopped beating, blood stopped pumping. Surely, if Patrick had died as quickly as everyone seemed to believe, there'd have been little time for a bruise of any kind to form. I hesitated to say any of that to Teddy, though, because I didn't want to suggest that his dad might have lingered in pain. I struggled to think of something more innocuous to say.

"What made you so sure it was your dad?"

"His running pants." Teddy wrinkled his nose and grimaced. "They were melted in places and black from the smoke. But he was still wearing the step counter I gave him when I was, like, seven. Just a kid. I got it at a Giants game, and it was orange with the logo on it. They gave out thousands of them."

"He must have loved it," I said. "Not only because it was a collector's item, but because you gave it to him. I can't tell you how many trackers like that Max and I have sent through the wash or lost. Your dad must have taken exceptional care of that one because it was a gift from you."

Teddy smiled and fell silent. No one spoke for the remainder of the drive home.

But as Tess's house came into view, I gasped. A Santa Clara County sheriff's car had pulled onto the front lawn with its lights flashing. News vans were back in full force, ready to film what was sure to be the top story on this evening's local news with teasers played incessantly throughout the day.

Chapter 12

Fire safety precautions differ depending on geography and style of home. National campaigns for home fire safety are held in October, which is a good time to brush up on all your safety programs. Similar programs for wildfire preparation begin in May. Need a personalized checkup to help a family member part with an accumulation of stuff? Contact a professional organizer or your local fire department.

From the Notebook of Maggie McDonald
Simplicity Itself Organizing Services

Monday, August 7, Afternoon

Sheriff's Sergeant Nguyen read Tess her rights. She barely had time to give Teddy a quick kiss, a hug, and her assurance that everything would be okay before deputies hustled her into the back seat of a squad car and sped away. The rest of us made an effort to stand between the cameras and Tess, but I doubted we'd shielded her completely.

I phoned Forrest, who promised to meet her at the county jail and do his best to get her out as quickly as possible.

Jason confirmed that the district attorney's office planned to charge Tess with first-degree murder sometime during the next forty-eight hours. "I suspect they may add additional felony counts, so the death penalty comes into play," he said, as though he was merely thinking aloud. "They do that to coax confessions and plea deals."

Teddy turned pale, moaned, and swayed a bit before Max caught hold of his shoulders and steadied him physically, if not emotionally. Jason's face filled with horror. "Teddy, I'm so sorry. I should not have been speculating. Let's go inside. I'll fill you in." He turned to me. "Get him a soda with plenty of sugar. If they don't have that, then juice or some other quick-energy food."

Jason was in full-on command mode. I jumped to do his bidding. Teddy needed shoring up, inside and out. As I dashed to the fridge, I heard Jason ask, "Teddy, when did you last eat? Never mind. It doesn't matter."

Brian and David were next in the spotlight. "Get your friend some food, then join us if you want. Food first, though."

I sensed that Jason was giving us all jobs to steady us, especially the boys. Their faces mirrored the terror in Teddy's, though I wasn't sure whether they empathized with his pain or if they were coming to grips with the fact that Teddy had effectively lost both of his parents in the last two days. I glanced at Max, and he nodded. Soon, if not right away, we needed to make sure our boys understood the extensive preparations we had in place to care for them should the unthinkable happen and the two of us were no longer around. They needed to know that people, money, and resources would kick in to help them at a moment's notice. That was our job as parents. To make our children feel safe, no matter what. Going into this weekend, Max and I had thought the fire was the only thing we had to fear and protect them from. But since then, the stakes had grown so much higher, threatening not just Tess, but Teddy, our two boys, and life as we knew it in Orchard View. If our town and neighborhood was one in which someone who knew the affable Patrick Olmos could cold-bloodedly kill him, would it ever again feel like a safe place to live and raise our children?

Tess often seemed stern, but she was a marshmallow on the inside, willing to drop everything to help her family, a client, a neighbor, a friend, or even a needy stranger. If someone like Tess could be arrested for murder, what did that say about our town and our sense of safety? Deputies had bundled Tess into a squad car and destroyed what was left of Teddy's tattered sense of security. And Jason, chief of the Orchard View Police Force, had let it happen, right under his nose. Jason hadn't had any choice, but Teddy was a white, upper-middle-class suburban kid with the often-overlooked blessing and privilege of expecting law enforcement to serve and protect. That trust had been breached, possibly forever.

I made up my mind. Anyone who put that look of terror and abandonment on a child's face, who destroyed his world and forced him to grow up prematurely, must face the full wrath of the justice system. I would see to it. I'm not a vigilante. I believe in the rule of law and that it's the purview of the courts to pass sentences on criminals. But I also think that sometimes, law enforcement and our legal system could use a bit of a helping hand in the form of background information available only to insiders. And that insider would be me—with a little help from my friends.

Jason filled us in as Teddy sipped at a red can of soda that was also bringing color back into his cheeks.

"After the sergeant and sheriff's deputies left this morning, they obtained another warrant for the shed out back. There they found a pickax—one of those tools that looks like a pick on one end and a sharp hoe on the other, stashed in the shed. It was one of the tools the medical examiner had suggested might have injured your dad. It was missing from the garage." Jason spoke quietly to Teddy, but the rest of us strained to hear every word.

It would have been an easy matter for the detectives to determine what tools were missing from the garage. Patrick was compulsively organized. He'd installed a pegboard and positioned his tools on specialized hooks. Using a technique perfected by Julia Child for her kitchen implements, he'd outlined the silhouette of each tool with a thick permanent marker. Anyone, including the sheriff's deputies, could tell at a glance whether a tool was missing or misplaced.

"They didn't have the paperwork required to search the shed on their first visit, but when they returned—" Jason began.

"No no no," Teddy interrupted. "It's my fault." He shook his head and buried his face in his hands. "Mom had nothing to do with it. My fingerprints will be on it." Brian and David looked to me for an explanation of what was happening. I patted the air, signaling that they should back off and calm down. We'd have to wait to see how this played out. Was Teddy confessing? But why? And how? Hadn't he been home in bed when the murder occurred? Could he prove it? If he hadn't been asleep, how could he have made his way up the ridge on his own? He couldn't drive, and it was a tough climb on a bicycle.

"Teddy," Jason said. "What can you tell me about that pickax? Why was it in the shed instead of in its place in the garage?"

Teddy uttered a noise that sounded more like that of a caged and injured animal than a teenaged boy. He cleared his throat and reached for his soda, taking another brief sip as the rest of us waited, silently begging him to speak.

"It's got blood on it too." Jason's face remained expressionless, but the muscles in his face rippled as his jaw clenched. He waited for Teddy to say more.

"I got this big idea last weekend to redo the back garden. Mom had let it dry up during the drought, and she's been complaining about it. Dad planned to prepare the soil, but he hadn't gotten around to it." Teddy swallowed hard, and I took a moment to realize that Patrick never would get to the garden he'd wanted to plant for his wife.

"She's been spending a lot of time with her clients, so after our cross-country workout Saturday morning, I got a start on it. It was grueling, worse than any workout Dad's had me do at the gym. I couldn't break up the soil. Not for the life of me."

Jason smiled. "Adobe soil made great bricks and floors for the early settlers, but it makes terrible gardens. It's like concrete. There are some tricks, though, and I'll show them to you tomorrow. I bet we can get that flower bed fixed up so it will be the garden of her dreams when your mom gets back."

I wasn't sure whether Jason was indulging in a police technique to help Teddy relax into saying more, or whether his words were genuine and meant to comfort. Knowing Jason, it was probably a combination of the two. "But what about the blood?" Jason asked Teddy.

"It was stupid. Dad warned me not to garden in my bare feet, but..." Teddy bit his lip and stared at his feet. He'd kicked off his sneakers when he entered the house. His white crew socks were crusty and brown at the toe. I wondered when he'd last thought to change them. "The pickax slipped and slammed into my toe. It hurt like—well, toes aren't nearly as hard as that stupid clay."

"Is that why you were limping at track practice?" Brian asked.

Teddy frowned. "You noticed? I was sure I could hide the pain so no one would know. It was so stupid."

Brian beamed. "Busted."

Teddy grinned back.

Jason lifted his chin in the direction of Teddy's less-than-hygienic socks. "Can I take a look? You take off the socks, though. I'm not touching 'em."

Teddy complied, and Jason knelt to examine his toe. "That's nasty. You did it when?"

"Saturday morning."

"Too late for stitches, then. But I prescribe a bath with plenty of soap and soaking for that wound. After you're clean and dressed, maybe Maggie can check it out and get it bandaged up for you. I've got emergency medical training, but I'd feel better if it got signed off by a mom. If we can't get the cut cleaned out, we might have to take you to the ER. You up-to-date on tetanus shots?"

Teddy, Brian, and David grabbed for their upper arms and winced. "We needed them for the cross-country team," David said. "You never know what you might step on."

Jason nodded approvingly. "Bath. Now." Teddy set down the can of soda and obeyed, limping visibly now that his injured toe had been outed.

Jason made a show of sniffing the air, made a V with his fingers, and pointed them at Brian and David. "Showers for the two of you too. Take turns. No fighting. Master bath. Now."

I stared at Jason in awe as Brian and David did his bidding without complaint. "What?" he said, feigning confusion. "I was a teenaged boy once. I get it. Is it possible for them to have too many showers? Did they even take them earlier? Chances are, they forgot." He dropped his voice to a whisper. "It will give us a chance to talk without worrying them. But first, I need to let Forrest know about the blood, the pickax, and the explanation for it. It may help us to get Tess home faster."

His optimism cheered me. But I hadn't reckoned with the momentum a murder investigation gains when a solution is at hand. Nor how easily evidence can be made to fit a proposed scenario once a suspect is in custody.

Chapter 13

Batteries and a hand-cranked radio are nearly always included on lists of materials to include in your evacuation or shelter-in-place kit. But in today's world, when we rely so heavily on our cell phones, I'd also recommend a car charger, extra cables, and a backup power source in case your battery dies when the power is out.

From the Notebook of Maggie McDonald
Simplicity Itself Organizing Services

Monday, August 7, Early evening

While Jason talked to Forrest and took calls from his men, I phoned Elaine and invited her to dinner. When she asked what she could bring, I didn't hesitate. "No food. Everyone brought casseroles last night, and the fridge is bursting. We've got enough zucchini and tomatoes to feed a regiment. Can you bring over whatever tools you have that might be useful in breaking up soil for a garden? I'll explain later, but Jason wants to show the boys how to prep a flower garden."

"Jason? Jason Mueller? *Our* Jason?" She laughed. "When the eighth graders had to grow plants for biology, Jason's died. He got a second chance, and that seedling died. When an enterprising group of students began selling home-grown weed, he was the one kid I didn't suspect."

I'd temporarily forgotten that Elaine had been a teacher, and then the principal, when Jason, Patrick, and Max had been in middle school. Her stories were a source of great hilarity for Teddy, Brian, and David.

I whipped up a quick dinner of spaghetti and salad, using up most of the tomatoes that had been left on the porch and a huge handful of fresh basil that had somehow survived in Tess's drought-ravaged garden. Elaine arrived as Max was setting the table, pouring wine, and not-so-surreptitiously sampling the desserts the neighbors had left.

Keeping busy seemed to be helping all of us tamp down our worries, though every time I heard a car drive up the street, I peeked through the front window hoping it was Forrest, bringing Tess home.

But by the time we sat down to dinner, we had to face the reality of Tess's empty chair. Jason made a noble effort to distract us as he dug into his spaghetti. "This is amazing, Maggie. A treat. Fresh basil and tomatoes?"

I jerked my thoughts away from Tess, but I must have taken too long to respond. Jason glanced at each of us in turn, then spoke firmly. "Look, everyone, we have to eat. How would your mom feel, Teddy, if she came home tonight and found us dead from starvation? She'd kill each of us all over again, I'm sure. Slowly, painfully..." Teddy picked up his fork, twirled it in his spaghetti, then put it down. "Have you heard anything from Forrest? Er, Mr. Doucett?"

Jason held up one finger as he finished chewing a crusty heel of piping-hot sourdough slathered with butter. "Does everyone want an update? Otherwise, I can debrief Teddy separately..."

Elaine, seated next to Jason, gave him a little shove, and noises of protest came from every other person at the table. Of course we all wanted to know.

Jason thought for a moment, earning him another round of protests. "Sorry. I'm not trying to add suspense. I'm organizing my thoughts. There are two questions I think we need to answer. First, why did they arrest Tess? Second, how soon can we bring her home?"

Teddy grabbed the back of his neck. The tension was damaging more than his appetite and mood, poor kid. And it was contagious. I tilted my head and rolled my shoulders to ease cramped muscles.

Jason cleared his throat. "Max, you wanna take notes? Get me back on track if I get lost." Max sat in the corner of the table near the windows, blocked in by Teddy and our boys. I hopped up and rummaged through Tess's kitchen drawers until I located a pad and pen. I handed them to Max.

"The sheriff's deputies cast a wide net to track down Patrick's killer. That's important. Teddy, they aren't targeting your mom. Television dramas often have us believing that they always look at the person closest to the victim. Some nincompoops from the neighborhood were going on about that the other night. But that's not true, and it's no way to run an investigation. Sergeant Nguyen knows that." Jason polished off a glass of iced tea, and I held up a pitcher of water. He pointed toward Max's beer bottle and raised his eyebrows. After I handed over a frosty bottle I'd pulled from the fridge, he continued. He spoke slowly but firmly, and his take-charge attitude seemed to soothe the boys, each of whom had managed a few bites of their dinner. I leaned forward with my elbows resting on the table, neglecting my own meal to hear every word Jason uttered.

"They've got teams interviewing neighbors, friends, coworkers, members of his running club, parents and kids from the high school cross-country team." David, Brian, Max, and I looked at one another, confused. No one had questioned us, though Max and I often drove kids to races and practice and Brian and David were both on the team.

Jason cleared his throat and regained our attention. "Apparently, people from more than one of those groups informed them that Tess and Patrick were separated and that they fought all the time. At least one person said that Patrick was having an affair, and was thinking of moving out of state with his lover, taking Teddy with him."

I gasped and pushed my chair back, only half-aware of the protests everyone else was making. Teddy flushed and his fists clenched. Jason placed the flat of his hand on the table next to Teddy without touching him. "Look, I understand what you're all saying. I know about Patrick's apartment..."

We *all* knew about the family's unusual living situation. Tess and Patrick had maintained mostly separate households since early on in their marriage. But they weren't separated. Patrick often spent weeks on end at the house, and Tess and Teddy sometimes slept at the apartment, particularly in the summer, when they could take advantage of its air-conditioning and pool. The fact of the matter was that Tess, at home, was a bit of a slob. Her home was clean but messy and cluttered. The kitchen cupboard doors were often open, there was toothpaste in the sink, and clean but unfolded laundry often covered their sofa. Empty iced tea glasses were often left out. Breakfast dishes didn't make it from the table to the kitchen. Patrick, on the other hand, had drawn the outlines in the garage indicating where each tool should be returned after undergoing a thorough cleaning and oiling to prevent rust. He folded towels before returning them to the towel racks, sorted his dirty clothing by color, and promptly picked up anything he found on the floor and returned it to its proper location. Much of the time, the couple's love for one another and their son could overcome the differences in their personalities and housekeeping habits, but when they found themselves overstressed by the pace of Silicon Valley living, they expressed their love by escaping to their own spaces. Patrick and Tess would be the first to pronounce the arrangement weird, but it was an experiment they claimed had saved their marriage. And no one who knew them could argue with that.

"Tess explained that to Sergeant Nguyen, as did Stephen and I when he interviewed us. Forrest will go over that with them too." Jason reassured us, but I still wondered who knew about the intricacies of the couple's marriage and felt compelled to present it as a conflict between them. I wrote a note on my pad to follow up on that line of investigation. If we could discover who'd tipped off Sergeant Nguyen, we might find someone who held a grudge against Tess or Patrick. But would that lead us to a killer? Pauline Windsor, for example? I shook my head. Pauline was too self-centered. I doubted she'd leave her enormous and comfortable home in the middle of the night for anyone. Was a workplace conflict behind the murder? No one was more competitive than Tess. Could one of her colleagues think she'd muscled in on a sale they felt was rightfully theirs? Silicon Valley real estate had the highest stakes imaginable. And where money was concerned, tempers ran hot.

"That's garbage," Teddy spoke through clenched teeth. "Who said that?"

Jason shook his head and continued to explain. "Sergeant Nguyen didn't tell me where he'd heard that stuff about your mom and dad's relationship. And honestly, right now, I don't think he gives it much credence. He may have arrested your mom following pressure from top brass at the county. It's an election year." Jason rolled his eyes. "Nguyen seems professional. He's impressed by the number of loyal friends your family has in the community and was a little afraid that if he gave me names, he'd have a vigilante nightmare on his hands."

Max scoffed. "Orchard View is not the Wild West, and this isn't the nineteenth century."

"Nguyen knows that," Jason said. "The prosecuting attorney will have to turn over any evidence they have to Forrest's team, if we get that far. Let's wait and see what Forrest accomplished today. The summation of the evidence I already know about is that someone, probably with their own agenda, has cast doubt on Tess's story. A pickax that could be the murder weapon was 'hidden'" —Jason held up two fingers of each hand to make air quotes as he spoke the word— "in the shed. And Tess does not have anyone who can corroborate her whereabouts for the window of time in which Patrick might have been attacked."

"That makes no sense," Teddy said. "There was plenty of time for my mom to get rid of that tool after Sergeant Nguyen left. If, that is, she even knew it existed." He shook his head. Tess rarely had time for or interest in gardening.

"Jason, you said Patrick *might* have been attacked?" I asked. "I thought the sheriff's office confirmed it was murder?"

Jason took a long swig of beer. "You're too sharp. This conversation is worse than any press conference I've held since I became chief." He turned toward me. "You're right, officials have confirmed it was a homicide. What they're not sure of is whether Patrick was attacked and later died from his injuries, or whether the blow that killed him was simultaneous with his death."

Jason's face softened as he focused on Teddy. "You doin' okay, bud? This is stuff no son ever wants to hear about their dad."

"You've already told us that people are saying my dad cheated on my mom. I know he's dead and that someone murdered him. How can it get worse?"

"Right," Jason said. "But if you need a break..." He peered at the rest of us. "Or if anyone else does, say the word. This is tough stuff. Even the most hard-boiled detectives need to take time-outs. There's no shame in that."

"What's the story on when Tess is coming home?" I asked, shifting the subject away from the details of Patrick's death to focus on a more positive topic.

"We can't be sure," Jason said. "Forrest said we should be prepared to have them keep her at least overnight. Maybe forty-eight hours. But then she has to have an arraignment hearing, at which the judge will decide whether there is sufficient evidence to charge her. If he decides to go ahead, he'll set bail or hold her over for trial without bail—"

I interrupted. "And what are the chances of that?"

Jason's brow furrowed. "For her to be held without bail, you mean? Tess has no record. Forrest will argue against locking her up for the lengthy period that's required to prepare a murder trial. That would essentially leave Teddy an orphan, which is cruel and unusual punishment for both Tess and Teddy, neither of whom has been convicted of anything. But what I think may not be the same as what a judge will decide."

Max leaned forward. "Forrest is good," he said with a half shrug that gave me the impression he considered Tess as good as released already. "And if she needs help getting the bail money together, we'll pitch in." We all nodded so enthusiastically we resembled a line of bobbleheads, and I laughed in spite of my worries.

"Is there anything more we can do to help?" Elaine asked. "Anything besides looking after Teddy and each other, I mean? I know the neighborhood. Max and Maggie know the team parents—"

Max interrupted, "I know a number of the people Patrick worked with. I'll keep an ear to the ground in the tech sector—"

"And we can keep an eye on social media," David added, lifting his chin to include Brian and Teddy.

Jason rubbed his chin, considering David's words carefully. "I want to talk about that. Tess reminded me about that web page you saw accusing her of the murder."

"Can you get them to quit it?" Teddy asked.

"Definitely, once we find out who's behind it. I want to know what motivated them to put it up in the first place, how they heard about Patrick's death, and where they found the photos. As dreadful as the page made Teddy and all of us feel, it may prove to be an important clue to locating someone who wanted to hurt Patrick. Can you take a look at the page again and tell me if you know where any of the images originated? Or if the words sound like something written by anyone you know? Or if they emulate language from a television show that a lot of the kids at school watch? I'm trying to determine whether setting up this web page was a bratty kid stunt, a stupid adult thing, or something more organized and sinister."

I watched as Brian turned to David and mouthed a name. I thought it was *"Rebecca,"* and I was about to question them, but then Teddy spoke, and I forgot about the website. His expression turned dark. "Wait, I thought of someone else," he said. "Someone who *seriously* wished Dad would disappear."

Chapter 14

How much is enough? Experts recommend stocking a three-day supply of food and essential items in your emergency evacuation kit. If you plan to shelter-in-place, they suggest stocking at least a two-week supply of essential items.

From the Notebook of Maggie McDonald
Simplicity Itself Organizing Services

Monday, August 7, Evening

Teddy had our attention, and my pen was poised to take notes. But then he hesitated. "I don't know. I don't like to say bad things about people without proof, but this guy..." He shook his head.

Elaine jumped in. "Teddy, it's important to uncover the truth. If someone is responsible for your father's death, we need to find out. And if he's not, I'm sure he'll still want to help the investigation in any way he can. It's essential we tell the police our suspicions, all of them, no matter how tenuous the connections." She spoke confidently, but turned to Jason for further confirmation.

"Elaine's right," Jason said. "There's a vast difference between tattling or gossiping and providing the police with a lead. We handle interviews with considerable delicacy." He *tsk*ed. "Those police dramas you see on television? The ones with the table pounding and chair flinging, and throwing suspects to the ground? I've never done that. Speaking softly in a conversational tone and requesting help seems to work pretty well, even with the toughest crooks."

"Okay, well, there's this guy," Teddy said. "He works with my mom. She calls him her assistant, but he acts like he's her partner..." Teddy's voice trailed off, and he shook his head. "I don't know why I don't trust him. If I say that he dresses too fashionably and works long hours, he doesn't sound so bad. But there's something..."

"His name?" Jason asked.

"Robert Wu."

"I can reach him at your mom's office number?"

Teddy nodded. "Mom defended him, saying he had a savvy business sense, especially when it came to the big investors from Taiwan and mainland China. But"—he shuddered—"he seemed kinda..."

"Smarmy?" I suggested.

Teddy bit his lip. "What's that? Shady? Or slimy?"

I looked to my boys to translate. They spoke both "mom" and "teen." Their eyes twinkled as they agreed with Teddy's suggested synonyms.

"My dad didn't trust him, either. Robert needed to be the smartest dude in the room and he put my mom down. A few weeks ago, I heard her speaking to him on the phone, using her super-polite voice—the one she uses when she's really mad." He looked up to see if any of us knew what he meant. I certainly did. Her polite voice made me sit up straight, even when she was using it on someone else.

"Do you know what the argument was about?" Jason asked.

"No, but he always called at night—not *late* late, but later than most people think is okay. He'd want my mom to show a house or talk about this book he wanted them to write to 'strengthen their brand,' whatever that means. Dad thought Robert would be a lot happier if my mom was childless and unmarried."

"He thought Robert had personal designs on your mom?" Jason chose his words carefully, but made it clear that the answer was important.

"Did I think he was hitting on her? Definitely." Teddy cleared his throat and turned away from Jason.

"Was your mom interested?"

"Gross!" Teddy leaned back in his chair, held up his hands in a gesture that said, "*That's enough.*" His face would have matched the color of a stop sign if he'd held one.

"Sorry, but I had to ask."

"I get it," Teddy said, ducking his head.

Jason focused on the rest of us. "I'm not sure any of you understand completely. Maggie's been tangentially involved in some murder cases before, but none of you have been this close to it. Teddy's going to need every ounce of protection and emotional support you can muster." Jason's face showed pain and apprehension and convinced me he spoke from vast experience.

"I'm fine," Teddy said, his voice defensive.

"Hear me out," Jason said. "I know that you're strong, capable, smart, coolheaded, and mature. But you don't know what's coming. If you thought that website was cruel, it's nothing like the questions that will come, the things you'll hear about your parents, and the statements otherwise well-meaning people will make in front of you. There are lots of cops who can't work homicide—not because of the grisly scenes, but because of what the investigations do to families and entire communities. A good investigator paws through the most personal details of lives that aren't as stable as the one you have with your family. We dredge up old hurts and forgotten wounds. I want you to know that it's going to be bad so that you don't feel like you're failing somehow if you find it difficult to handle. I need you to know that I'm on your side, and so is everyone else. Call one of us before the pressure gets to be too much. I don't care what time it is or what day it is. You call me, and I'll answer. Got that?"

Teddy nodded.

"You sure? This is your most important job right now."

"Does that mean I can skip track practice?"

"Nice try." Jason's smile reflected Teddy's, and the teen's shoulders relaxed. I felt mine do the same. If Teddy was comfortable enough to trade banter with Jason, he'd likely be able to ask for whatever help he needed.

As quickly as the atmosphere lightened, however, it plummeted again. This time, it was my youngest son whose voice broke hesitantly through the laughter. "There's someone else you should look at…" Brian began.

I wasn't sure how I felt about the kids coming up with the first real suspects. I'd found that adolescents had a finely tuned sense of justice and were more reliable than any lie detector at smoking out an adult who was skirting the truth. Were the rest of us naïve? Inattentive? Or had we failed to consider the secrets of some of our closest neighbors?

"His partner, Katherine."

"Partner, as in business?" asked Jason.

"No. No. His running partner. She treated him like he was supposed to be her coach or something."

"But how do you know her?" I asked, examining David and Teddy to measure how they felt about Brian's suggestion and whether they knew Katherine.

David leaned forward. "Bri's right. There was something weird about her. Like, she'd join us on team training runs, but act like we were crowding her time with Patrick."

"Is that normal? For adults to join student practices?" I wasn't sure how I felt about that. The twenty-four-hour news cycle, being friends with law enforcement, and having kids of my own made me hyperaware of the dangers of child predators.

Brian shrugged. "It's not like Rancho San Antonio is private property. It's a heavily used public park. Tons of runners train at the same time we do. They aren't necessarily working out *with* us."

"After school? During the workday?" I heard a little too much alarm in my voice, so I leaned back in my chair, took a sip of water, and tried to dial it back. Jason saved me by jumping into the discussion.

"Tell us more about Katherine. How did Patrick meet her?"

"Work, maybe, or the running club?" Teddy said, referring to the Orchard View Road Runners, of which Patrick had been a founding member. It was a loosely organized group intended to provide safety and companionship for runners of varied abilities after they'd left organized scholastic sports behind. Patrick and some other members of the Stanford team had pulled the group together upon graduation. They'd picked up additional members over the years through work connections and word of mouth. Patrick and some of the other athletes competed in masters races from time to time, but it was primarily a fitness and recreational group. I saw their team jerseys frequently when I was running errands around town.

"Women join for safety reasons," Jason said. "They feel more secure if they're running in groups, particularly in the more remote areas."

"But Katherine—" David hesitated, but continued after Brian and Teddy leaned forward to urge him along. "She always ran next to Patrick, even if he was obviously coaching someone from the team, which was, like, his job when he was with us, right? Once, he and Teddy were trying to work out some schedule conflict, and she edged herself right into the conversation."

Teddy snorted. "We call her the 'ghost' because she wears super-thick sunscreen. The mineral stuff with zinc. I think she'd had skin cancer. All those scars, right?"

"Like, when Emily wears it, it's cool, right?" David said, waving his hand in front of his face. "With the colors, like face paint. But on Katherine, it was just—weird." Emily's name was coming up in conversation around our house more and more frequently. I'd have to ask Tess if she knew anything about her. Parents like Tess, who'd lived in the area all her life, knew so many kids from sports, Mommy and Me classes, preschool, and every year of elementary school. To learn as much as those parents already knew about the local kids and local customs, I'd have to be more than a helicopter parent. I'd need to be tethered to my kids 24/7—not something any of us was striving for.

Jason pulled my attention back to the matter at hand. "Is she married?"

"Emily?" asked David, his face flushing.

"No, Katherine," Jason said. The kids looked at each other with eyebrows raised, communicating telepathically, or at least on a wavelength inaudible to adults. They conferred aloud, but their words were muffled. Finally, they shrugged as one and David spoke. "Maybe. There was a guy we saw pick her up sometimes. He had a van with one of those super-cool wheelchair lifts." David had a fascination with anything mechanical, and with the clever adaptations that made life easier for people who might otherwise consider themselves disabled.

"We saw her with this other person too. An older lady with white hair. Kinda round. Short."

"Do you know the names of either of these people?" Jason made a note with a stubby pencil in a dog-eared notebook that harkened back to the days of the early TV detectives, like Columbo and Sergeant Joe Friday from *Dragnet*.

The boys shook their heads, but Brian then sheepishly added, "We called them Mr. and Mrs. Claus."

"Don't worry. We'll find their names. And you've given us more information than we had a few minutes ago. But...why do you think we should look into Katherine?"

David seemed to have been silently appointed the group's spokesperson. "There was something off. Like, she wanted Patrick to herself. She got antsy when he talked to anyone else, and especially tense when both Patrick and the wheelchair guy were around at the same time." He waved his hand in the air as if waiting to be called on in class. "Sean. His name was Sean. Sean Philips. And her last name was McNamara or something. If they were married, they had different last names. He was old too. Older than Katherine."

"Way older," added Brian. "More like Mrs. Claus's age. Maybe he's married to her?"

I glanced at Max, and we communicated silently in our own way. It was time to get the boys moving. Jason was adept at reading subtle cues and must have agreed with us. "You guys want to go for a run? You missed your training last night and this morning." He glanced at me for confirmation. "I'll go with you, if it's okay with your mom. Just to make sure you don't get waylaid by gossipy neighbors or news vans. We'll take the dogs."

So much for my hope to get us moved back home today. One more night at Tess's house was in order. The boys leaped up from the table. "Dishes," I prompted, and they gathered up their plates and silverware before bumping and caroming down the hall to get their gear together. Tomorrow, I promised myself, we'd move this herd back up the hill to our house, where we'd have more space and freedom from the news crews.

Max had gotten a great start on the dishes by the time the boys came out and stood on one foot or the other as they tied their running shoes. "When you get back, get your stuff together, and we'll load up what we can. Tomorrow you can sleep in your own beds." He reached out an arm to encircle Teddy. "Maggie and I will act as your mom and dad for as long as you need us to be. You and Mozart can crash in the third-floor suite if you want. Or in Brian or David's room. But you're coming with us, no matter what, so you pack up your gear too, okay?"

Teddy's face revealed a series of expressions, showing he was grateful, embarrassed, reassured, and fearful about how long the situation might last.

Brian, as usual, broke the tension. "Great. Just what every teenager begs for. More parental supervision." His goofy face and melodramatic sigh made us all laugh. Jason ushered the boys out the door, and they stretched in the front yard. The sound of their friendly banter and the slap of their shoes on the pavement began loudly and then faded in the distance.

I turned to Elaine and Max. "Let's look at that list of suspects," I said. "I've got a plan."

Chapter 15

If you have children who'll need to be picked up from a school, camp, or day care, be sure you know each organization's identification requirements. In the chaos surrounding an emergency situation, volunteers may be told to rigorously enforce rules. And those volunteers may not recognize you or your children.

From the Notebook of Maggie McDonald
Simplicity Itself Organizing Services

Tuesday, August 8, Morning

A perfectly organized plan is no match for the reality of modern life. The night before, I'd hoped to divvy up our growing list of suspects, sharing the names and investigating responsibilities with Max and Elaine. In the end, the list and task of delving into the background of the people we'd identified as possible culprits was all mine. Today, Elaine would be held captive awaiting service on her aging air conditioner, so she agreed to comb through cyberspace gathering as much information as she could from the comfort of her own home.

Max was in charge of our move back home. I hesitated to drive one of the cars to begin my investigation. Without the extra hauling capacity of my SUV, I feared it would take far too many trips to transfer all of our belongings and everything that Teddy would need to feel at home. Max reminded me that he and the boys were perfectly capable of completing the job without my help. The Olmos cats had suffered enough disruption, and would remain in their own house, where Elaine would check on them daily. The boys and the dogs might be a tad squished in Max's car, but the journey between Tess's house and ours was only a few miles, and they'd all be fine.

Eventually, Max convinced me. I waved good-bye and set off. Robert Wu, Tess's purported second-in-command, was first up on my interview list. I decided to drive to the real estate office directly, rather than speaking to Robert over the phone. In my experience, most people found it tricky to say no in person.

Tess had given me a tour of her building a year ago, soon after we moved to Orchard View. She'd bought the property about ten years earlier. Originally built in the 1920s, it was centrally located downtown with plenty of nearby parking. While the working aspects of the building, including plumbing, electricity, and connectivity, were twenty-first century, the ambience was stable, comfortable, old-school California, designed to project an air of tranquility and comfort. I parked about two doors down and walked past a children's bookstore and a jeweler toward the real estate building.

As I entered a peaceful courtyard, a young Asian man with one foot out the front door shouted instructions at someone inside. He let the door swing closed behind him, lifted the strap of his computer bag to his shoulders, and took a step forward before he noticed me and stopped abruptly.

"Sorry!" I apologized for startling him. "Mr. Wu? Robert Wu? Tess Olmos's colleague?" That last word came out with a bit of a squeak I hoped wasn't noticeable. I'd started to say "assistant," but based on what Teddy had told us, that might put Robert on the defensive before I even began. "Colleague" was a more neutral word.

Robert smiled widely, stepped forward, and held out his hand, looking down at me from the raised redwood deck one step up from the courtyard. "Good morning, Ms.—"

"McDonald. Maggie McDonald. A friend of Tess's and the Olmos family. Do you have a moment?" I glanced around the courtyard. A fountain tiled in cobalt blue and yellow Italian ceramic bubbled quietly with what a sign identified as recycled water. Lavender, rosemary, and other drought-tolerant plants filled beds that surrounded the courtyard, while two of the corners sported cushioned garden chairs and low tables that seemed to invite conversation and relaxation. Tess had intended that her clients feel at home from the moment they decided to consult her.

I lifted my chin toward the nearest seating area, where a paperback book, coffeepot, and mug gave the impression that someone had stepped away moments earlier.

Robert scoffed, shifted his computer bag, and held out his right hand. "That's staging. Tess's idea. Let's step inside, and I'll see what I can do to help. Are you interested in listing a local home? Trading up?" His eyes were shining, and he stepped closer to me. Too close. It was a demonstration of the type of behavior that Teddy had struggled to describe. And no wonder. It was a creepy combination of avarice, unwanted sexual attention, superiority, and condescension. I squelched my desire to kick him in the shins, or worse, and looked up in what I hoped was a disarming fashion.

He opened the door and invited me inside, where the décor continued the theme of a welcoming home. The room was appointed with wood flooring, a Persian rug, and two soft beige armchairs that sat in front of a white reception counter trimmed with crown molding.

Robert nodded to the receptionist. I smiled and took a half step forward. The receptionist shook her head slightly and examined the desktop. I knew her well. She'd been a guest in my home, and I'd been present at the birth of her son. I felt hurt and confused by her apparent snub, but I honored Ketifa's wishes. I winked at her and gave her a look that I hoped communicated something along the lines of *"What's up? We'll catch up later, yeah?"*

Robert ushered me toward a comfortable arrangement of sofas and chairs surrounded by glassed-in conference rooms. Stairs to the left rose to what I knew to be the heart of the business's operations, where phones, computers, and printers hummed, and agents worked in banks of modular desks designed for efficiency and ease of use. Clients never saw the upper floor, which was as streamlined as the downstairs was homey. But it reflected the needs of agents who needed to plug in, meet colleagues, and make calls.

"Can I get you some coffee? A latte? Biscotti?" Robert examined his fingernails. Without waiting for an answer, he shouted to Ketifa, "Kitty! Coffee service for two." He sat without adding a please or thank-you to his request.

"Kitty"? Was Ketifa now using a nickname? It seemed so unlike the Ketifa I knew...

"How can I help? We're the premiere—" Robert's question tugged me away from my focus on my friend.

I chose a seat on a taupe sofa. "No. No. I love my house and have no plans to move. I'm here about Tess."

Robert frowned and pushed at his cuticles with a fingernail, then smiled using as few facial muscles as possible. No wonder Teddy had sensed friction between his mom and Robert. Tess had built a successful business focused on providing stellar service to her clients and the community. Being a good neighbor was good business in her book. And it had paid off. Neighbors who'd once asked her advice regarding home repairs, for example, often turned to her when it was time to sell.

That service-focused notion was apparently one Robert had yet to master, or that he'd learned and discarded now that Tess was temporarily out of the picture. I'd already learned so much about this guy, and I had yet to ask him a question. It seemed my interview was off to a roaring start.

"You said you were a friend of the family." Robert brushed invisible lint from his thigh. "So you know that she's been arrested and is in jail." He failed to hide a smirk. "Please tell Tess that I've got everything under control here. I'm handling her clients and mine, and was actually on my way to meet up with a prospective seller." He lowered his voice. "One of those dot-com guys up in the hills. He's taken up flying and wants to move to Atherton, closer to the Palo Alto Airport. I'm hoping to handle both the sale and the new purchase." He didn't rub his hands together with glee, but he appeared to want to, desperately.

"I won't keep you. It's just—" Now that I was here, I wasn't sure how to begin.

"Go on. How is Tess? It's so sad. How is poor Timmy holding up?" Robert uttered all the socially acceptable words of concern for the bereaved, but he seemed more interested in fussing with a hangnail on his thumb.

"*Teddy* seems to be doing well, under the circumstances. He's upset about his father, of course. But he's confident Tess will be cleared. As I'm sure, you are. It's just these rumors—"

"Rumors?" Robert watched my face carefully, as if he feared his helpful-friend-and-colleague performance was fraying around the edges. It was.

"What have you heard?" I asked, leaning forward.

Robert rubbed his thumbnail over his bottom lip and didn't say anything for a moment, but then shrugged and mirrored my conspiratorial posture. "At one time, I feared that Patrick was getting in the way of Tess's ambitions. He seemed to have a tight hold on her schedule. I had plans for taking this business to the next level and collaborating with Tess on a book that would establish us as the experts in real estate here on the Peninsula." He patted the side of his computer bag. "I've got the outline ready to go, but Patrick thought she was already spending too much time at work. She was always reshuffling her schedule to look after Teddy whenever Patrick flaked out."

I pursed my lips and shook my head. I knew that the schedule shifting he described was a challenge for any good parent, mother or father, who was raising kids in a demanding modern world. If it wasn't a universal problem, companies like Microsoft, Apple, and Google wouldn't be making so much money on their calendar and scheduling apps.

"I take it you have no children," I said, making a supreme effort to keep the judgment out of my voice.

Robert shook his head. "No children, no spouse, no girlfriend." He smirked. "No boyfriend either, for that matter." I fisted my hands. How could Tess have put up with this smarmy know-it-all?

"I had plenty of time and energy to devote to this business and would have poured my heart into it, if Patrick hadn't discouraged Tess from capitalizing on my ideas. I never thought Tess would actually kill him. But she was frustrated. It was so sad that she had to fight her own husband for the right to pursue her dreams."

My forehead wrinkled, and no matter how hard I tried to force those muscles to relax, they insisted on telegraphing my confusion and disgust over the portrait Robert was painting of Tess's life. I soaked in the homey atmosphere of the real estate office, knowing that the décor was all Tess. There was no sign of Robert's money-grubbing input, not on this floor anyway. Perhaps his influence was more visible upstairs than down.

He waved his hand quickly. "Oh, I know that the story was they were happily married. But separate residences? Seriously? Who does that when they are 'happily married'?" He waggled his eyebrows and leered. *Ick.* "Word was, he was having an affair. And bidding for a management position at his company's outfit in Texas. He'd travel less and be able to buy a mansion for what he was paying on that tiny condo in Mountain View."

Anyone who knew Patrick would know the gossip Robert had repeated was a lie. I bristled at the negative portrait he painted of the life of my dearest friends. Luckily, Robert didn't notice. He rubbed his chin and stared into the middle distance. "She called here a lot. The girlfriend. Worked with Patrick and would relay messages for him. Now, that was weird. What kind of secret girlfriend is so brazen that she calls the wife at work?" He shook his head. "It was straight out of a steamy soap opera."

"Do you know her name?"

"Kate something. No. Katherine. Katherine McNamara. I met her once. Red hair, reed thin, pale as a sheet, and with scars." He ran his left hand over his right arm and grimaced. "Like she'd been an addict. Or one of those cutters." He made slicing motions on his forearm. "I don't know what those scars look like, but they could have been from self-harm, you know?"

I'd had enough. "So you think Tess killed Robert because of this woman?"

Robert looked shocked. "Of course not. How did you get that impression? I'm only pointing out that the circumstances fit well enough. I can understand why the police or sheriff or whoever is interested in Tess." He checked his watch. "I have to go, if there's nothing else."

I tried to retract my claws and relax the muscles of my face. "I'm sorry. I misunderstood. Can you think of anyone who might have wanted to hurt Patrick? Or at least sideline him for a while? Maybe someone who tried to get him out of the way temporarily, but it went wrong? Could killing him have been a mistake? I've heard it might have been an accident." So far, Robert had become my top candidate for the person who wanted Patrick sidelined.

He spoke so softly that it took a moment for his words to penetrate my meandering thoughts. "...think of anyone who might have been willing to hurt Tess like that. Maybe Patrick was a problem, but anyone who knew Tess knew she doted on Tim—er, Teddy. Hurting Patrick would hurt Teddy, and that meant hurting Tess too."

Rats. If Robert sincerely believed those words, that would scratch him off my list of suspects. But what if his remorse had come *after* the murder? After he'd seen the terrible impact Patrick's death had on Tess and Teddy? He could have realized how badly he'd miscalculated. I shuddered. The mind of a killer was a dark place. Not for the first time, I wondered why I was spending so much time there. I didn't entertain the question for long. I had to find Patrick's killer and free Tess. She needed to be home with Teddy. She wasn't the killer. And that meant someone else was. Someone else who deserved to face the full force of Orchard View justice.

Robert cleared his throat and examined his watch again. He stood.

Seated, I felt a disadvantage I corrected immediately by standing myself. "I'm so sorry to keep you," I said. "I was lost in my thoughts. Do you have a card? Can I call or email you if I think of any other questions?"

Robert reached for his wallet, pulled out a business card, and handed it to me in a smooth and practiced motion, then pulled it back. "But why are you asking these questions? Isn't that a job for the sheriff's office? Or the Orchard View Police? I hope they wrap this up quickly. It's terrible for property values."

Horrified by the way he was harping on money when his supposed friend and colleague was in such terrible trouble, I snatched the card from his hand and tucked it in the front pocket of my backpack. I held out my hand to shake his. "Thank you for your time. I know I'm holding you up. May I sit in in the lobby for a moment? I need to check my email and make a call before I get back behind the wheel."

Seeing a chance to make a graceful exit seemed to please Robert. He shook my hand firmly. "Please make yourself at home. That's what all this is for." He turned and extended his hand in an arc to indicate every part of what Tess called the "customer room." "Ask Kitty for anything you need. She never did bring that coffee." He made an angry *tsk*ing noise and stomped off. Just before he rounded the divider that separated the lounge area from the receptionist's desk, I thought of another question and called out his name.

Chapter 16

Cell phones and other devices may not work properly or consistently following a disaster. If you'll need a map to walk or drive to safety, stash a paper one in your emergency kit and glove box.

From the Notebook of Maggie McDonald
Simplicity Itself Organizing Services

Tuesday, August 8, Morning

"Robert, sorry. Wait. I don't suppose you can provide Tess with an alibi, can you? Were you working with her either Saturday night or Sunday morning?"

Robert flushed, though I had no idea why. My question wasn't embarrassing. Of course, I was really asking for *his* alibi, but I'd couched the query in a way that concealed my objectives—at least I hoped it did. I waited for an answer without speaking.

"Er, I was working all weekend. Showing houses, making phone calls. When I wasn't with clients, I was at home. I don't think I saw Tess. Kitty would know. She keeps my schedule and my charge sheet." He turned without waiting for a response.

After I could no longer see him beyond the partition, I could still hear the angry, dismissive tone he was using to berate Ketifa for, I assumed, being late with the coffee. The *thud* of a palm on glass followed, indicating he'd used far more force than necessary to open the door, and he'd almost certainly left a handprint marring the otherwise spotless door.

I decided to check in with Elaine and was rummaging in my backpack for my phone when Ketifa appeared from behind the divider with a tray containing two steaming mugs and a plate of what looked like handcrafted biscotti.

"Do you mind if I join you?" she asked. "My neighbor makes these, and they're gastronomical." She tilted her head. "Somedays I don't feel like sharing them with...him." She cleared her throat. "I'm sorry. I couldn't help but overhear his nonsense about Tess. I was steaming. Withholding biscotti is as petty as it comes, and I'm not proud of it. But, here." She set the plate on the coffee table and pushed it toward me. "I don't mind sharing with you."

Ketifa was twenty, but she was wise beyond her years and she lived in a galaxy distant from Robert's self-centered worldview.

I hugged her, then held her at arm's length. "You look strong, fit, and rested. Not like a new mother at all. How are you? And how is baby Sabih? You have pictures, I'm sure."

Ketifa whipped out her phone and showed me photos of her seven-month-old son, who exuded intelligence, energy, humor, and health. Which meant, I knew, that he'd be a handful for any young mother, particularly one who was far from home and alone. Her husband was missing in action, but not by choice. Army investigators believed he'd been wounded and captured in the confusion following an air strike in Nangarhar Province near Jalalabad.

"And are you still living at Moffett Field?" Though Max and I had hoped that Ketifa would board with us after Sabih was born, the young woman was fiercely independent. Once Stephen had helped her receive the benefits to which she was entitled, she'd found a roommate who served in one of the Army Reserve units still based at Moffett Field in Mountain View.

Ketifa shook her head, took a sip of coffee, then picked up the plate of biscotti. "You have to try these. An Italian lady who lives downstairs from us makes them. She speaks a bazillion languages and is in one of the army's psychological operation units. I suspect this is one of their secret weapons."

I took one, broke it in half, and nibbled. My eyes widened as the flavors exploded. Vanilla, almond, cinnamon, a hint of citrus, and other spices I could only guess at.

"Delicious, right? I'll give you some to take home to your guys. I think she should quit her army gig and bake these full-time." While Ketifa talked, I kept busy trying to identify the cookie's complex flavors.

I brushed the inevitable crumbs from my lap. "But if you're not at Moffett, then where?" Affordable housing wasn't easy to come by in the Bay Area, and I couldn't imagine Ketifa would willingly give up her adorable apartment.

"Oh, I still have the apartment," Ketifa said. "But Susan—she's my roommate. She's getting serious with her boyfriend, so when Tess offered me this job, and the chance to house-sit one of those downtown apartments, I jumped at it. Susan's paying my half of the rent so I can afford Sabih's day care." She sat up straight and beamed. "Everything's within walking distance—grocery, work, day care, and the mosque."

"You know you have a home with us anytime. But I can't match this deal for convenience. You like working with Tess?"

"Oh, Maggie, can you help her? I can't believe the police took her." Somehow, when Ketifa said those words—"the police took her"—I was reminded that the police in many nations, and even within some American communities, were not as uniformly helpful as Paolo and Jason and the rest of the Orchard View Police Force. In many places on our planet, being "taken by the police" could mean disappearing forever. I reached out and took Ketifa's hand to reassure her. Her fingers were cold and she shivered, despite being covered head to toe in a modest but still trendy charcoal-grey outfit that announced both her religious affiliations and her identity as a fashionista.

"It'll be okay. Forrest is working on it." Ketifa had met the lawyer and me at about the same time, shortly before Sabih was born.

"And Teddy? He's Sabih's favorite babysitter." Ketifa passed me her phone to show me a picture of a sleepy baby curled up in Teddy's lap, as the older boy read from what appeared to be a physics text.

Ketifa sighed in what I assumed was frustration, because I was feeling similar emotions. There were no words for the trauma Teddy and Tess had experienced. We reached for the plate of biscotti at the same time.

"You came here to help Tess," Ketifa said. "Did you get the information you'd hoped for?"

I bit my lip and massaged the tense muscles in the back of my neck. "I'm going to have to think about that. Most of what I learned from your coworker wasn't in what he told me, but in the scurrilous gossip he chose to believe—and in the way he gleefully repeated it. He's no friend of Tess's, is he?"

"No friend of Patrick's, that's for sure. With Tess? There, it's complicated. He's a mess." She shook her head. "A pitiful excuse for a grown man." "'Kitty'?"

Ketifa smiled and patted her hijab, a pretty black and red floral scarf. While she'd previously favored a rainbow of vibrant colors, her current outfit echoed the color scheme Tess so often wore. Modest, fashionable, and businesslike, it suited her.

"He *claims* that 'Ketifa' is too difficult for him to pronounce." She waggled her eyebrows. "More likely, he doesn't like the feel of an Islamic name on his tongue. Like, if he uses it, Immigration will break down the door and arrest both of us. What a dork."

"Are you afraid?"

She snorted. "Of Robert, or of Immigration? Neither of them. What'll they do, deport me? Where to? My great-grandmother was born in Iowa and built bombers during World War II. It's not like Muslims suddenly landed here after the World Trade Center attack. It's so stupid. Like, if I was a terrorist, would I run around in my hijab? No. I'd dye my hair pink and dress like a hipster so I could go anywhere and no one would notice me." She brushed crumbs from her lap. "But you didn't come here to listen to my family history. How can I help Tess?"

"Robert mentioned this Katherine McNamara—"

Ketifa snorted again in the midst of taking a sip of her coffee. I handed her a napkin, and she wiped steamed milk from her face before answering. "What an idiot. Katherine and Tess are friends. They helped me paint my apartment. Katherine likes to run, you know, for exercise. But she's a software engineer, and she works those crazy hours. She runs with Patrick and the kids for safety and fun, not because she has designs on Patrick. As if." She shook her head. "I mean, they're both great people, but she's got a husband, Sean." At the mention of Sean's name, Ketifa rubbed her chin, and her expression changed in a way I didn't understand. Whatever it was, the micro-expression disappeared quickly, making me wonder whether I'd imagined it. Was she afraid of Sean? Disgusted by him? Concerned? I didn't know. But something about him apparently bothered her.

Before I could ask a follow-up question, Ketifa reached for her phone and began scrolling. "Let me set up a meeting for you with Katherine. You'll like her. Robert has twisted ideas about her...probably projecting his obsession with Tess. You can form your own opinion, and see if she has any ideas about how we can help Tess and Teddy. She's probably spent more hours—*innocent* hours—with Patrick than anyone else outside his family, since she worked with him and ran with him."

While Ketifa waited for the phone to ring, I headed to the restroom. As I walked toward the back of the building, I could hear her voice lift in a way that told me she'd connected with someone she liked and trusted. Though her words were businesslike and direct, laughter threatened to break through at any moment.

Ketifa was still chatting with Katherine when I returned. "Hang on a sec," she said, pushing a button to mute the call. "She's invited you to lunch at the office, can you make it?"

I took a moment to consult the not-always-reliable calendar in my head. I was pretty sure I didn't have any appointments for the rest of the week. Early August was a quiet time in Orchard View. Most people were away on vacation, and no one needed my organizing services. I kept a calendar on my phone, but it would take so long to access it that I might seem rude and I didn't want to put Katherine off before I'd had an opportunity to meet her.

"Twelve thirty?" I asked. Ketifa consulted Katherine, thanked her, and ended the call.

"She'll text you the address. She'll meet you in the outdoor lunch area, at a table with a green umbrella. Here's her picture." Ketifa showed me her phone, which displayed a snapshot of Katherine with her arm around Patrick at the end of a race. Others milled about in the photo. The pair were laughing and happy, with fondness for one another they didn't try to hide. To someone else, their closeness might indicate a romantic relationship, but I detected a fuzzy ear in the bottom of the picture that I suspected belonged to Mozart.

"Did Tess take this picture? Is that Mozart's ear?" I raised my eyebrows in question.

Ketifa nodded. "Tess takes tons of pictures for work, and they instantly upload to my phone and computer. She's supposed to change the settings after work, but she usually forgets, so I get lots of pictures of her family and friends." Ketifa shrugged. "Either she trusts me, or she's not taking pictures of anything she needs to hide."

"So, no selfies of her with a murder weapon?"

Ketifa smiled, sort of. "*Ick.*"

"*Ick* is right. On that note, I think it's time for me to leave." I thanked her for the biscotti, invited her and Sabih to dinner, and told her that Teddy was staying with us at least until Tess returned. "I'm encouraging them both to stay as long as they like," I added. "Those news vans are everywhere. Tess and Teddy don't need that hassle on top of everything else they're going through."

I added Katherine's address and cell phone number to my list of contacts, then followed my phone's GPS directions. Though the office was less than five miles away, it would take me nearly a half hour to get there. I checked my watch. I had enough time, just.

Chapter 17

Establish a backup plan for your pets. If you evacuate to a shelter, that shelter may not take animals, and local kennels may also be under evacuation orders.

From the Notebook of Maggie McDonald
Simplicity Itself Organizing Services

Tuesday, August 8, 12:30 p.m.

I turned into an expansive shaded parking lot in an area of Mountain View dominated by Google; its parent company, Alphabet; and spin-offs of both organizations. These days, it was often difficult to tell where one high-tech company ended and another began. Products, people, and buildings were interdependent and intertwined.

I found a parking spot not too far from an outdoor patio filled with round tables of varying sizes shaded by umbrellas in bright colors. A woman matching Katherine's photo approached me, balancing on a pair of crutches while struggling to get her long auburn hair under control in the gusty breeze.

She wrangled her hair into a lopsided ponytail, and we shook hands. "I tried to get a table with a green umbrella like I said I would, but they were all taken. Are you okay with more shade?" When I agreed, she led me to a table under an all-weather overhang. She nodded toward a bright red fleece jacket slung over the back of one of the chairs. "It gets brisk out here close to the Bay, and not everyone's dressed for it. You can borrow that if you get cold."

We hustled inside to pick up our food, and I asked Katherine about her foot, offering to juggle her tray and my own. "I'll get help from one of the servers," she said. "They have to offer. It's part of the Americans with Disabilities Act. They've also got some wheeled tray tables around here somewhere, if I can locate one."

She glanced around, then pulled a plastic tray from a stack at the end of a cafeteria line. She handed it to me and pulled another one from the stack for herself.

"What are you hungry for?" she asked.

It wasn't an easy decision. The food at many Silicon Valley companies was legendary, an important perk designed to attract and retain employees. Most offered locally sourced produce. Choices here ranged from healthy versions of comfort food to ethnic options and sushi. I was overwhelmed, but Katherine helped me out. "The fish tacos are to die for, or we can do build-your-own omelets or wraps." We both chose the tacos with delicately fried white fish, avocados, and fresh mango salsa on corn tortillas as good as any I'd tasted. While Google and its offshoots were famous for lunchtime fare that was served from dawn to well past dark, this was the first time I'd eaten here. There was no awkwardness about who would pay. The food was available before, during, and after traditional work hours at no charge to employees and their guests. At the end of the line, a server appeared, as if by magic, to carry Katherine's tray to our table.

Once we'd settled into our seats, we enjoyed a few moments of silent appreciation for the food. But in short order, Katherine wiped mango juice from her chin and eyed my rapidly disappearing meal. "We can get more if you like."

I shook my head. "This is plenty. I apologize for my overly enthusiastic appetite."

Katherine waved off my apology. "No, no. We tend to get jaded about the food here, so it's great to be reminded how special it is."

"I'd wondered whether a free employee café could really live up to the hype, but this truly is 'unmatched epic foodie cuisine'." I did the air-quote thing. "I read that somewhere, but I'm not sure where."

"We can go drool over the dessert tray in a bit, but in the meantime, how can I help? I'm still in shock over the news about Pat. I keep expecting him to run in, apologizing for being late. How are Tess and Teddy doing? Are they holding a memorial service? I'd like to attend."

Katherine's barrage of rapid-fire questions matched my much-maligned style of speech—spitting out sentences as fast as I could without filtering my thoughts or giving anyone else a chance to respond.

She began to apologize, but I shook my head. "Never mind, I think I've got it." I kept track of my responses by touching the index finger of my right hand to the extended fingers of my left. "Tess and Teddy are doing... okay. They're both as tough as they come, but this is a terrible blow."

"Salt of the earth. I'd expect nothing less, but is Tess really alright? I mean, Patrick, and now jail."

"So you're aware Tess is a person of interest. I haven't heard from her since her arrest yesterday. Her lawyer says she's doing fine, though, and that her biggest problem is that she's worried about Teddy."

"Can we visit her?"

I frowned, and my voice cracked as I answered. "No. Apparently there's a weeklong adjustment period during which prisoners can't receive any visitors without special dispensation from the warden—dispensation he's not inclined to grant."

"Whackadoodle."

We laughed, then took turns rattling off a series of increasingly ridiculous synonyms that matched the truly unhinged decision of the sheriff's office to arrest our friend. Our laughter edged into tears as our grief for Patrick broke through the lingering shock. We'd bonded over the laughter, but we were still brand-new acquaintances. I sensed that Katherine was as wary of giving in to a public display of grief as I was.

I wiped my eyes with a napkin as surreptitiously as I could manage.

"That fire, and all the smoke," said Katherine, pretending the poor air quality was the reason our eyes were tearing up.

I sniffed the air. "It's close to being contained, which is great, but they're still fighting to extinguish the blaze inside the borders of the fire. We need rain. And calm winds."

Katherine lifted her glass in agreement, and I returned to answering her series of questions. "I haven't heard anything about a memorial service yet. Nothing will happen while Tess is in jail. I'll pass along whatever I learn."

"How do we get Tess out of the clutches of the sheriff's minions so that she can take care of that beautiful boy of hers?" She punctuated her sentence with a firm pat on the table, then rummaged in her bag, pulling out a bright yellow Google pen and a pad of lined paper.

Shivering either from the increased breeze off the nearby San Francisco Baylands or from the enormity of what we were undertaking, I welcomed the comfort of the fleece Katherine had offered. It was enormous, like wearing a blanket. Katherine pointed at the jacket with the end of her pen. "It's huge," she said. "But it fits everyone." She held the pen poised over the pad of paper. "Where were we?"

"Who *really* did it?"

Katherine leaned back against the bright red cushions and sighed. "It's that simple, isn't it? That simple and that difficult. Who would want to hurt Patrick? And by extension, his gorgeous family."

"I talked to a guy this morning who seemed convinced Tess did it."

Katherine gasped, but I couldn't look at her. I watched a distant group of employees cheer as one of them spiked a volleyball, outfoxing the opposing team. "This guy, Robert, thinks Tess killed Patrick because he was having an affair. An affair with you." I sucked in my lips as if to stop myself from hurling any more dreadful words Katherine's way, but I watched her face as they hit their target. At first, her pained expression reflected the wound my words had inflicted. But then she laughed.

"Robert? That officious money-grubber? Tess's wannabe sidekick?"

I smiled slightly over her apt description, but said nothing. We'd already detoured into near-hysteria once, and I didn't want to go there again. I needed to make progress on this investigation, fast. "Exactly. He seemed to have a lot of hostility for Patrick. Do you think Robert could have done it? And then thrown suspicion on Tess to prevent everyone from suspecting him?"

Katherine bit her lip and intertwined her fingers as she considered the question. "Maybe. There was certainly no love lost between them. Robert was jealous of the time that Tess devoted to her family, so he despised Patrick, but he didn't like anyone else Tess spent time with, either. If more of Tess's friends disappear, I'd look to him, but he's so wrapped up in the real estate business that I can't see him taking the time to bump someone off. Not unless he could figure out a way to make Patrick's death put money in his pocket." She shook her head and sat back in her seat. "Nope. Not Robert. If he did do it, we could prove it with his time sheet."

"Time sheet?"

"Another one of his goofy ideas to improve office efficiency. He wanted everyone to keep detailed records showing which projects they were working on every fifteen minutes, like they'd do in a law office. Patrick told me about it, oh, about two months ago, I guess. Tess let him make a presentation to the office, but then made the time sheets optional. Robert was the only one who followed through."

"Good to know. But at the moment, looking at time sheets sounds like a big fat bore, and not very helpful. How would we know they were truthful?"

"Right. If I had to fill out a time sheet, it would be like 'bungee jumping at nine,' 'hot date with major movie star at ten'—totally fake."

I smiled at Katherine's sense of humor. I liked this woman.

"Too much joking?" she asked. "These are dark times."

"And when do we need laughter more?"

We sipped our drinks in silence for a moment.

"I have an alibi, by the way," Katherine said.

"Your foot?"

She frowned, glared at the foot, then stared off into the distance. "I spent most of the afternoon, evening, and into the night in the emergency room on Saturday. ERs are so slow when your condition isn't life-threatening. Don't get me wrong. It's good that they take people with life-threatening illnesses first. But it was ages before I got anything for the pain. They gave me an ice pack, but I think I did some real damage to my dental work, gritting my teeth through the agony. My sister-in-law was there with me. She deserves a medal. She kept me distracted and supplied me with coffee and chocolate, both of which have surprisingly powerful painkilling properties in a pinch. I nearly kissed the nurse who finally brought me a pain pill." She took a sip of her coffee, then glanced at her phone. "Too soon for another dose. Do you have any ibuprofen?"

I rummaged in my purse and handed her a bottle. She shook out three. Or maybe four. I wasn't sure, but it seemed like a lot. She swallowed them with the last bit of melted ice from her drink.

"What happened?"

She winced and put her foot up on a neighboring chair. "A stupid fall on my hardwood floor Saturday morning. I'm a klutz, and I'm sure I've twisted my ankle worse than that a hundred times before. On stairs, stepping off a curb, or on that equestrian trail at Rancho San Antonio near where Patrick was found. The horses make a mess of the mud after the rains, and then it hardens. It's treacherous when you're running. This time, though, the culprits were just my slipper socks." She shook her head. "At least I'd just had my toes done." She wiggled her brightly painted toes, which sported pink polish that was nearly a perfect match for her cast. "My husband treated me and my sister-in-law to a full-service spa day on Friday. Massage, manicure, pedicure, salt scrub, meditation lounge, the works. I took the day off work, and he hired a limo to take us there and back, so we didn't have to drive afterward, when our brains were mush."

I made the appropriate envious noises and pantomimed the motion of crossing her off a list of suspects.

"There's Debra, though..." Katherine's voice startled me.

"Debra?"

"Debra Mah. She works with Patrick and me. But honestly, if she wanted to kill anyone, it would probably be me. Robert isn't the only one who thought Patrick and I were having an affair. Tess, Patrick, and I laughed it off, but Deb was sure all the juicy rumors were true. And I could so easily see her bumping me off so she could have Patrick for herself."

Chapter 18

Pay attention to warnings issued by emergency personnel and government officials. Obey signs prohibiting admittance to restricted areas.

From the Notebook of Maggie McDonald
Simplicity Itself Organizing Services

Tuesday, August 8, Afternoon

Katherine phoned Debra for me and explained that I was a friend of Patrick's who was devastated by his death. "She's working on a memorial project for him and wants to interview people from every sphere of his life. You know, to build a complete portrait of the great man he was." She was laying it on pretty thick, it seemed to me, but Debra was apparently eager to help.

Katherine muted the call. "She's leaving early today for an appointment. Can you meet her tomorrow, here at Google for lunch?"

I nodded and waited for her to end the call.

"Twelve thirty, tomorrow afternoon, right here."

I shook her hand. "Thank you so much. I'm sorry we didn't meet under better circumstances. May I contact you again if I have more questions?"

Katherine rummaged in her backpack, pulled out a rumpled business card, brushed it off on her shirt, and handed it to me. "Sorry. I don't use my cards much. They get a bit grubby sliding around in the pockets of my bags."

I held the card at arm's length and squinted. "I think I can make out the contact information, so it's fine."

"My husband's meeting me here in a bit. He wants to pick up some stuff from the employee store and needs my badge to get the discount. Let me walk you to your car."

I protested, but Katherine insisted that the parking lot was on her way back to her office. We paused halfway there so that I could return the fleece jacket Katherine had loaned me. I tucked it into her backpack, a gallant act I hoped would save her an awkward moment on her crutches. But I nearly toppled her over when a large forest-green van screeched to a stop next to us. I instinctively took a step away, still holding on to Katherine's backpack, pulling her off balance. She fell back into my arms, and I quickly righted her, apologizing profusely. Disaster averted. Then I lifted my hand to shield my eyes from the glare reflecting off the shiny finish of the van that had caused the trouble.

Katherine knew the driver. "Ah, Sean," she said. "This is Maggie McDonald, a friend of Tess and Patrick's. Maggie, this is my husband, Sean, and my sister-in-law, Fiona."

We waved at each other, making polite but awkward gestures. It turns out it's difficult to greet someone when you're separated by the door of a van that's blocking traffic. I did a quick scan of the parking lot, which was decidedly short on empty parking spaces. "Nice to meet you both. I'm leaving if you want to nab my spot."

Sean smirked. Fiona laughed aloud. "No need," said Sean, pointing to the bright blue handicap placard hanging from his rearview mirror. "I get one of the primo spots by the door, marked by the banner of my people, the great white rolling chair."

Their good humor was infectious and dispelled the dour mood that still lingered from my conversation with Katherine about Patrick and those who might want to kill him. It wasn't until I reached my car that I turned, suddenly realizing that Sean and his sister, Fiona, both significantly older than Katherine, were undoubtedly the "Mr. and Mrs. Claus" whom Brian, David, and Teddy had mentioned.

I'd also met Sean briefly on Sunday at Tess's place. "Mr. and Mrs. Claus" were apt nicknames for the siblings. They both had clouds of curly white hair, and the rosy cheeks and ready smiles I associated with the great Saint Nick. Sean sported an impressive beard. I tried to remember what the boys had said about Sean. Was it favorable? Suspicious? I shook my head, hoping a few marbles might fall into place.

My phone rang, and for the first time in a long time, I was able to answer it using the buttons on my steering wheel without hanging up on the caller.

"Max, it's good to hear from you. Are you and the boys settling in, or do you still have nine hundred trips to make? I'm on my way home if you need me to pick up a load of stuff or the dogs or something."

"We've got that in hand, but the boys are still antsy. We're thinking of taking a run, or at least a walk, up the hill to check out the fire damage. And if it's not too creepy, Teddy wants to see if he can get a sense of where his dad died."

"I can see that, I guess."

"Me too. But we'll play it by ear. Once we get near the trail, it may seem like too much, too soon. In any case, we'll get some more exercise, so everyone sleeps better tonight."

"You're a good man, Max McDonald."

"As I keep reminding you, Maggie. As I keep reminding you."

By the time I reached home, Max and the boys had taken off with the dogs. Dogs weren't typically allowed on the Rancho San Antonio trails, but Max might have assumed that, since the parking lots were closed, and the vegetation had burned, there wouldn't be any people or wildlife up there for Belle and Mozart to disturb. My husband typically followed laws to the letter, but at unpredictable times he'd surprise me by flouting rules I expected him to follow. We'd been married for many years, but he still held many mysteries. It kept things interesting.

I'd had time to unpack groceries, start a load of laundry, and consider taking a closer look at the fire damage myself when I heard them outside the back door, laughing.

I stood on the porch and surveyed my guys, who'd launched a full-scale water war to combat the soot that covered their skin and clothing.

"Can you get us some buckets, Mom?" asked Brian.

"And soap. Lots of soap," Max added.

"What about the shower down in the barn?" I suggested. "And the washing machine down there? It may take several cycles to get all that soot out of your clothes."

Max called up, "We were told that going up there was a super-bad idea and that we should wash this soot off as soon as possible."

"It's okay, Mom. Don't freak," David said, skipping the eye roll and filling his voice with empathy and reassurance. "As long as we wash it off, we should be safe. Firefighters are repeatedly exposed to carcinogens. And poison oak." He paused to scratch at his skin, as though the words themselves had set off a reaction. "We got stopped before we got too far up there anyway."

"How's your breathing, Bri?" I asked. My youngest son had intermittent trouble with asthma. Smoke often triggered a flare-up. He'd been symptom-free for so many months that not one of us had thought about protecting him from particulates now that the fire and smoke had mostly moved on.

Brian dashed to the bottom of the steps, then took a deep breath in and blew a long, hard breath out to demonstrate that he wasn't wheezing and was able to use every cubic centimeter of his lung capacity. I felt my shoulders relax. I gave Brian a thumbs-up, and he beamed. Brian was remarkably patient with my tendency to go from normal levels of parental concern to DEFCON One when his breathing was involved. I knew it annoyed him, but he didn't remember the long nights we'd spent in the hospital when he was an infant and toddler.

"There's shampoo in the cabinet under the sink in the barn bathroom. I'll bring down a change of clothes and a load of dog towels—maybe you could use them and spare the new ones on the shelves down there?"

Scruffy towels in our house were marked with Belle's name and were kept in a basket by the back door, ready to wipe down her feet and coat during the rainy season or sop up unexpected kitchen spills.

Nearly a year ago, after our barn had burned down, we'd rebuilt it, matching the original footprint and design on the outside to speed the project through the planning commission. On the inside, though, we'd included two bathrooms; one was downstairs with a washer and dryer that came in handy when we were working in the garden or on other messy projects nearby. One day, we hoped to convert the loft to a small apartment. That day, however, was not yet here.

Watching the boys, Max, and the two dogs trooping down the hill toward the barn, looking for all the world like nineteenth-century coal miners, I was glad we'd sprung for an extra-large water heater in the remodel. That crew was going to use up every gallon of hot water we had before they were scrubbed clean.

Less than an hour later, they trickled back up the hill slowly, first Brian, then the older boys, followed by Max with the dogs. I was getting dinner ready, and they stopped to chat and pull munchies out of the fridge in quantities that might staunch the appetite of a small army, but that I knew would barely hold them until dinner.

"I ran the first load through twice. Unless the boys' track team changes its colors to blue and gray from blue and white, though, they may need to be washed a third time. Don't let me forget them."

"Set a timer?" I was a big fan of timers. The trick was remembering why I'd set them. Max grabbed a digital one that I'd affixed to the fridge with a magnet.

"An hour should do it," he said. "How did your interviews go?"

I filled him in on what I'd learned from Katherine and Robert, told him about meeting with Ketifa, and about my lunch date the next day with Debra. "Nothing earthshaking that will get Tess released, I'm afraid. How about you? Did you discover anything new on your jaunt? How did Teddy feel about visiting the spot where his dad died?"

Max shook his head. "We didn't get close. As soon as we hit the old PG&E service road, a ranger truck pulled up, and the biggest dude I've ever seen told us the park was closed due to the fire danger. Suggested we head back where we belonged. Didn't say anything about the dogs, though."

"Did you get a fine?"

"No, he was focusing on trying to keep people safe. Warned us about washing off the soot, but also said to be watchful for wildlife. With so many of them burned out of their homes—rattlers, mountain lions, deer, coyotes—they're regrouping. And outside their established territories, they're skittish and more dangerous than usual." Max began clearing the table. "Interesting guy, though. Kon Sokolov. Huge. Six foot five, and maybe three hundred pounds, all of it muscle. He could fight a grizzly and win. He's a first-generation Russian immigrant, and his granddad worked at Chernobyl. Died young. Kon wants to avoid similar environmental threats, so he leads a super-healthy life. He eats organic, home-grown vegetables. Passionate about ecological issues. Joined the U.S. Army right after high school to earn money for college, trained as a sniper, which he hated, but has been working for various branches of environmental or outdoor recreation groups ever since he got out."

"You got his full life story. How long did you talk to him?"

Max ignored me. Part of our family lore was that Max could walk into a roomful of strangers and learn everyone's life story in fifteen minutes flat. He rummaged through the pockets of his cargo shorts. "Somewhere here I've got the numbers he gave me to text if we see any hot spots flare up, or anything else we think the authorities should check on." He pulled out a crumpled slip of paper, smoothed it out on the counter, and hunted for a thumbtack to affix it to our kitchen message center. He frowned, which affected my mood in much the same way that a passing cloud darkens the earth.

"There are more tacks in the drawer if you can't find one on the board," I said, guessing what was amiss.

"It was something else Kon said. Something that worried me."

Chapter 19

During fire season, safety awareness is as important on the trail or in wilderness surroundings as it is in fire-prone residential areas. Be aware of potential threats in your immediate area, and heed recommendations from officials. In periods of extreme fire danger, make alternative plans.

If you see smoke or a fire, hustle back to civilization and notify authorities immediately. Never try to escape a fire by travelling uphill. Heat and flames rise.

From the Notebook of Maggie McDonald
Simplicity Itself Organizing Services

Tuesday, August 8, Evening

"Kon Sokolov is the ranger who found Patrick," I reminded Max. "Paolo told me on the way home from the medical examiner's office on Sunday."

"I'd forgotten," Max said. "But he asked if we knew the guy who died. Kon said he doesn't normally approve of 'helpful civilians,' because they get in the way and put themselves at risk. But then he told me Patrick was different. Both of them had been keeping an eye on an illegal marijuana cultivation area. It had diverted water from one of the natural springs on the downhill slope west of the ridgeline."

"West?"

"Right. Close to where Kon found Patrick."

"Did you ask if he thought the growers had a hand in Patrick's death?"

"He gave me one of those looks that told me he wouldn't answer even if I did ask. He warned me those guys are big-time bad news. The rat poisons they use to protect the crop is nasty stuff that's been outlawed for decades and hurts deer, raptors, coyotes, and mountain lions. They divert springs and dam creeks, which damages the entire watershed. Their fertilizers make the algae grow in the ponds and kill off the fish. Up and down the food chain, they create barren deserts out of some of the richest and most beautiful habitats in the world. And then there's all the garbage and sewage generated by the guys who look after the plants. They pack in supplies, but they don't bother to haul out their trash."

"Take a breath, professor. I get it."

"Sorry. I didn't mean to lecture." Max picked up a mug and the carafe from the coffeemaker, which was empty. He measured out a new batch and waited while it brewed. "Those illegal farms are dangerous for people too though. Kon made sure the kids knew what to look out for—irrigation pipes where you wouldn't expect to find them, heavily used trails that aren't marked on any map, piles of garbage in remote areas, and unexpected erosion. Wander into territory these growers have staked out, and they'll defend it with lethal force."

"I thought we were talking about public land. Doesn't all that property between here and the next ridge belong to the county?"

"Exactly. But when the bad guys claim it for their own, it's not safe to argue. I don't want the boys, or you, going up there right now—not unless you're in a big group or have the dogs with you. No solo meditation walks, okay? Kon says California Fish and Wildlife guys call the shots on when they round up the growers, eradicate the crops, and restore the streams. That's slated for later in August."

"Why wait?"

"I'm not sure. Something to do with the harvest. Maybe waiting means the bad guys don't have time to replant." He shrugged. "The problem is that the closer it gets to being picked or cut or whatever they call it with weed, the more valuable the plants are and the more fiercely they're defended. These guys actually carry assault rifles, according to Kon."

"Assault rifles? What's the range on those things?" I glanced nervously out the window toward the hill and the mountain beyond it. "And how far is that ridge from here, a mile?"

"More like three-quarters, as the bullets fly. Do you know how many summer camps are within range up there? Kon didn't want to guess, but it's a lot. Hundreds of kids. Maybe thousands. He was glad they'd been evacuated because of the fire."

"Yikes. Is it safe for us to be in the backyard? What about between the house and barn? Are the dogs safe?" My voice rose in panic.

Max pushed his hair back from his forehead. "As long as we don't look like we're threatening their livelihood, I think we're safe. But do you know who runs those illegal grows?" he asked.

I shook my head, knowing I didn't want to know but that Max would tell me anyway.

"If Kon is to be believed, and I think he is, it's the big cartels from Mexico, Colombia, and points south."

"But why here? Why in our sleepy little town with our sleepy little summer camps for sleepy little kids?"

"It's like everything else in California since the dawn of time. Land. Land and water. All national, state, and county land is free to those who don't respect public property or the health of the environment. Growing it here cuts their distribution costs and eliminates any need to bother with drug-sniffing dogs at the border. They still smuggle in their dangerous pesticides, but no one on the border is looking for those."

I shuddered and was tempted to close the blinds on the kitchen windows. Who knew how many desperate people in the drug trade had put us in their gun sights over the last year? Previously my biggest fear had been stumbling over a rattlesnake on a hike. But apparently there were far more lethal snakes out there than rattlers.

After dinner, we let the kids take off to play video games or to plan their backpacking trip to the coast, assuming conditions would one day materialize in which it was again safe for them to make the trek. Their health and safety, which included their mental health, was paramount right now. None of us, especially not the boys, thought doing dishes and cleaning the kitchen was the best way for anyone to heal their grief. Besides, after the increasingly frantic and crazy events of the last few days, Max and I needed to regroup and plan.

When Max came back to the house after taking out the dogs and the garbage and shifting the laundry down in the barn, I was still drying the dish I'd plucked from the rack before he'd left. "You've been pondering," he said as he took it gently from my hands and put it away.

"Do you think we're looking at this all wrong?" I asked.

"How so?"

"We've been focused on who wanted Patrick out of the way. Who had a grudge against him."

"Right."

"Do you think it could be something else entirely? I mean, we agree that everyone we know liked Patrick. So, assuming there was a rationale for injuring him and leaving him for dead, we're missing some other motivation—something other than hatred."

"I'm with you so far, but what other reason could there be?"

"There was that case in Texas years ago when a cheerleading mom killed the mother of her daughter's rival to ensure that her offspring had a lock on the top spot on the team."

"The problem is that if anyone wanted Patrick's coaching spot or Teddy's position in band, cross-country, or soccer, all they had to do was say so. Teddy or Patrick would have been happy to share their responsibilities or give them up entirely."

Max was right. Neither Patrick nor Teddy was particularly competitive. They were happy being in the midst of things, organizing fun activities, and making sure everyone was included. Jostling for position wasn't for them. "If it was a competitive thing, though, Pauline Windsor would be the one I'd question first." A kernel of an idea began to sprout in my brain, but I tamped it down, for now.

"Agreed. Pauline wasted no time in accusing Tess, did she?"

I shook my head, bit my lip, chose another bowl from the drying rack, and considered another possibility. "What about corporate espionage?"

"Elaborate."

"Do you know what kind of engineering Patrick did? Did he work on one of those super-secret projects with a code name? Like the early iPhone team? Could someone have been stalking him to learn his secrets?"

"And then pushed him off the ridge?" Max's voice was filled with skepticism.

"Bear with me. There's been talk in the news lately about high-tech companies that poach engineers from competitors. And questions about the legality of nondisclosure agreements. What if someone wanted to get around all that? What if they'd been trying to overhear phone calls or steal Patrick's laptop and things went too far?" Max was drying the silverware and tossing it in the drawer. Loudly. "Is it too much like a Hollywood caper movie with a Silicon Valley twist?"

Max nodded. "I've never thought much of the supposed logic behind that nondisclosure stuff, though as an academic I observed it from an objective distance." Up until a year ago, Max had been a professor of computer and software engineering at a small private university in California's Central Valley.

"But wouldn't it shorten development time for some of those hot consumer products if you could steal the technology instead of creating it on your own? Wouldn't it give your company a leg up while hobbling your competitor?"

"In theory, yes. But look at it as a practical matter." Max rubbed his chin and took on a professorial look and stance. "In any technical field or in the arts, ideas bubble up all the time. They're built on concepts that came before. Chances are, more than one person will have a breakthrough at the same time, right?"

"Of course," I said.

"But even if ten people had the same idea, each person's ability, resources, and vision would mean the implementation would vary."

"Like at back-to-school night, when they post artwork done by thirty kids with the same assignment and identical materials. No two paintings look alike."

"Precisely. And the problem is magnified when you consider that most people with a good idea won't be able to turn it into a product. Maybe they're missing the funds required, or the expertise to resolve an intermediate step. Or, as happens often, completing a small-scale proof-of-concept project satisfies their intellectual curiosity, but when it comes to manufacturing, marketing, and sales, their interest fizzles."

"You're saying it takes a team?"

"Exactly. And it takes the right team. That's one of the things I've learned about managing engineers since I joined Influx. They aren't interchangeable cogs. When you get the perfect mix of talents and interests, a team can do incredible things. But distract them, remove a guy like Patrick who turns a hodgepodge of talent into a team, or throw in a troublemaker, and you've got nothing."

I pushed my hair back from my forehead and sighed, "So, no matter how valuable the technology is, stealing it wouldn't get you far?"

"Right."

"Then why are the business pages full of news about takeovers and lawsuits related to patent infringement?"

"It's not unusual for companies to come up with similar solutions to market problems." Patrick tossed a spoon in the drawer, then pulled it back, held it up to the light, and buffed it with his towel before adding it to the others in the drawer. "Patents and licensing are a significant profit stream for every big company. But lawsuits are expensive too. That's why corporations settle so many lawsuits before they get to court. Forget the big Hollywood crime and conspiracy scheme. The easiest and least expensive way to nab technology someone else has is to phone them up and ask how much they want for it. The two parties whip up a license agreement, and everyone goes home happy. Happens all the time."

I wasn't ready to let my theory go. "But what if you took out the star player? What if Patrick was the key? Could someone have tried to recruit him, failed, and then indulged in the sort of thinking that creates a deadly love triangle? 'If I can't have him, no one else can have him'?"

Max looked pensive and sat down at the kitchen table, his eyes fixated on a corner of the kitchen ceiling. I finished putting away the few remaining dishes, set up the coffeemaker for the morning, and refilled the cat bowls with fresh water and kibble.

He sighed. "In a logical world, it doesn't hold water, Maggie. Despite what you read in the business pages, we need to compare notes with suppliers throughout a project, particularly if we're asking them to rush advances in their technology so that we can piggyback our next idea onto theirs. And we know we aren't their only customer. Developing products fast and first isn't the only key to success. Making sure the products are reliable, easy to use, and available at the right price is critical—among a great mix of other elements. Most good companies, the ones that will be around for a while, know it can actually be more profitable to be the second or third to release a product, if you take the time to make sure your version is better than anyone else's."

"So, bottom line, crime doesn't pay?"

"There's a reason clichés become clichés."

"Still, logic doesn't rule out a madman who decides murder is the best way to resolve a problem, does it?"

"Or a madwoman," Max said.

That idea I'd buried earlier resurfaced, and I glanced at my watch, trying to decide whether I had time to pursue it this evening.

Chapter 20

Overplan your hike. Hike with others. Stay together. Leave information listing your route, travel partners, and your expected date and time of return.

From the Notebook of Maggie McDonald
Simplicity Itself Organizing Services

Tuesday, August 8, Evening

The kids came barreling down the back stairs, followed by the dogs, temporarily ending my efforts to flesh out my seedling idea.

From the foot of the staircase, David slid across the smooth tiled floor in his stocking feet, skidding to a stop at the table and plopping his laptop in front of me. "Look at this. We found a route that doesn't go into any of the burnt areas and is upwind from the fires. What do you think? Can we pack up our stuff and go tomorrow?"

I examined the three beaming faces of boys who'd plotted out their version of the perfect backpacking trip. Their first without adult supervision. I hated to burst their bubble and was thankful when Max did it for me. He slid the laptop to his side of the table and refreshed the screen, scrolling to follow their route.

"Great job, guys. This looks like a terrific plan. But—"

The boys moaned as one and looked deflated. "No fair!"

"Didn't you hear what Ranger Sokolov said about the Central American drug cartels?" I asked.

Their eyes grew large, and they pulled chairs up to the table, eager to hear more. "Drug cartels in Orchard View?" David scoffed. "Have you been listening to talk radio?"

Max shook his head. "The boys and the dogs had already headed back down the hill when the ranger and I had that conversation."

Max filled the kids in on the information he'd gleaned from Kon about the dangers lurking right outside our back door from criminals, wild animals, and poisonous snakes. At the mention of snakes, Brian lifted his feet from the floor and rested them on the bottom rung of his chair. Teddy grimaced. David, who had been lobbying for a reptile-filled terrarium since he'd spoken his first words, grinned.

Max made a valiant attempt to sidestep the drama. "Look, the state parks, the Open Space Preserve, the camps, everything is closed in case they need to get fire crews in there. The wind can shift in a heartbeat. Keep this plan. It's a good one. But save it for after it rains and the danger has passed."

The boys seemed disappointed but resigned to their fate. "Are there any cookies left?" Brian asked, changing the subject. I convinced them to bring their clean laundry up from the barn before they decimated our snack supply.

While they were gone, the phone rang. It was Forrest with bad news.

"I can't get Tess out," he said. "They arraigned her today. She's been charged with first-degree murder and held over without bail."

"No! Not Tess. On what grounds? She's a *mother*, not a flight risk."

"Apparently she recently renewed passports for her and Teddy, but not for Patrick. The prosecuting attorney argued that meant she'd planned to kill Patrick and take her son out of the country."

"That's ridiculous. Tess and I took care of that together right after school got out. She needed to renew her passport. Patrick gets his taken care of at work. We took the boys to get their photos in one fell swoop. I did mine, too. You know how it is, if you don't renew those things when you're thinking of them, you forget. We wanted to make sure the boys had current passports for any trips they might go on in high school or college."

"Tess told me, and I reported that to the judge. Everyone's been renewing passports because of the rumors swirling about changes to Homeland Security legislation and the Transportation Security Administration requirements. But the judge wasn't buying it. I've argued cases in his court before. He's got a rigid and narrow view of legal precedents. I'm not sure he believes in bail for murder or any capital offense."

I cringed at the reminder that Tess had been charged with murder, which carried the possibility of a death sentence in California. "Can she appeal?"

"She can. And I've already submitted the paperwork. But our chances of winning are slim. I don't know any recent cases where bail appeals have been granted."

"Can we visit or phone her? She must be eager to check on Teddy."

"She can call out from the jail, but you can't call in. I've set her up with the calling card she needs. The best thing to do, I think, is to make an appointment with her to call at a time when Teddy's sure to be here. I can relay a message to her for you."

"But what about visiting?"

Forrest was uncharacteristically slow to respond. I was about to ask whether we were still connected when he sighed and answered. "Go online to the Department of Corrections. You and Teddy can fill out a request to be approved visitors. The paperwork is supposed to take three days to go through, but with budget cuts, processing now takes at least a week. And none of the inmates are allowed visitors for the first week anyway. I hope to get her out of there before a week's time, but it wouldn't hurt for you to complete the forms, just in case we run into a snag."

I winced when Forrest used the word "inmate" to describe Tess and was glad Teddy wasn't listening in on the call. But rather than mentioning my discomfort to the lawyer, I thanked him for the update, ended the call, and turned to Max.

"I heard," he said. "Do you want to tell Teddy or should I?"

I sighed, feeling as deflated as the boys had moments earlier. "And we thought putting the kibosh on their backpacking plans would burst their bubble."

We talked it out with the boys, encouraged them to think positively, assured them that Forrest was working hard and that Tess was hanging tough. She would not linger in jail any longer than any of us could help it. We applied liberal amounts of ice cream and cookies to the problem, after which, the boys began to droop. Whether it was due to adrenaline withdrawal following the dreadful news, the cumulative effects of grief, lack of sleep, Max's concerted efforts to keep them active, or an extra helping of carbs, the biological imperative had caught up with them. When we followed them up the stairs twenty minutes later, they were sound asleep.

I'd feared my wide-ranging thoughts and worry over Tess's predicament would rob me of sleep, and I was right. Within seconds of my head hitting the pillow, my brain accessed and downloaded a giant file containing new threads to pursue. Max must have experienced a similar phenomenon. "I forgot to tell you about the chains," he said. "They were cut."

"Chains?" I sat up, turned on my bedside lamp, and squinted at him. His eyes were closed, and it took me a moment to verify that he wasn't talking in his sleep.

"Sorry. The chains on the gates at the entrance to the PG&E trail. They were cut. Anyone could have driven a car up there. Or a truck, anyway. A car would probably bottom out on the ruts. But a truck could do it. The rangers' trucks do."

"Did Kon tell you that?"

"Yup. I wouldn't have noticed, otherwise. Hikers, mountain bikers, and horses can bypass the gates." Max was speaking more clearly and was fully awake now.

"Could firefighters have cut the chains when they came in to strengthen the firebreak? They wouldn't have wanted to wait for a ranger."

Max shook his head. "I asked. Law enforcement, firefighters, and rangers all have keys. Unfortunately, so do a number of the volunteer groups who help maintain the trails. An astronomy group unlocks the gates when they hold observing parties for the public. I suggested Kon get a list to Sergeant Nguyen of everyone who had access. None of them would have needed to cut the chain, so we can rule them out."

I bit my lip. "That's an awful lot of keys floating around, most of which probably aren't secured. And as you say, anyone could get up there by going around the gate, as long as they didn't need a car up there. So, who would have needed to cut the chain?"

"Someone who wanted to get away in a hurry? Someone who was hauling supplies into the growing areas?"

"But wouldn't they have been afraid of being heard or seen?"

"That's just it. Kon heard a truck. At about three thirty in the morning, shortly after he was awakened by a gunshot."

I shook my head as I tried to make sense of the ideas bouncing around my brain like the marbles in a pinball machine.

"Never mind that, though. I gave some more thought to your idea about corporate espionage. The way to make it pay off in a hurry is through insider trading. Personnel responsible for setting release dates for products are prohibited from benefiting from that knowledge. But someone outside the company could make a fortune on publicly traded stocks by stealing a laptop that contained information about product release dates."

"Afterward, they could toss the computer or surreptitiously return it, with no one knowing what they'd done."

"Exactly."

"Do we know whether Patrick had that sort of a job?"

"No, but the fact that we didn't know actually tells us something. In my experience, any techie who routinely avoids talking about work is either unemployed or sworn to secrecy."

"You think he was a *spy*?"

"No. Well, yes. Maybe. I'm saying that neither one of us knows anything about what Patrick did, beyond that he was some kind of engineer. Maybe there was a reason for that."

"He was kind of nerdy, worked long hours that were extraordinarily flexible, didn't wear a tie, and knew his way around a computer. But did he or Tess ever actually tell me he was an engineer? I don't think so. Maybe." My sleep-robbed brain refused to grab hold of any reliable memories.

Max turned and patted his bedside table, searching for something. He stopped, let out a sigh, and turned back, his face flushed.

"What?"

"I was hunting for my phone. I was going to check with Patrick so we could set the record straight. And then I remembered."

I wrapped my arms around him and hung on tight.

Hours later, I still couldn't sleep for thinking about our theories. Theories that were leading nowhere. I slipped into my Ugg boots, pulled a sweatshirt on over my pajamas, and checked on the kids. Belle looked up when I peeked in David's room. I left the door partway open so she could nose her way out without waking him if she decided to follow me. Holmes was camped out at the foot of Brian's bed. She stretched and tried to follow me downstairs to the kitchen without appearing to be the slightest bit interested in my activities.

I made chamomile tea with honey to reduce my caffeine load, but quickly gave up and started the coffeemaker. I defrosted a tray of cinnamon rolls for breakfast. There was nothing quite so comforting, in my opinion, as waking up to the smell of cinnamon and melted sugar.

But then I got to work. I use lists for organizational purposes, but writing tasks down also helps me organize my thoughts. If what I'd learned from Katherine and Robert yesterday was going to help Tess, I needed to make notes in a format that would be legible to other people. I made a note to ask David to help me set up a Google document or other online tool that each of us could add to as we learned more.

And then I wrote out a script to help me tackle one of my toughest jobs yet. I wondered if come morning, I'd be brave enough to venture into enemy territory. I gave myself a fifty-fifty chance, but I wanted to be ready for anything.

Chapter 21

Hiking safety means having the clothing, footwear, and supplies you'll need for your entire venture, which may mean packing or wearing a range of layers in areas or seasons prone to inhospitable or fluctuating conditions. It's surprising how often that same level of organization and preparation pays off in the life of a suburban Silicon Valley mom.

From the Notebook of Maggie McDonald
Simplicity Itself Organizing Services

Wednesday, August 9, Morning

In the morning, I e-mailed copies of my notes to Paolo and Forrest, saying I'd phone them later. Max poured himself a cup of coffee, wrapped a cinnamon roll in a napkin, and took off for work. He hoped to stay for a meeting and then work the rest of the week from home.

I waited for the kids to get up, but then decided that sleep was the best thing for them. I left a note saying they could reach me by cell phone, then took off to run a few errands before meeting with Debra Mah for lunch. I stuffed my script in my pocket, scolding myself for not tackling the hardest project first. I'd get to it, I reassured my inner critic, after I was sure my target was awake.

I met Debra at the same outdoor eating area where I'd met Katherine. I scanned the crowd as I approached the café. Debra stood, waved me over, and introduced herself.

"I hope you don't mind, but I ordered lunch for both of us," she said. "It will be here soon. I didn't know what you liked, so I got you the same thing I ordered for myself. Low carb. High protein. Everyone wants to be healthy. I'd like to make this quick so I can still get in a Pilates session before I get sucked back into my project. I hope you don't mind."

I shook my head, smiled, and sat down at a table that, unlike yesterday, was fully set with plates, utensils, and ice water. Though she'd repeated her apology, I had the sense that Debra didn't care what I thought. And I was annoyed. With little sleep and too much caffeine, I was looking for a comfort meal. Either a repeat of the zesty fish tacos from the day before, or one of the bubbling pizzas with fresh herbs cut to order that I'd spotted yesterday. And maybe a dark chocolate dessert followed by a quick catch-up nap. My inner toddler threatened to throw a tantrum. I marshaled my more grown-up resources and tried to focus on the reason I was meeting Debra: solving Patrick's murder and setting Tess free.

"That's efficient, Debra. Thank you. I know your time is precious, and I appreciate your agreeing to meet with me." I cringed inwardly. I sounded like I was reading from a customer service training manual.

Debra took a long swig of her ice water. "Where would you like to begin? Katherine said you wanted to know more about Patrick."

"I do. Maybe you could tell me first how your job connects to his?" I was hoping she might accidentally reveal some information that would answer the questions Max and I had tossed around the night before and determine, once and for all, whether he might have owned a computer with information worth killing for.

Either Debra was on to me, or the company had trained its employees well. "I can't talk about that. I thought you wanted to know more about Patrick outside of work."

"Did you spend a lot of time with him? Or with Patrick and Tess? Were you friends as well as colleagues?"

Debra bit her lip. "I was friends with Patrick, but I didn't know Tess. I never saw her with the team. That's how I knew Patrick—through the Road Runners. We tried to run together as much as possible. I was a top runner in college, and I want to get back to it. Patrick had been working with Katherine a lot, but she hadn't made a commitment to her running or training. She wasn't a Road Runner, but that didn't stop her from putting demands on our coach. It wasn't right. I'm committed to my running, and I should have priority over her. I teach martial arts classes and self-defense, so I'm not like those simpering women who match their Lycra shorts to their socks and sneakers. I don't see running as a fashion show."

Debra folded her arms and leaned back in her chair, looking smug.

"You and Patrick saw a lot of each other..." I said, hoping she'd fill in the blank so I wouldn't have to. I feared she'd balk if I asked directly about whether she had a romantic interest in Patrick.

She waited me out, and I caved. This interview stuff was harder than it looked in the movies. "It sounds as though you relied on Patrick."

"I did. Well, as much as he relied on me. It's hard for him to find running partners who are up to his level." Our food arrived. Debra dug in, but I poked my fork at the lumps on my plate. While yesterday's fish taco had been fresh and worthy of a four-star restaurant, today's "spinach egg-white omelet" resembled nothing so much as a small green hockey puck. A pile of steamed vegetables added color and real texture, but the presentation didn't do nearly enough to overpower the image of the hockey puck. I picked up a steamed green bean in my fingers and chewed, thinking about how to wring more information from Debra.

"Do you know what he was doing up on that ridge at night?" I asked, opting for a more direct approach. "Or who might have wanted him dead?"

"Well, I don't want to get anyone in trouble..." Debra began. I perked up and leaned forward. I'd found that when people used that particular phrasing, they usually meant the exact opposite of what they were saying.

"But Katherine..." Debra tried to make a show of hesitating to rat out her coworker, but her body language told me she was eager to dish.

"Yes?" I smiled and raised my eyebrows, hoping to encourage Debra by mirroring her expression.

"She was so jealous of my work with Patrick, both here and on the trail. I mean, she was married, but you wouldn't know it by the way she flirted with him and monopolized his time. He's supposed to be supporting members of the club, but he spends more time with Katherine and the high school track team than he does with us." Debra's words took on an increasingly whiny tone, and her face grew pinched.

"Is he compensated for his time with the team? I mean, is there fraud involved in the fact that he's officially your coach, but you can't get the training hours you need?" Debra's description of the purpose of the Road Runners differed from what Katherine had told me. She'd described it as an informal group of people who loved running and occasionally competed. Debra made it sound more cutthroat than an Olympic ice-skating qualifying round. I couldn't reconcile what she said about Katherine "not being serious" about her running with her assertion that Katherine monopolized Patrick's time. But I was learning a lot, so I didn't call her on the contradiction.

"It sounds like you and Katherine were the last people who might have wanted Patrick out of the way."

Debra tilted her head from one shoulder to the other, as if weighing the truth of what I'd said. "I certainly didn't kill him. I can't speak for Katherine." She sniffed.

"So, you must have an alibi for Saturday night."

"I called Katherine during the day, but her husband said she wasn't at home. He told me that she was indulging in spa time with her sister-in-law. But she'd told *me* earlier in the week that she was taking a personal day on Friday for that, so one of them was lying. Katherine does stuff like that."

"She's a habitual liar?"

"Maybe, but in this case I meant that she enjoys expensive, self-indulgent jaunts. Maybe her husband feels guilty since he's in a wheelchair or something, but he sends her to Palm Springs and has large flower arrangements sent to her work. He even took her to Paris for a weekend last year."

"What's their story?"

Debra looked around as if trying to determine whether anyone was close enough to eavesdrop. "Sean works off-site as a marketing engineer. Visiting customers. I've heard people here complain about his work ethic, but he wins all these awards from the company and the community. Raises money for kids sports, mostly. He was a member of the 1980 Olympic team—the one that didn't go to Russia."

"So he's a lot older than Katherine."

Debra stabbed at the last piece of broccoli on her plate.

"I'd guess maybe fifteen years, at least. Sean tried out for the 1984 team, but tripped near the finish and didn't qualify. I think that's when he messed up his legs. Or maybe there was already something wrong, and that's what caused the fall. I don't know the whole story. You'd have to ask him, or Katherine."

I pulled a pad of paper out of my backpack and made a note on it. I shivered as a gust of wind came up off the San Francisco Bay. I should have brought a sweatshirt. I noticed that, unlike Katherine, Debra hadn't brought an extra jacket for her unprepared guest. "Why were you trying to reach Katherine on Saturday?"

"I wanted her to give up her spot on the Road Runners. Like I said, she wasn't serious, but she was taking up too much of Patrick's time. Patrick wasn't that serious about his running, either, to tell you the truth, but he was the best coach the Road Runners had, and I wanted the best."

Something about Debra's statement didn't ring true. Hadn't she just said that Katherine wasn't part of the official Road Runner group? It wasn't worth the effort to untangle her statements now. I forced myself to focus on clarifying whether Debra had an alibi. "But you couldn't reach her."

"Right. After that, I went for a run on the high school track to blow off some steam. I guess we'll both have to look for another trainer now." Debra sighed heavily, as if she thought someone had killed Patrick solely to inconvenience her. "I ran into some of the other Road Runners there. When it got too dark to see, we went out for a beer. Well, they each had a beer. I had water. We talked about needing more coaches for the Road Runners."

"Would any of those other runners have wanted Patrick gone?"

"I don't think so. As I said, we had a severe shortage of coaches."

"Can you think of anyone who'd benefit from his death?"

She shook her head and began to gather up her belongings. A cafeteria attendant collected our plates. Thankfully, Debra didn't seem to notice that I hadn't touched the green hockey puck.

"Sorry," she said, without sounding the slightest bit contrite. "I have to get to that Pilates class. The teacher's good, but she's a bit of a flake. If she doesn't show up, I'll have to teach it myself."

I shrugged myself into my backpack, frustrated by my failure to glean any information from Debra aside from my conviction that I'd like to avoid her company in the future. I thanked her for her time and started toward my car when she called my name. I turned and saw her running toward me. She took a moment to catch her breath. "You might want to look at Sean, Katherine's husband. After all, Katherine spent a lot of time with Patrick—another man. Sean could have been jealous. Maybe those lavish trips were an attempt to woo her back? Maybe he envied Patrick's mobility? Could he have been overcompensating because he was in a wheelchair? I think he was looking for another coach for her too. I overheard something like that at one of the Road Runner get-togethers."

I thanked her again, and watched as she took off at a sprint. I shook my head. I was no expert, but I was a track mom and Debra didn't seem to have the athletic form I'd expect from an elite runner. And she'd been out of breath when she'd mentioned Sean. Surely someone who was training for long distance races would have more stamina after jogging only a few yards. I was missing something. But was it important? Debra hadn't provided much of an alibi for the time of the murder. That could mean she was guilty, or that she didn't know when Patrick had been killed.

She'd implicated Sean, but Sean was wheelchair-bound, limiting his options as a murderer. Besides, he seemed like a nice guy. The kids called him Mr. Santa Claus, which seemed to imply he was jovial and harmless. But later they'd said something was off when it came to Katherine, Sean, and Sean's sister, the woman they called Mrs. Claus. I needed to follow up on that. What was wrong with this trio of family members? Could it have led to murder? I made a note of the things I needed to discuss with the boys, including setting up an appointment for Tess to call.

I scrolled through my phone for emails and texts and noted that it was only one o'clock. The kids hadn't called. I had time to make a short visit to Sean and double-check his alibi, assuming he was at home and lived close by. Debra had implied he was employed by the same company, but that he worked from home. Without much hope, I searched the Internet for Sean Philips. To my surprise, his name popped up with an Orchard View address about five blocks away. Many tech people I knew worked hard to hide their personal information from search engines. It took frequent monitoring, and an in-depth search would still reveal their data. Still, I was surprised that Sean's name came up so quickly. I clicked on the third link, which showed a Fiona Philips and Katherine McNamara living at the same address, so I was sure I had the right guy. Maybe my luck had turned. I decided to take a chance and drive to the house. Fiona might be as much help as Sean. Chances were, one of them would be home. If not, I'd call and make arrangements to meet them another time.

My stomach rumbled, and I stopped on the way to get a latte and a chicken wrap. The "spinach omelet" at lunch didn't resemble any egg I'd ever tasted, and I didn't like meals that pretended to be something they weren't. Life was too short to trust dishonest food.

In Orchard View, moving five blocks in one direction or another doesn't change much about the neighborhood. I had no trouble finding Sean Philips's address. It was an ordinary house on an ordinary street, one block off a six-lane boulevard that connected cars traveling between Highways 101 and 280 at a much higher speed than the original roadway engineers had intended.

Their one-story ranch was beige, with darker beige shutters and a marine-blue door. Their yard and gardens had not yet recovered from the drought and still sported bare patches of rock-hard adobe soil and a drought-era sign promoting water conservation. It read, "Brown Is the New Green," but the letters were almost too sun-faded to decipher.

The green van Sean Philips had been driving when I first met him was parked in the driveway. The glare of the shiny waxed surface threatened to give me a migraine and triggered the distinct feeling that I was missing something important. But what?

Chapter 22

In California's warm, dry summer weather, it can be tempting to hike on well-maintained trails wearing shorts and sandals. But even heavy-duty sandals designed for hiking can prove dangerous to those who startle a napping pit viper. Long pants and hiking shoes are a wiser choice.

From the Notebook of Maggie McDonald
Simplicity Itself Organizing Services

Wednesday, August 9, Early afternoon

Fiona resembled Mrs. Claus more than I'd remembered. She answered the door in a red-and-white striped T-shirt, white slacks, and red tennis shoes. With one foot out the door, she called good-bye to an unseen Sean before she looked up, startled to see me. "Whoa! Sorry. Maggie, is it? Katherine introduced us, right? I was expecting a friend who is driving me to ballroom dancing this afternoon." She leaned forward and peered past me, up and down the street, then down at her watch. "I still have a few minutes. Please come in. Can I get you a glass of water?" She raised her voice. "Sean, Katherine's friend Maggie is here. You remember. We met her at Kath's work."

I stepped inside. "I have a few questions for you. About Patrick. I don't want to keep you. I can wait with you outside if you think your ride will be here soon."

Fiona seemed flustered. "When I heard the bell, I just assumed I'd lost track of time, but my friend won't be here for another half an hour. Please come in."

Sean rolled in through a wide hallway. He was sitting in a lightweight chair, much like those I'd seen wheelchair marathoners use. He wore gloves and had a towel draped over his shoulder. "I'm sorry about the sweat. I was working out. I need to keep the muscles that still work strong and flexible. Were we expecting company? Don't you have to leave soon, Fiona?"

"This is Maggie. Remember? From Kath's work?"

"But you don't work with my wife," Sean said, scowling. "You were meeting Katherine for lunch."

"Right," I said, stepping forward to shake Sean's hand. "I have a few questions about Patrick Olmos. His wife, Tess, is one of my best friends. And their son is a friend of my kids'."

"I'm so sorry for your loss," said Fiona. "Please, have a seat." We traded polite phrases while Sean wiped sweat from his face. Eventually, I felt able to ease into my interview questions.

"Obviously, as Tess's friend, I don't think she killed Patrick. I hope to exonerate her and bring the real killer to justice." Fiona and Sean glanced at other, nodded, and turned back to me, so I continued, "The Patrick Olmos I knew had no enemies, and I can't imagine why anyone would want to kill him. Nor can I think of him creating a problem for anyone. At least not a problem so large they'd be drawn to murder as a solution. But I'm wondering if you'd seen another side of him. I'm talking to as many of his friends and associates as I can think of."

"But surely the police are investigating. Wouldn't it be safer to leave it to them?" Fiona's face was lined with confusion and concern. "I wasn't acquainted with Patrick, except, of course, as Katherine's running partner. Sean may have known him better."

Sean pursed his lips. "Patrick and I were classmates at Stanford. I introduced Katherine to him and encouraged her running as much as I could. I used to coach her myself. But I had some injuries...and here we are."

"Do you know of any reason why someone would want to kill him?"

"Of course not. We had words from time to time over Katherine's training. I didn't think Patrick pushed her hard enough or enforced her health regimen enough. She should be following a stricter diet, but Patrick let the kids bring junk food to practice, and he never discouraged her from taking part." He seemed disgusted. "I told Katherine that if she wanted to get serious about her future, she needed to look at triathlons or marathons, and forget this cross-country trail running stuff. Quit her job and train full-time."

"She was that good?"

"She could have been. She still could be." Sean shrugged. "She was prepping for Olympic events when I met her. Back then, the business climate and her level in the company made it easier for her to train and simultaneously work in a field like software engineering, where the hours are flexible. It's getting more and more difficult now for her to do both. She has to decide soon."

"Can she afford to quit?" I asked, blurting out the words before I realized I was saying them out loud.

Sean appeared horrified, and I couldn't blame him. "That's none of your business, is it?"

I shook my head. "No, it certainly isn't. I apologize."

Fiona stood, and Sean pointed his wheelchair toward the door. It was a clear indication I should leave. I'd blown this interview, but I tried one more question anyway.

"Sean, do you have any idea what Patrick was doing up on the ridge the night he died? If the police were to ask you about your whereabouts, would you have an alibi?"

Sean's lips thinned in anger, and his fists clenched. "I think it's time for you to leave," he said, nodding to Fiona before spinning his chair around and shooting back down the hallway.

Fiona held out her hand, inviting me to walk ahead of her to the door. "Let me grab my purse, and we can wait outside for my friend," she said. "My brother has a temper."

"Do you know if he has an alibi for Saturday night or early Sunday morning?" I asked.

Fiona looked pensive. "I was in the emergency room all night with Katherine, but I assume Sean was here. He doesn't go out much in the evenings. He takes his training seriously, goes to bed early, and as you heard, has no patience with those who want a more balanced life."

"Is there a way to prove he was here?" My questions were more direct and abrupt than Fiona deserved, but Sean had given me way more pushback than I'd expected, and I was taking it out on Fiona. Fiona was politely pretending not to notice. That, or she didn't care. Maybe living with someone as demanding and brusque as Sean had made her immune to inappropriate behavior in anyone else. Or had Sean been having an unusually bad day? Was I overreacting because I'd skipped lunch? It was hard to know.

"I'm not sure," Fiona said, and it took me a moment to remember what we'd been discussing. Sean wasn't the only one who'd let his temper derail him. "His equipment is computerized, and he keeps meticulous records. The machines talk to his training apps. I suppose the police could get a warrant for that data if they needed it." Fiona sighed. "Look, I'm sorry he was so rude. I'm not apologizing for him, that's up to him. But I don't like to see people treated badly. The truth is, Patrick and Sean didn't get along. Sean was jealous of Patrick's athletic talents and annoyed that Patrick squandered them. But Sean may have been the only person who saw things that way. Patrick used his gifts to keep himself fit, have fun, and teach other runners, particularly the next generation. He was generous with his time, and that didn't sit well with Sean. When Sean ran, he ran for himself and drove himself as hard as he could—with great success. He wanted that same level of achievement for Katherine and Patrick. They had other goals, and Sean found that hard to live with."

How hard? I wondered. Were powerful feelings, tremendous disappointment, an unbound temper, and limited ways to work off anger a recipe that added up to murder? And did it matter? Surely wheelchair-bound Sean couldn't have killed Patrick, particularly up on the ridge with the rutted trails and slippery hillsides. And with a fire approaching? It had proven a deadly mix for Patrick, and surely it would have been even more dangerous for Sean, no matter how nimble he was in his chair.

I was getting nowhere. I'd learned a little bit more about Patrick and the people he lived and worked with, but I was no closer to exonerating Tess. All my chief suspects had alibis. I phoned Forrest, Elaine, Paolo, Stephen, and Jason from the car and invited them to dinner, hoping their investigations had been more successful, or that our pooled information would point to a breakthrough. Jason, at least, could update us on Sergeant Nguyen's investigation, possibly giving us a lead on what our next move should be in our attempt to debunk official theories of the crime.

Discouraged and hot, I cranked up the air-conditioning and flicked on the radio, only to hear: "We turn now to the peninsula, where a wildfire continues to burn in the hills between Orchard View and the coast. According to the National Weather Service, the weather pattern is expected to change late this evening, causing mixed reactions from area residents."

The announcer went on to explain that the wind would shift to an onshore flow, bringing cooler and damper coastal air into the afflicted areas. In a plus for the fire crews, that wind was likely to push the fire back over already-burned acres now short on fuel. But that could spell disaster for us. That same wind would bring heavy smoke back into the valley, making breathing a challenge for infants, older people, and anyone with respiratory issues, including Brian. It would also put our house smack in the middle of the zone with the biggest threat levels. I needed to consult with Max and learn what Cal Fire was recommending as far as evacuation readiness was concerned. But I had time for one more errand.

I asked Siri to text Max and the boys to tell them we'd have guests for dinner and that I'd be home within the hour. If the fire forced us to change our plans, I'd text everyone I'd invited. Our guests and my family would know we'd be having chili for dinner. I had quarts of it in the basement freezer, the contents of which had resisted thawing when the power went out. It was my go-to solution for serving meals to large impromptu gatherings. A tad heavy for a hot summer evening, but I'd lighten it up by offering a cold salad, fruit, and refreshing drinks, with ice cream to follow.

I looked up an address on my phone and asked Siri for directions. The property covered an acre of land in the hills, about a half a mile from our house. At least I'd be close to home, in case I needed to dash back there to lick my wounds.

Pauline's car wasn't in the big circular driveway when I pulled through the Windsor family's ostentatious gateposts, but she could easily have stashed her car in one of the six bays of the expansive garage to the left of the main house. I parked the car, looked over my script, took a deep breath, and let it out. With any luck, my target would be home alone.

Three stairs led up to a covered porch flanked by stone benches. I rang the bell. I was about to turn away when I heard steps on the tiled floor inside. A thin hand pushed aside the sheer curtains covering the sidelights. I listened to a series of locks click and watched the oversized doorknob turn.

Chapter 23

Parents should prepare emergency medical information for themselves and their children. In the past, we kept cards in our wallets. Now there are phone apps that serve the same purpose. Information should include: prescriptions and medications; insurance details; organ donor status; chronic conditions; history of illnesses and surgeries; allergies; family history; immunizations; and emergency contacts, including doctor, pharmacy, hospital, dentist, friends, or family. Teens should carry their own medical information.

From the Notebook of Maggie McDonald
Simplicity Itself Organizing Services

Wednesday, August 9, Afternoon

Rebecca, Pauline Windsor's only child, opened the door. She was Teddy's age, but looked much younger. Her pale blue eyes were swollen and tear streaked. Her normally shiny blond hair was lank and stringy. What looked like melted ice cream had dripped and left splotches on her stretched-out T-shirt.

I was shocked by her appearance. I'd once heard Brian refer to her snidely as "Orchard View Barbie." Any other time I'd seen her, the description would have been apt. This girl had won the genetic lottery. But today wasn't the first time I'd had an inkling that something was very wrong in her world.

She sniffed and rubbed her eyes. I said nothing. Faced with this forlorn waif, my carefully prepared plan turned to vapor. Rebecca took a step backward as if threatened by my silence.

"Rebecca, I'm Maggie McDonald, Brian and David's mom. Is anyone home with you?" I winced. One of the first rules suburban teens learn is never to tell a stranger if they're home alone. I backpedaled. "Never mind. I'm sorry. Can we talk for a moment? Maybe out here on the porch?"

Rebecca stepped forward without replying. She left the front door open and sat on one of the benches. I took the seat opposite.

"You're not a happy girl right now, are you?" I asked gently.

She hesitated, and I spotted a hint of the bravado and defiance that might protect her from whatever had wounded her so badly. But then it vanished. She half-sobbed and shook her head, examining her dirty bare feet.

"Do you know why I'm here?"

She started to shake her head, but in the end, she confessed, "You know what I did."

"I think so. It's more important, though, that *you* know what you did. You hurt Teddy badly. You spread lies about his parents, not just to their friends and neighbors, but to the world. That's a hurt that 'sorry' doesn't cover."

Rebecca flushed and moaned, then started sobbing. I moved quickly to her side and hugged her. I didn't want to. I'd come here prepared to treat her as though she and her evil deed were the same. I didn't like her mother. I didn't care for what I'd heard about Rebecca, that she was snobby and manipulative. And I hated what she'd done with the vile website she'd created. But in the end, my nurturing instincts saw a little girl who was hurting nearly as badly as Teddy was.

But my loving nature only took me so far. After a moment, I moved away from her a bit, and I searched through my backpack for a tissue.

I handed it to her, and she swiped at her eyes, then blew her nose. "How do you plan to fix the mess you've made?" I asked.

"I've already taken it down. When I first built it, I thought it was funny, edgy, and clever. Then I saw Teddy's face when he found the page, and I realized how sick and awful it was. And how big. It's like I created this giant blob that just kept growing. I don't know how to stop it."

"I'm not sure you *can* stop it, completely. It's out there now. Too many people have taken screen shots and posted them on social media." I let my words sink in for a moment before throwing her a lifeline. "Do you want help?"

"*Is* there help?"

I answered as honestly as I could while I dug into my purse. "I'm not sure. But if anyone can help, he can." I flicked the corner of Paolo's card and handed it to her. "If you're mature and responsible enough to admit what you've done, accept the consequences, and do everything in your power to set things right, Paolo Bianchi can probably help. But it's up to you to call him. Will you do that?"

She sniffed. "I think so."

"I won't tell anyone about our conversation, as long as you contact Paolo within the next twenty-four hours. But if you don't, I will report you to the chief of the Orchard View Police Force. What you did comes with criminal penalties."

Rebecca, to her credit, sat up straight, squared her shoulders, and looked me in the eye. "I'll call him right now."

I stood, smoothed my T-shirt, and nodded. "Good." I turned and stepped off the porch, heading toward my car. I'd completed my mission. But then I paused and turned. "Rebecca?"

Her shoulders shook with tears, but she looked up.

"Take a shower first. Put on clean clothes. Make your bed. The new you starts now. You can leave a message for Paolo outside regular work hours, but don't delay too long. Fixing this will make you feel better." She nodded, and I turned away but called to her again when I reached the car.

"I'm sorry something has happened that has made you so angry. Eventually, you're going to have to deal with that problem too. If you need help, get it. But don't let it define you. Don't let this mistake define you. You've got a mess to clean up, that's certain. Try to let your efforts to fix the problem become the new Rebecca."

Finally, I felt like I'd finished what I'd set out to do this morning. Whatever happened to Rebecca, I'd lightened my load and lifted some of the pressure from Tess, Teddy, and everyone who cared for them.

As I pulled out of the driveway, I sent up a little prayer, or a wish. I hoped that Rebecca would have time to do what needed to be done before Pauline got wind of her daughter's crimes or her plan to repair the damage. If I knew Pauline, she'd try to explain the problem away and help her daughter dodge the consequences. And that wouldn't do anyone any good. For the first time, I wondered if there was a Mr. Windsor, and if so, whether he was the kind of dad who could provide his daughter with a moral compass.

But my work was done. For now.

On my way back to the house, I stopped by the grocery for a quick resupply of necessary items, I looked forward to getting home, taking a quick shower, and getting caught up with the kids.

After unlocking the kitchen door and putting two heavy sacks of food on the table, I called to the boys for help bringing in the remaining groceries. Holmes and Watson snaked around my ankles meowing for food, but there was no accompanying sound of the dogs' toenails scrambling down the back stairs and no calls of greeting from the boys. Assuming they were down in the barn, I went outside to grab the last load of groceries from the car, calling down the hill. But I heard nothing in response, and no sounds to indicate that they'd had trouble hearing me over whatever it was they might be up to.

Figuring they must be out for a walk with the dogs, I stashed the perishables in the fridge and the freezer as quickly as I could, pulled the chili out to thaw, and checked to see that we had enough ice for a party. Everyone who was coming tonight was a regular in our house, so setting up for the gathering was routine. Time for that shower.

I washed my hair twice in scalding water to remove the soot and the persistent feeling of having become soiled in probing the lives of my neighbors. I dialed down the temperature to soothe my irritated skin. For the next few minutes, I thought I could almost hear my skin slurping up the moisture.

I was drying my hair when my phone erupted with a series of chirps, telling me I had messages from my weather app, texts, emails, and voice mails. It's the way life works. I'd spent the morning leaving messages without any response. But then I stepped into the shower for ten...or maybe twenty luxurious, self-indulgent minutes, and the world demanded my attention.

I flicked through the messages. They included the same fire news I'd heard on the radio and RSVPs from everyone I'd invited to dinner. A local update with more detail than the one from the weather service showed that various areas of the hills were still under mandatory evacuation. Others, like our neighborhood, were deemed relatively safe, but everyone was cautioned to pay attention to shifts in the weather, to the warnings, and to our emergency preparedness. That text included phone numbers to call for more information, including services for those who needed help evacuating. I sniffed the air, wondering if the smoke I smelled was residual from the earlier burn or a sign that increased winds had coaxed the fire to jump its containment lines. I couldn't shake the edgy feeling that disaster was again stalking us, just out of sight.

Then a text message came through from Max:

*Heard from boys? I've been texting all day. No
response. What's up? Wondering if they want to do
Baylands run this evening. Cooler, cleaner air.*

What had been a small hint of worry blossomed into a nagging fear. Where *were* the boys? It wasn't like them to go anywhere without leaving a note, though I had enough experience with grief to know that a death in the family can disrupt everyone's thinking and their ability to follow long-engrained practices, like some of our family rules: Leave a note or text when you leave home. Return parental texts immediately. The principal at Brian's middle school, April Chen, shortened the rule for easy consumption by young teens with short attention spans: *If they're worried, you're toast.*

So, no note. But no dogs, either. The boys weren't here, and they weren't close by, or the dogs would have heard me calling earlier and brought everyone home.

I looked for clues. Their cereal bowls were in the dishwasher, which was nearly as unusual as no note. No food left out, crumbs on the table, or plates in the sink meant they'd either left after a late breakfast, or taken food upstairs to play video games. Food upstairs was unlikely. We didn't have a rule against it, but it wasn't a habit we encouraged. I dashed back up the stairwell to our spare room/den where we kept our TV and the online gaming paraphernalia. The room was relatively clean and tidy, which told me they hadn't been playing in here today. So where? I thought for a moment, and my heart sank. They'd been so keen to go on their backpacking trip. Could they have ignored our prohibitions against the overnight hike and set off anyway? I flew up the attic stairs and leaned against the wall, breathing hard when I spotted their rolled-up sleeping bags and backpacks scattered around the upstairs hallway, partially packed. My faith in my children and their judgment was restored, but my fear for their whereabouts grew. I glanced out the attic window to the barn, but couldn't see their bicycles. I doubted they would have taken them anywhere. Normally, conditions were perfect in our hills for both road biking and mountain biking. World-class athletes, avid amateurs, and recreational cyclists all frequented both streets and trails. And, of course, like teens anywhere who didn't yet drive, bicycles were our kids' preferred mode of transportation. But the air-quality was still dreadful from the fires and as far as I knew, Max hadn't brought Teddy's road bike up the hill. It was worth checking. I shot off a text to Max:

Still checking on whereabouts of boys.
Did you and the boys pack Teddy's bike?
If not, can you bring it up tonight?

My whole family laughed at my texting skills. I was a slow typist. My sentences were too long, and I used too much punctuation. I laughed along with them. Texting wasn't a skill I felt I needed to practice. Nor did I desire to converse like a fifteen-year-old regardless of the communication medium.

I checked the laundry, the floors of their rooms, and the pile of shoes by the back door in an attempt to figure out what sort of gear they'd taken with them. I gathered an inconclusive mass of information. Their track clothes and the trail running shoes they normally wore to cushion their feet from rocks and protect their ankles on the deep ruts were still covered by soot from yesterday's excursion and parked by the door. Pool towels and board shorts hung on the line outside, equally covered by soot, which precluded a last-minute invitation to a neighbor's pool. The nearest community pool was closed for the duration of the fire emergency.

I texted them again, then phoned, listening for text alerts and ringtones. Nothing. Could the stress of the past few days have caused them to allow their phones to run out of charge? *Ridiculous.* Their phones were their lifelines. While Max and I frequently found ourselves holding dead or dying phones, the kids had grown up with the habit of recharging their electronic gear and were more consistent with that chore than they were about brushing their teeth. They even owned backup chargers they carried with them, just in case.

My anxiety climbed. I'd exhausted my ideas. It was time to enlist help. Using the same group list I'd used to invite our friends to dinner, I broadcast a message that I hoped set the right tone—mildly alarmed, eager to be reassured, but not yet freaking out:

Teddy, Brian, David not checking in. Out
somewhere with dogs. Are they helping
you? Do you know where they are?

Jason was the first to phone back. "I don't like this, Maggie. I've already alerted my troops and nearby jurisdictions."

Chapter 24

Expect the unexpected. Even if you're familiar with the area in which you're hiking, be aware that unexpected detours due to washed-out trails or roaming wildlife may require you to rethink your route. Plan accordingly with a map or GPS system.

From the Notebook of Maggie McDonald
Simplicity Itself Organizing Services

Wednesday, August 9, Afternoon

"It's not like your boys to take off without letting folks know where they are, especially now." Jason said. "You're their connection to safety and security. With the fire, and Patrick's death, and Tess being in jail, they wouldn't risk breaking the rules or even stretching them."

"So, what do we do?"

"I'll send out an alert."

I gasped, thinking he meant an Amber Alert for a missing child. It was a term I associated with abduction and grave risk to a minor.

"Sorry. Poor choice of words. I'll let my officers know we're looking for them. I'll let the rangers and firefighters and the sheriff's office know, too. The boys didn't leave a note, which, unless they've got some kind of teenaged brain fade going on, means they weren't planning to be gone long. That puts them in the fire areas, which means they are officially at risk."

My throat clenched, and I could think of nothing to say. My brain went from sane to frantic in only a few seconds, and horrific images raced through my mind.

"Don't panic, Maggie. I'm sure nothing's wrong. We'll find them quickly. If we don't, an Amber Alert would be appropriate because of the fire danger. But we're not there yet. Do you know what they're wearing?"

I shook my head, then remembered Jason couldn't see me. "I don't. Probably shorts and T-shirts, but I don't know for sure."

"That's fine."

"They have the dogs with them. Mozart and Belle."

"Even better. The dogs will protect them if necessary, and make them easier to identify. I'll hang up so you can pick up your calls from everyone else you texted. That was another smart move. Contact me if you hear from them."

Before I could thank him, Jason ended the call. I checked and saw that I had several messages.

From Elaine:

> *Haven't heard from them. Max called me. I'm*
> *coming up now with Teddy's bike. Tell him*
> *cats are doing well. Will alert April Chen.*

April was the principal at the middle school and another friend of the family. If the kids were at loose ends, she was another person they might have sought out. And she would have been happy to put them to work at school with any number of maintenance chores.

From Max:

> *I'm running the Find iPhone app.*

Like many families of teenagers, we had mixed emotions on the myriad of child-stalking apps available. If our ultimate goal was to raise strong, independent kids, we reasoned, was it right to stalk them? Did that say we trusted neither their judgment nor their skills? Weren't they entitled to at least the illusion of privacy? Was using an app a safety precaution or an overreach worthy of a helicopter parent? We'd asked the boys for their feelings on the matter. Predictably, they were horrified to think that we'd be able to pinpoint their location 24/7. So, we compromised. We installed the apps on everyone's phones, and we established a new rule. Every call or text from a family member had to be answered within five minutes. If a response didn't arrive, we were allowed and encouraged to activate the location app. So far, we hadn't used it, and I'd forgotten I had the capability. It terrified me that we were in this spot. If one kid didn't answer, that was worrisome. But we had three boys missing, and none of them had responded to texts. The implications were horrifying.

By the time Elaine arrived, I'd called a few of Brian and David's friends. Max had sent a text blast to the cross-country team. The few parents I reached wanted to hear about Tess. My heart raced as I fended off their questions and focused on clues to the kids' whereabouts. Most local families were out of town for summer vacation trips, and no one I reached had seen the boys or knew where they might be. Everyone assured me they'd keep an eye out and call with any news.

I hugged Elaine and then apologized. I was covered with sweat and smelled of fear. My reserves of equanimity had been low following Patrick's death, and now they were nonexistent. Elaine took my phone and texted Max to come home. He texted back that he was already on his way, though stuck in traffic.

Max and Stephen arrived simultaneously, and entered the kitchen with eager expressions as if convinced I'd have great news for them. Stephen had brought Munchkin, his mastiff sidekick, whose downtrodden and devastated expression matched that of Max and Stephen's as soon as they learned the boys were still missing.

Stephen kissed my cheek. "Can I look around? See if there are any clues you missed?"

I agreed immediately. "The more I worried, the less effective my searching became. Have at it." Stephen's preretirement experiences with the marines included law enforcement responsibilities. Both he and Munchkin had a search-and-rescue background. He also had an able group of veterans willing to help out at a moment's notice whenever people were in danger. I hadn't met them, at least not for more than a second or two. Wounds they'd sustained in America's multiple wars had made them shy away from strangers, but hadn't put a dent in their need to serve. One, named Rocket, had helped protect us a few months earlier when Ketifa and a friend were stalked by a dangerous ex-boyfriend.

Munchkin sniffed around under the table, then at Belle and Mozart's food dishes, and then near the hook where we kept their leashes. He sat at the back door, whined, and scratched gently, then glanced over his shoulder toward Stephen and sat, returning his attention to the door. "Munchkin's weighed in. Let me see what I can do," Stephen said.

He examined the pile of shoes near the back door, nudging them a little with his foot as if taking inventory. He nodded, then scanned the row of coats, jackets, and sweatshirts hanging on the kitchen hooks. Like me, he glanced in the sink and dishwasher, and then in the fridge. "They've been gone awhile," he said without turning around. He lifted the milk and orange juice cartons as if assessing their weight. "Otherwise they'd have cleaned you out."

Max smiled briefly, but his face was lined with tension and fear. His hand gripped mine, hard.

Stephen closed the refrigerator door and opened the freezer compartment. The rasping sound of scraping ice crystals affected me like fingernails on a blackboard as he sorted through the few frozen items that had survived the unexpected power outage and thaw during the evacuation. It seemed so long ago. And Stephen's progress seemed so slow and deliberate that I wanted to scream. Until he turned and held up one of the small yellow pads we used for grocery lists and notes to one another. Moisture had smudged the note, but it was still legible.

"Out for a run with the dogs," Stephen read aloud. "Will stay away from fire areas. Back soon."

I sighed with relief, though I felt foolish for having missed it when I'd put away the groceries. I guessed my inattentiveness showed how many routine household chores I performed on autopilot. We hadn't found our missing children, but at least we knew they'd left under their own steam. We'd narrowed down the area we'd need to search. I hadn't realized I'd feared they'd been abducted, perhaps by the same person or persons responsible for Patrick's death. But I must have subconsciously been sure that's what had happened, or I wouldn't have found myself so relieved now.

"How did you know where to look?" Max asked.

Stephen grinned. "I didn't. But I should have. Isn't that the cliché? That people under stress put their cereal in the fridge and the milk in the cupboard? Keys in the vegetable crisper?"

I shook my head. "I was looking for clues in the usual places. Looking for things in unlikely locations makes more sense."

Munchkin whined.

"In a minute, Munch," Stephen said, turning to Max and me. "Do you have their computers?"

Max rubbed his chin, looking confused, but I knew at once what Stephen was getting at. I ran up the back stairs two at a time, and came back with two laptops. David's was covered with stickers from musical groups he followed. Brian's was pristine with a red plastic protective cover. "If we look at their browser history, we can see whether they consulted any maps that could pinpoint their location," I said, breathless from my run and swirling emotions.

I handed both computers to Max, who was adept at making any electronic device cough up what it hid from the less tech-savvy, like me. Max opened David's laptop. "He would have taken the lead on deciding where to run." Max spoke mostly to himself. His knee jiggled. He gritted his teeth. His fingers typed so quickly the sound of each tap melded with the next to create a single sound. I held my breath and tried to refrain from unnecessary pleas for him to hurry. There was no one better at squeezing information from a computer, and no one more motivated.

The kitchen clock's audible *tick* set my teeth on edge. Munchkin sighed and dropped to the floor, his head sinking to rest on his front paws. Until Max punched the air with his hands.

"Arastradero Preserve! It's accessible from here, dogs are allowed, and it's outside the most likely paths of the fire, even if the wind changes."

Stephen was already punching numbers on his phone. "I'll let Jason know so he can alert the appropriate authorities."

I ached to run out the door and drive, walk, or fly toward the kids. Munchkin was equally antsy. Normally reserved and stately in his behavior, he bounced from one front paw to the next, whining and snuffling the bottom of the back door.

"What can we do?" I asked Stephen when he finished the call. "Stay here? Stay by the phone? Go?"

I was talking too fast to be intelligible, but Stephen got the message anyway. "One of you should stay here, definitely," he said. "They could be on their way back and arrive just after the rest of us leave. But if the reason we can't reach them is that they're in trouble or hurt, one of you might as well go to the trailhead, so you're close by when we find them. And we *will* find them. All the fire teams are searching, including the helicopter that's tracking hot spots. Kon Sokolov, the ranger, is following the PG&E trail in that direction—"

"They won't have gone that way," Max interrupted. "Kon warned them off yesterday, and so did Maggie and I."

Stephen held up his hand. "Stay with me. Kon wants to rule that trail out. It's the fastest way to Arastradero. He'll talk to anyone he runs into... firefighters, law enforcement, errant hikers, and ask about the boys. But he's also got two guys on ATVs who'll set out from here. We'll find them,

Maggie. I want to drive to the Arastradero trailhead and work backward from there with Munchkin. He's not a tracking dog, but he's friends with Belle, Mozart, and your boys. That connection means the dogs will detect each other long before we do."

I could read Max's thoughts as well as I could my own. We both wanted to be where the boys were. We wanted to be together. We wanted to be the first to find them. I cursed physics, which dictated each of us could be in only one place at a time. My shoulders drooped.

"Go with Stephen, Maggie," Max said. "I'll stay here by the phone and get everything set up for dinner. Those boys will be hungry when we get them home." Already texting, he added, "I'll cancel tonight's dinner too. We don't need to be entertaining right now. Our friends will understand."

I gave him a quick hug and grabbed a sweatshirt, water, energy bars, and a flashlight, in case our search went beyond sunset. I glanced at my watch, trying not to think of the dangers lurking beyond the fire—mountain lions, rattlers, members of the drug cartels, assault weapons.

Stephen made an effort to distract me. "Take Munchkin's leash," he said. "We'll go in my car. My radio is tied to Jason's phone, and I've got rescue equipment in the trunk."

My eyes grew wide in fear. Stephen elaborated in a slow, quiet, and calm voice. "Rescue equipment—like blankets, water, more flashlights. We're fine. They are too. Let's go get them."

He'd almost convinced me that I was overreacting when I heard what sounded like a series of gunshots echo through the canyons on the far side of the ridge.

Chapter 25

There's not much humans can do to prepare for an encounter with rattlesnakes, except to know their enemy. Snakes are shy and will not attack unless threatened or startled. Most bites occur when a combination of testosterone, alcohol, and drugs are present in large quantities. Fifty years ago, snake bite first aid included ice, elevation, cutting the wound site, and sucking out the poison. Today, experts recommend against all of those procedures and advise seeking medical attention immediately. Phone ahead when you're en route to the hospital.

From the Notebook of Maggie McDonald
Simplicity Itself Organizing Services

Wednesday, August 9, Late afternoon

I jumped into Stephen's SUV.

I reminded myself that every public protection agency in the county was doing all they could to find the boys. Every member of those many teams was more experienced than I was. And the boys were sensible. I knew they'd stick together and look after one another. Those were the thoughts my rational brain repeated over and over like a mantra. My lizard brain, my mama bear instinct, and every other part of me fought panic and terror.

Long purple shadows on the golden hills proved an unwelcome reminder that the clock was ticking.

When we reached the trailhead, Stephen led the way at a steady pace that I sensed was slower than he'd travel if he was alone. I was tempted to let him go ahead without me, but I couldn't do it. I wanted to go faster, but my lungs were already straining on the steep uphill climb. Stephen must have anticipated my thoughts, or else I'd said the words aloud without realizing it. "It's okay, Maggie. This isn't a race. We'll find them. Chances are, they've forgotten the time. Or their phones are out of charge. It's not like them. I know that. But we've had a rough couple of days. None of us are acting normally—whatever that is."

I knew that Stephen was trying to distract me. And if we'd been searching for just one kid, I would have had an easier time believing him. But could all three of them have forgotten to charge their phones? Unlikely. Something else was wrong. Something serious. Something, I was sure, that stemmed from the terrors Kon had outlined for Max. My eyes scanned the edges of the trail for rattlers, the hillsides for smoke, and the trees for mountain lions, though any cat that heard us or spotted us was likely to freeze as it lay in wait—or slink off quietly after deciding we weren't worth the trouble. Mountain lion sightings in Orchard View were relatively rare. There were no more than four or five a year in the area. Attacks were far less frequent. But anything could happen.

The same went for rattlesnakes. They were shy and tended to avoid people, attacking only when surprised or threatened. Most deadly bites occurred when a mixture of elements was present: immature men, alcohol or drugs, and young snakes who expelled all their venom in one bite. Older snakes were wise enough to conserve their energy and their weaponry. They'd strike in warning without injecting venom when a target was too big to eat. With smaller prey, they'd inject just enough poison to subdue. My knees quivered in fear, and I turned my ankle on a rut. After a few quick, hopping steps, my ankle recovered, thank goodness. Could something like that have happened to the boys? Their young ankles were more pliable than mine, but their workouts were faster paced.

I scanned the hillside. Dark-leafed oaks disappeared into darker clefts in the undulating hills. Arastradero was much more open than the county land closer to our house, but hills and gullies made it impossible to see very far ahead.

Munchkin barked and strained at the leash—unusual behavior for the well-trained dog. Stephen paused to unhook his leash. I heard what could have been Belle's answering bark, and Munchkin surged ahead. Stephen turned toward me. "I don't think it's far now. He's acting like he's found a friend."

I must have looked skeptical. Stephen added, "If he were responding to a threat, he'd have a ridge of hair standing up on his back like a Mohawk. He's a scaredy-cat too. No Mohawk means friendlies."

Stephen sped after Munchkin, but waited for me to catch up when Munchkin left the trail to bound uphill toward a wooded area, with only his tail visible above the long grass.

I followed at a breathless run, hoping that any rattlers had slunk away, terrified by the pounding footsteps of the large man and his dog.

Belle exploded from a concealing clump of trees and other vegetation and, like a sheepdog, circled behind me, bumped at the backs of my legs, and barked, urging me forward. Once inside the shady copse of trees, I stopped to catch my breath. All three boys huddled against the trunk of a tree. Brian's cheeks were tear-streaked. David's revealed pain. Teddy clutched Mozart's head to his chest. They stared across the clearing as Stephen raced to the side of a man pinned down by Munchkin. The man's hand gripped a gun. He dropped it and raised his hands above his head, wincing.

I sank to my knees and gathered all three boys in a giant hug. They were alive. A more careful examination could wait a moment or two. I followed the direction of their wide-eyed stares to take in the man Munchkin held down with one paw. In a moment, my brain took in enough details to alter my initial assessment of the situation. The stranger wasn't fending off Munchkin's attentions, but reveling in them as he laughed. He wasn't scrambling for the dropped firearm, but pushing it away to protect Munchkin.

Stephen picked up the scary-looking black assault weapon and examined it. In one smooth motion, he ejected a curved block slightly larger than a cell phone and planted it deep in the thigh pocket of his cargo pants. He flicked a few latches, ran his hands over the spotting scope and tripod-type legs, grimaced, and slung it onto his back as nonchalantly as if he'd been picking up a grocery bag.

"Did you disarm it?" I asked.

"It wasn't loaded."

The man on the ground eyed Stephen carefully but seemed unafraid. After the gun was safely stowed, he sat up, pushing Munchkin's head and tongue away from his face. "Your mother?" he asked in hushed Spanish. It was one of only a few phrases I could understand. The boys nodded without speaking. In urgent tones, the man rattled off a paragraph's worth of words I couldn't translate. The vocabulary words required when one's children are held captive by a gun-wielding member of a drug cartel weren't covered in any of my high school Spanish classes.

I'd let Stephen and his law-enforcement training sort out the stranger and his motives. I shoved Belle aside so I could examine the boys more closely. I touched Brian's tear-stained face and hugged him, firmly. "It will be okay," I assured him. Belle licked his face. "Are you hurt?" He shook his head. "Mozart...and David," he whispered, forcing out the words. I couldn't be sure whether his raspy, wheezing voice was the result of fear or an asthma flare, or both, but I handed him his inhaler from my pocket. Normally, he would have carried one with him in the pocket of his shorts. But as Stephen kept reminding me, there was nothing ordinary about today or any of the immediately preceding ones.

He took a few puffs, closed his eyes, and relaxed a little against the tree behind him, waiting, I knew, for the adrenaline-like drug to open the passageways in his lungs and relax muscles that had tightened and made breathing shallow and painful.

I watched for a few moments as his face relaxed and his lips changed color from purple-gray to a dusty mauve. He'd need another dose before he was ready to go anywhere, but the drug appeared to be working. I moved on to David.

"Brian says you're hurt? Where?"

David made a dismissive *tsk*ing sound. "I'm fine."

"Why does Brian think you're hurt?"

Teddy leaned in. "It's his foot. Could be broken."

I scooted back to examine his ankle. David pulled on my sleeve. "Don't. Look at Mozart. Rattler."

I gasped and whipped my head around to stare at Stephen in alarm, then back at Mozart. I wasn't prepared to leave David and his injury to examine the dog. Nor did I know anything about doggy first aid. Did Stephen? Had he heard David's words?

Stephen left the side of the disarmed stranger, and sank to his knees on Teddy's left side. He patted Teddy's leg in a reassuring gesture, then held Mozart's head between his enormous hands as the dog whined softly. He tilted the dog's head as if trying to catch the light. Without turning toward me, or releasing the dog, he said softly, "Still got that flashlight, Maggie? Hand it to Teddy."

I did as I was told, pulling a small LED flashlight from the pocket of my jeans. "Teddy, shine it where you think he was bitten," Stephen said. "Did you see the rattler? Was it a big 'un or a little guy?"

Teddy turned on the light and pointed it at the dog's snout. His hand and his voice wavered. "Pretty big. I saw the snake and went to grab Mozart's collar, but he was too fast. They were both too fast. Mozart jumped in front of me, snarling, and the snake coiled and struck."

"Big around as my arm," added David, holding out his hand to demonstrate.

"That's good," Stephen said. Though I wasn't sure whether he meant the snake or the way that Teddy was holding the flashlight. "There's not a lot of swelling, and his eyes are clear. He's hurtin', no question, but my guess is that he's more worried about you than he is about himself. Has he had the vaccine?"

Teddy looked to me, confused.

"He has," I said. "Both he and Belle had it in the spring. Doc Davidson recommends it for dogs who live in the hills or who run with their owners in areas like this one. We haven't seen a rattler yet in our yard, but I'm sure they're there. Or nearby, at least."

"It's still an emergency," Stephen explained. "We'll get help for him quickly. But a rattler as big as David's arm has been around awhile. He probably didn't waste much venom on Mozart, since this dog is too big for a rattler to eat. Mr. Grandpa Snake was protecting himself by warning Mozart off. A baby snake would have freaked and poured out all his venom at once." He ruffled Mozart's ears and patted Teddy's leg. "Good job, bud. Let me check out David, and then we'll make some calls."

It took Stephen one step to move from Teddy to David. I scooted out of the way, comforting Belle and Brian. Belle licked Stephen's face and seemed relieved to relinquish David's care to an expert. Stephen palpated David's ankle, glancing at him occasionally to assess his pain level. "What happened?" he asked.

David flushed. "The snake. I heard it and jumped back. My foot caught on some loose shale at the edge of the path. My balance was off, and I twisted. Landed in a wild rosebush. I've been picking thorns out of my butt ever since." He winced. Stephen patted David's knee. "You'll live. But your cross-country season may be over. We'll get you checked out."

He reached for his phone, glanced at it, then swapped it for a small radio with a long rubber-covered antenna I hadn't known he was carrying. Short, unintelligible crackles came from the radio. Stephen listened, then calmly made similar staccato utterances of numbers and jargon that meant nothing to me. He stashed the radio in a pocket and translated.

"They're sending a helicopter to take David, Brian, and Mozart to Stanford. Jason will meet them and transport Mozart to the emergency vet in Palo Alto."

A moan escaped my lips, and Brian trembled. Belle growled softly.

"No panicking," Stephen said, looking stern. "It's rush hour. The wind is coming up, and so is the fire danger. The helicopter has been looking for the boys and needs to head back to the airport anyway. The hospital is on the way. I don't think anyone's injuries here are life-threatening, but I'd feel better with an expert opinion."

He examined each of us as if measuring our fear. "There's some bad news too. There won't be room in the chopper for Teddy, Maggie, or Belle. But we'll get your mom back to you as quickly as possible."

A short burst of Spanish came from the man under the tree. This time, Teddy responded. Then he translated, saying about the last words I'd expected to come from a guy who, minutes earlier, had been holding an assault weapon.

Chapter 26

When you live in rattlesnake country, your emergency preparedness efforts need to include the possibility of a snakebite for both humans and dogs. Dogs are prone to bites due to their habit of sniffing to investigate anything strange to them, but there are remedies. A canine vaccine may help battle the effects, but expert opinions vary, and vaccinated dogs bitten by rattlesnakes should still be considered a veterinary emergency. Check with your vet for his or her recommendation. Rattlesnake avoidance training classes using positive reinforcement have been helpful (but not foolproof) in teaching dogs to steer clear of the deadly creatures. Rattlesnake aversion therapy using shock collars is controversial and generally not recommended.

From the Notebook of Maggie McDonald
Simplicity Itself Organizing Services

Wednesday, August 9, Late afternoon

Teddy translated for the rest of us. "Martín wants to know if he can come too. Says he'll watch the dogs while the doctors look after us. But he's hurt too. A gunshot wound to the arm. He needs a doctor."

Stephen spoke to the stranger in Spanish, then knelt to examine him.

"Okay," Stephen said. "Martín goes on the chopper too. Again, not life-threatening, but that wound needs a serious clean out and antibiotics."

"Wait," I shouted. "What's his story? Did he fire those shots we heard? Was he firing at my kids? He's not getting on that chopper or going anywhere with us until I know more. Ask him. Why was he aiming an assault weapon at my kids and their dogs?"

Stephen and the dogs tilted their heads. Shortly, the rest of us heard the helicopter. It was like an episode of *M*A*S*H*. Spinning blades stirred up dust, and the noise was deafening. We squinted and covered our ears. Brian pulled his T-shirt to cover his nose and mouth and filter out the pollen and dust.

Stephen shouted answers to questions barked by the EMTs. Brian, David, Mozart, and the man with the gunshot wound were scooped up by medics in black jumpsuits with red stripes on the arms and legs.

Stephen clapped me on the shoulder and mouthed the words "*Trust me.*" I frowned and bit my lip. There was no time for the answers I needed. The stranger was unarmed. I did trust Stephen. The boys and Mozart needed medical attention. The rational part of my brain forced me to nod and smile encouragingly to the kids. I squeezed in a quick wave and thumbs-up to both boys before the chopper was gone.

The silence that followed was deafening, interrupted by chirps from birds and insects getting ready for bed. Would Brian and David be okay, swallowed up by the enormous Stanford University health care system? Would I survive being separated from both of them in an emergency? I had to phone Max. Panicked, I began slapping my pockets, hunting for my phone.

How would I explain to Max that our children were sharing a medevac helicopter with a man who'd held an assault weapon on them?

"They'll be fine, Maggie. And I'll get you there as soon as possible." As usual, Stephen left me with the comforting but also creepy feeling that he'd read my mind. "You can call Max on the way. Ready, guys?" He turned to Teddy, Belle, and Munchkin, the only remaining members of our little band. I stood, gathered a jacket I thought might be Brian's, attached Belle's leash, and followed Stephen back to the car. It was barely dark enough to require the use of a flashlight, but I deployed mine anyway, for comfort. Under other circumstances, it might have been pleasant to hike through the quiet preserve, listening to the evening sounds and watching the sun set, the rise of the planets, and the emergence of the stars. But not now.

I ran to catch up with Stephen. "So, what about that assault weapon? Who was that guy? And why on earth did you decide it was okay to put him on that helicopter with my kids? You heard the shots, Stephen. And that man had a bullet wound. He'd been in a gunfight. A *gunfight.* Like the Wild West. Was his gun empty because he'd poured all his ammunition into someone else? Why wasn't he in handcuffs? Did he hurt the boys? What happened? Why didn't they call?"

Stephen turned and put his arm around me, but kept us moving forward. "The boys were in a dead zone with no phone service. I made the emergency calls on my radio, remember? As for the rest, it's a long story, Maggie. Let's wait 'til we get to Stanford, and I'll fill both you and Max in while we wait. There'll be lots of waiting. There always is. For now, I'll tell you that I heard enough to know that Martín is a good man who protected your children. Think for a moment. Did they seem afraid of him?"

I sighed. Stephen was right. The boys, though injured and fearful, had not seemed afraid of the stranger. And the dogs hadn't leaped to protect us from him, either. I forced myself to breathe out hard and inhale slowly to keep from hyperventilating. Teddy caught up with me and held on to my sleeve. If he'd been a few years younger, he might have held my hand. If I'd been his actual mother, he still might have. As it was, the teen had a death grip on my hoodie, creating wrinkles that time might never iron out. I put my hand over Teddy's, soaking up the comfort that came from reassuring someone else. "Stephen says the boys are in good hands and we'll have answers soon," I told him. I wanted to tell him that everything would be okay, but so much had already happened that wasn't anywhere close to okay. I doubted he'd believe me.

Back at Stephen's SUV, he pulled a magnetic emergency light from the passenger seat and slapped it on the roof, then activated a siren I didn't know he had. "Seat belts," he said, putting the vehicle in gear without waiting to be sure we'd buckled up. We were only a few minutes from Stanford.

I called Max. He'd already received a call from Ranger Kon Sokolov relaying the news that the boys had been found and were on the way to Stanford Hospital for the treatment of injuries that were not life-threatening. After he verified that I was uninjured, he said he'd meet me in the emergency room and ended the call.

Now that there was nothing left for me to do, I took quick shallow breaths, and my hands shook. I grew sweaty and choked down sobs. I checked on Teddy, who looked pale. He grabbed my hands. Belle leaned against Teddy. Munchkin, confined to the flat back cargo area, put a giant paw on Teddy's shoulder. Stephen checked the rearview mirror, then reached for a padded cooler on the floor. He tossed it to me.

"Sugar," he said. "After the adrenaline rush. Tank up. I don't have time to deal with either one of you fainting on me."

I unzipped the cooler and handed Teddy a soda, watching and waiting until he'd taken a sip. "You too, Maggie," Stephen said.

Stephen pulled the SUV up near the emergency room entrance and parked. A teenager who moved like a cop, even in jeans and a faded T-shirt, ran to the car. "The chopper arrived," he said when Stephen rolled down the window. "I can't tell you anything about the patients except that the doctors say they're in good shape. The chief's taken the dog to the emergency vet and said he'd be back as soon as the vet says Mozart's stable. The EMTs pumped him full of fluids. He was wagging his tail."

"Thanks, Todd. Good man. You willing to park the SUV for me?"

"If I don't, Chief will kill me."

"Can't have that." Stephen tossed him the keys. "See you inside?"

Todd nodded.

I held Belle's leash in one hand and Munchkin's in the other, wondering what to do with the dogs while I checked on Brian and David.

Teddy stepped forward with his hand outstretched. "I can wait out here with them while you go in."

"Nope," said Stephen. "They're medically necessary for the recovery of those patients inside." He took Munchkin's leash and strode confidently toward the door, flashing an ID at the guard on duty and the clerk staffing the registration desk inside the door. Both officials seemed to know him and waved him through, smiling as Teddy, Belle, and I followed. From the busy waiting room filled with uncomfortable patients and worried families, we toddled after Stephen like baby ducks after their mother. He led us through two sets of double doors into a small, quiet lounge. Max and Elaine looked up as we walked in.

"Any news?" Max enveloped me in a hug. Belle and Munchkin made the rounds, sniffing pockets for treats. Elaine put her arm around Teddy and held him close.

"They couldn't tell me anything outside," Stephen said. "Patient privacy. Have the kids seen a doctor? A nurse?"

Max shook his head. "Like you, we've heard nothing yet."

"Hang tight," Stephen said. "Let me see what I can find out."

As if summoned by the words, a young man in scrubs and rubber clogs opened the door. After stepping aside to let Stephen out of the room, he leaned in through the doorway. "I'm headed to the cafeteria. You guys need anything? I've asked volunteers to freshen up the coffee supplies, but if you need sandwiches, comfort food, anything, say the word."

I shook my head, still feeling overwhelmed. The room's walls insulated us from the hospital bustle and confusion, but the muffled public address announcements, coupled with the incessant *click*, pause, *click*, pause, *click* of an industrial clock, put me on edge. The smell of antiseptics mixed with burnt coffee, stewed cabbage, and other earthier and more pungent fragrances. Those odors, combined with the unmistakable smell of human fear, forced me to wrestle with my instinct to run.

Why were we getting special treatment? A lounge to ourselves? Was it because the boys' situation was more critical than anyone had let on? Had something terrible happened on the way here?

"Whoa, Maggie. You turned a little gray there. Let's sit you down. If you fall and break something, it won't help anyone." Max led me to a chair and sat beside me, holding my hand.

Elaine pulled up a chair for Teddy and another for herself. She filled a pink hospital emesis basin with water for Belle and another for Munchkin. "Be as tidy as you can, please. Slurp carefully." She pulled a plastic bag of cookies out of her voluminous quilted bag, then handed each of us a gingerbread man and a bottle of water.

I grabbed Elaine's hand. "Thanks so much for being here." I wanted to say more, but I didn't know what to say or where to start. I needed to tell Max about the boys and the stranger with the gun, but how could I when I didn't have any of the information yet myself? Elaine filled the conversational void.

"Where else would I be?" she asked. "I dropped Teddy's bike off at your house, and was keeping Max company while he waited for news. When we heard the boys were on their way here, we both jumped in our cars. No discussion."

I started to tell them what little I knew about the boys' injuries when Stephen returned. We all looked up as he entered the room.

Elaine was the first to speak. "Don't just stand there, dear. Grab a chair and tell us what you know." Stephen did as he was told, and the dogs flopped at our feet. "Give me a sec. My thoughts are a jumble." He took a sip of water, then turned to Max. "How long have you been here? Have you seen the kids?"

"Not yet." Max looked around the lounge. "What is this place? I gave them my name at the registration desk and told them I was looking for Brian and David. They swept Elaine and me in here fast enough to give us whiplash. Are they alright? Is this one of those spaces where, you know, family..."

I knew where Max's thoughts were headed. The same place mine were. I feared we'd been isolated so that the hospital could deliver bad news in private.

Stephen gasped. "Oh. Not at all. Sorry." He chuckled, then grew serious. "This is where cops and their families wait. Special privileges for service personnel. Teachers, soldiers, nurses, cops—we do the same kinds of jobs.

Lots of stress without a lot of money. We support each other when times get tough, and there's nothing more grueling than the hospital. They stash us in here to keep us from overwhelming the waiting room. You can imagine what passes for chitchat when law enforcement officers get together, and it isn't what you want the general public to overhear."

"Now we've got that out of the way..." He rubbed his bald head, scratched his beard, then stared at the ceiling for inspiration. "Don't panic. I'm figuring out where to start, not how to break bad news. Both Brian and David are in pretty good shape. They were brought in on the chopper along with Martín and Mozart because they were off the main trail more than a mile from the trailhead and it would have been silly to send an ambulance or even transport them in the car when the helicopter was already nearby. The chopper put down right next to us and scooped up all four of them. Helicopter does not equal catastrophe. Are we clear?"

We nodded like a row of bobbleheads on giveaway day at the ballpark.

"I got the scoop on Mozart because he's not covered by patient privacy laws. He took a rattlesnake bite to the snout, likely from a big-old-grandpa kind of snake. His bite was intended to tell Mozart to get lost. If he injected poison, chances are it wasn't a lethal dose. Maggie said he's had the vaccine." Stephen turned to me for confirmation.

"Yes. In April."

"Good. Some vets don't think the shots do much good, but guys I know with dogs who've been bitten—mostly search-and-rescue dogs—swear by them." He reached out a hand to pat Munchkin, and Belle nudged her nose under his arm to share the love. "And we're enrolling all of you in the next positive-reinforcement rattler avoidance training class I can find."

"That's a thing?" Teddy asked.

"Yup. Works too."

The door squeaked open again, and I looked up, hoping for news on the boys.

"This is Todd." Stephen stood and introduced us to the police intern we'd briefly met outside. The young man pulled up a chair behind Stephen.

"Now the boys. Maggie's probably the best judge of Brian's state of health, right? He was having some breathing issues, and there's nothing like a mom for sizing up that kind of problem. Good move bringing the inhaler. A doctor is looking at him now. The doc in charge of the ER said he'll swing by in a few minutes and take you to him."

Max squeezed my hand. "He'll be fine," I said with enough confidence that I believed it myself. "He was wheezing less by the time the EMTs arrived, though he wasn't wasting his breath on talking. Wasn't smiling.

Distressed, but"—I scanned the room, noting the weariness and worried expressions—"aren't we all?" I sighed again. "My guess is they'll put him on an IV to get his fluids up, maybe put him on oxygen for a bit, and give him some prednisone to relax those breathing passages."

"And David?" Max had scrunched up his face in a way that suggested he was trying to look hopeful but couldn't quite manage it.

I tried to read Stephen's face. I knew nothing about orthopedics and only knew that David's ankle was swollen and bruised. The David I knew would have hobbled out on it without accepting assistance if it had been possible to do so.

Stephen frowned. "I told him he'd live. Beyond that, it's hard to say. Could be sprained. Might be broken. Either way, I think his cross-country season is over. Marching band might not be possible, either. But I don't know. Kids heal fast."

Max's expression turned dour as he absorbed the news. "With everything else that's been happening, cross-country's the least of our worries." He let out a long, slow breath and bit the head off his gingerbread man, then took a big slug of water. "So, what's next?" he mumbled with his mouth full. "What happened out there, and who is Martín?"

Stephen started to answer, but Teddy leaned forward. "I've got this part," Teddy said. "Brian and David were tag-teaming me to keep me busy and distracted. We knew we weren't supposed to run in the burned areas, go up on the ridge, or start our backpacking trip. We figured we'd follow the path system toward Arastradero and find the trailhead we'd use if and when we were allowed to do that trek to the ocean."

Teddy seemed hyperaware of our reactions, flinching at the slightest move from Stephen or Max. Elaine put her arm around him. "You're doing great, dear. Did you leave a note?"

Teddy nodded. Now was not the time to tell him they'd left the note in the place we were least likely to have seen it. Nor was it important to quibble about the contents and the fact that they hadn't revealed their destination or expected return time. We'd cover that in a few days, when it would sound instructive rather than scolding.

"We weren't going to be gone long. Maybe an hour or two. We didn't bring water or snacks or anything. Bad move." He *tsk*ed and shook his head.

"It's okay. We just want to know what happened." I tried to reassure him. "Sounds like you did everything right. You left a note and stayed together. You kept David warm too. To prevent shock."

Teddy took up the thread of his tale, "Part of the trail was shaded and cool, so we stopped for a bit. It was about that time we realized Brian was lagging behind and that his heavy breathing was because of his asthma, not because we'd been pushing the pace. The dogs were panting too. And we hadn't brought any water. We got nervous standing there, what with the things that ranger guy had told us about bad guys and mountain lions and snakes. David wanted to turn around, but Brian thought he'd feel better if he could get some water at the trailhead." Teddy took a long sip of water as if to demonstrate. "The rattler came after that."

Chapter 27

Consider a Personal Locator Beacon (PLB) that allows you to send a distress signal in an emergency. Used appropriately, a PLB can help search-and-rescue personnel find you quickly.

From the Notebook of Maggie McDonald
Simplicity Itself Organizing Services

Wednesday, August 9, Evening

Teddy shuddered. "The snake was around a bend where the trail headed into the sun, and it was hard to see. I heard Mozart and saw his hair standing up before I saw the snake. I wanted to hold him back, you know. Keep him safe." Teddy's voice broke, and his eyes grew distant. He switched to present tense as if events were unfolding in real time. "Mozart's protecting me. He barks, pounces, and then screams like the world is ending. Brian and Belle bump into me from behind." He glanced at his heel, where his sock had a bloody stain. "David's between us, but off to the right, closest to the snake. I can't see either one of them, but he yells. Loud. And then I see him. He's fallen. He tries to get up but can't, so he scrambles away from the snake."

Teddy turned pale and started shaking, then grabbed his elbows with his palms to hug himself. Elaine put her arm around him. "The dogs are barking. Brian can't breathe. David and I are shouting, and no one knows where the snake is..." His voice trailed off, and the room was silent, save for the loud ticking of the institutional wall clock. "We couldn't see anyone. That trail is usually so busy, but there was no one. I told Brian to check out Mozart and keep him quiet in case he'd been bitten. And I got David back up on the path. I don't know how. I couldn't see the snake anywhere, or hear him. We made so much noise he was probably long gone, but it felt like there could be snakes everywhere.

"We're just sittin' there on the trail, trying to catch our breath. Brian looks bad. David wants to show how he can move his toes. But he can't. I'm scared but trying not to look it, 'cause, you know, David's, like, fearless. But I look at his face. His eyes get big and he turns grayish. At first, I think he's going into shock. That foot must be bad. Get him warm. Get the foot up. Call 9-1-1. But then we heard gunshots." He stopped speaking and watched our faces as if gauging our reactions.

"We all heard the gunshots," Max said. "Were they close to you?"

Teddy shook his head. "It was hard to tell with all the echoes. And after the snake, it was like we didn't believe it. We all kinda froze and stared at each other. Ordinarily, I guess we'd have leaped for cover, but with the snake, none of us wanted to go anywhere that we couldn't see the ground. So we just froze. And then I hear this noise behind me, and I'm afraid to turn around. Both Brian and David are staring at something behind me, and Belle and Mozart are growling. I'm picturing some kind of werewolf or swamp creature or zombie—somethin' out of a horror film. I see Brian scrambling backward on his butt. So, I take a deep breath and turn around. And then I blink, 'cause I can't really believe what I'm seeing is real."

"Martín?" I asked

"Yup. Dirty, in fatigues, looking like something out of an action movie with this giant gun. *Giant* gun." He flung his arms wide, extending them to their full length, which was about double the actual size of the assault weapon Stephen had confiscated from Martín.

"But then he held out his hand to Belle, and she wagged her tail." He shrugged. "And Mozart didn't freak out like he sometimes does with strangers. Then Martín started speaking in Spanish, urging us to get off the trail and into the bushes and hide. He's super calm but insistent. Talking like a dad, except in Spanish."

Teddy took a drink from his water bottle. "He tells us bad guys will get us if we stay where we are. He points up the hill, grabs David's arm, and starts helping him up."

"Do you know what his story is?" Max asked. "What was he doing there? Where did he come from?"

"We didn't, not yet. But we trusted him. Belle and Mozart weren't afraid of him. And there were those gunshots. We already knew we weren't safe where we were." Teddy sighed.

Stephen jumped in to give him a break. "Martín gave the EMTs part of his story, and I picked up a little bit before we got him on the chopper. So far, it sounds like he was kidnapped in Nicaragua by one of the cartels. He's been here several years, he thinks. He knew he was in the United States but nothing more specific than that. The head of the crews in this area told them not to talk to anyone. If he tried to run or got sick, they'd kill him, and then kill his family back in Nicaragua. He's got two kids who were toddlers when he was captured. He doesn't know if they're still alive, but he's hopeful. One guy told him the kids were dead and they sold his wife to another drug lord, but he doesn't know if it's true."

Max cursed under his breath. I leaned into him and grabbed his hand. When had our lives become an action-adventure film? I wished I could change the channel to Animal Planet or a gentle British murder mystery. Something far away from here, where bad guys got what they deserved and good guys had it easier than life in Orchard View had been over the past week.

"But how was he wounded?" Max asked. "And who was shooting? Were they shooting at the boys?"

"Martín told the medics he'd taken advantage of the confusion caused by the fire to run away," Stephen said. "But in his haste to flee from the area where he'd been working, he stumbled onto another illegal marijuana garden by accident. The guys working that plot fired on him to chase him off. The bullet went through the soft tissue of his upper arm, but he should be fine as long as they can get the wound cleaned out and stop the infection."

"Did he shoot them? Was that why his gun was empty?" I asked.

Stephen shook his head. "Martín's gun hadn't been fired. He said it scares him and he never has it loaded. He took it with him when he ran, hoping he could sell it—or at least keep it out of the hands of guys who were likely to come after him. If they thought he was armed, he hoped they'd be less likely to shoot him."

The door squeaked open. An older woman in a pink smock came through and began fussing with the coffeepot until the aroma of warm, fresh coffee filled the air. On her heels was a doctor, trailed by a handful of white-coated young adults I took to be medical students, interns, or residents.

Consulting a tablet, the doctor spoke without looking up. "McDonald? Brian and David?" Her voice was flat, not lending itself to interpretation. Max and I stood and walked toward her.

As we approached, she raised her head and smiled. We made the appropriate introductions. "I'm Dr. Poppy," she said. "I'm the emergency room attending physician, but I'm also a pediatrician. Your boys are both great kids." She clicked the button on a ballpoint pen with her thumb as she spoke.

"How are they? Is Brian still wheezing?"

Dr. Poppy waved us to a seating area near the windows, as far away as possible from the rest of our group.

The doctor spoke softly but clearly and patiently, giving us time to ask questions. She punctuated her sentences with the clicking pen. "I've called for X-rays and an orthopedic consult for David," she said. *Click click.* "We're backed up, so I'm afraid it will be a while." *Click.* "We've got him on an IV for now, with fluids and some meds to manage his pain." *Click.* *Click.* "He was a little dehydrated, but it's mostly a precaution." *Click.* "We're icing the leg and keeping it elevated."

"Can we see him?"

The clicking continued. "I'll have someone take you back in a few minutes." She looked at us, then at the rest of our group, all of whom were leaning forward, eager for information. "Are these people with you?"

We nodded. "Friends and family."

"The boys were telling us about what happened to them, and we were going to call the police to investigate, but it seems you've brought your own." The doctor nodded toward Stephen. "We checked in with the Orchard View Police." She paused to check her notes. "And talked to Sergeant Bianchi and then Chief Mueller. They're taking care of the gunshot victim your boys came in with." She took a deep breath and shook her head. "So, your boys are my immediate concern. It sounds like it's been a rough few days for everyone, but especially for their friend Teddy. How's he doing? Does he need a consult? I'd like to talk to him for a little bit, just to make sure."

It took me a moment to shift gears from focusing on David's leg to considering Teddy's state of mind. Did he need a mental health consult? Probably. Maybe we all could use one. "It certainly wouldn't hurt to have someone on tap to call if he needs help," I said. "Or to talk to him about what kinds of services are available and how mental health counseling works. Max and I are his temporary guardians while his mom is"—I considered my words carefully but then settled on the truth—"in jail."

The doctor made a note on her tablet. "I'll do that, then. I've got a friend in pediatric psychology who can swing by while you're still here."

"But only if Teddy approves," I said. "I think it's important for him to steer his health care himself as much as possible."

The doctor clicked her pen again several times. Since she was making notes on her tablet, I wondered if she carried the pen simply to indulge this nervous habit. "Does he still go by Teddy? Is that a family nickname? Is it Ted to strangers?"

"Teddy. Short for Teodoro. It's a family name. Thanks for asking, though."

She smiled and shrugged. "I was Bitsy to my family until I was thirty-five. Those childhood nicknames are hard to shake. I like to give teens whatever help I can."

"And David?"

"Right. We'll pop him in a wheelchair with an IV pole and bring him in here to wait for the X-ray tech, radiologist, and ortho. You'll be happier if you're together, and we need his bed."

"Is his leg broken?"

She sucked on her lips, glanced at her watch, and clicked her pen again, a gesture that was now becoming annoying. "That's really for the ortho to say, but I'd be surprised if it's not. He seems like a pretty stoic kid. I would have said he was reserved before we gave him the pain medication. Now that he's more comfortable, though, he's cracking jokes and looking out for his little brother." She shrugged. "We'll need the X-rays to know for sure."

"So, a cast, crutches?"

She put her hand on my arm. "Try not to look too far ahead. We'll wait to see what the ortho says and go from there. Typically, if the break requires a cast, they'll splint the leg until the swelling goes down."

"And Brian?"

She clicked her pen. "He's on an IV too. We'll get him a breathing treatment and a chest X-ray. He's doing much better. His oxygen saturation is above ninety. We'll want to see it at least at ninety-five before we cut him loose, but he can hang out in here too. I want our respiratory specialist to check on him. Does he see a specialist for his asthma?"

I gave her the names of Brian's doctors, and we covered a few more details before Max and I were dismissed and she moved on to Teddy.

She stashed the pen in the breast pocket of her white doctor's coat, crouched at Teddy's side, and held his hand in a way that suggested she was checking his pulse at the same time she was offering comfort. She gave him a business card and some brochures, patted him on the knee, and stood.

She glanced at me, and I raised my eyebrows, but she shook her head. "I'll let you get it straight from Teddy. He's on top of things." She winked and gave me a thumbs-up. I let out a breath I hadn't known I was holding. I'd never been responsible for someone else's child before, not like this. The pressure was huge, and my expectations for myself were high, particularly with a kid I already adored and who was under such intense strain.

Before I had a chance to glean the details of Teddy's discussion with Dr. Poppy, Brian and David rejoined us, looking considerably healthier than they'd appeared when we found them on the Arastradero Trail two hours earlier. Two hours? I checked my watch and compared the wall clock with the display on my phone. I'd lost all sense of time.

The door squeaked open, letting in Jason along with the antiseptic smell and institutional sound of loudspeaker announcements. Behind him, a food service worker pushed a catering cart filled with sandwiches, snacks, iced drinks, bottled water, and cookies.

Jason's first words were for Teddy. "That Mozart's a trooper," he said. "He's in good hands. The vet on duty at the emergency clinic is a specialist in treating snake bites. He had the antivenom ready to go when we got there. Your pup looks a little like he's been in a prizefight, with his nose all swollen up, but he's feeling no pain. The doc's got him on some good drugs—painkillers, steroids, antihistamines, sedation, and a whole lot of fluids to help his body flush out the poison."

The news about Mozart gave us all a lift. Refueled and together, with our kids on the mend, our morale soared. The conversation overpowered the noises from the hallway that had earlier set my teeth on edge.

But my growing sense that our lives were back on a more normal track was thrown off balance when the door creaked open again, with a lower-pitched and more menacing sound. I looked up as Martín poked his head through the doorway, clutching his coat and biting his lip as if he was unsure of his welcome.

Stephen moved to greet Martín in Spanish that, to my ear, was spoken with a terrible American accent, much like that of a British actor pretending to be from Texas. Jason clapped a hand on Martín's back and pulled up a chair, encouraging him to join us with a few more quick words in Spanish.

Munchkin scrambled to accompany Stephen as he moved to the catering cart and began loading a plate with sandwiches and other snacks. Brian greeted Martín and thanked him, haltingly, in formal high school Spanish I found easy to follow. As the stranger asked after the boys' health and Brian inquired politely about his, however, it was Brian and Teddy's gestures and facial expressions that did most of the talking. They liked this man, trusted him, and were glad to know he'd survive his wounds.

Teddy, whose Spanish far surpassed that of the rest of us, quickly translated. "He's going to be fine. They didn't want to stitch up his gunshot wound because of the infection, but they numbed it, cleaned it, and shot him up with antibiotics."

Martín must have understood some English, because he picked a vial of pills out of his coat pocket, held it up, and shook it with a grin. Teddy laughed and added, "And gave him some more to take home."

"Where is home?" I wondered what I was asking. Where did he go from here? How would he remain safe if the cartel was after him? Where had he come from in Nicaragua? How would he get back?

Teddy translated my words for Martín, but Jason spoke up before the man could formulate a response. "We found a cop in San Jose who's from the same village and speaks the same dialect as Martín, which is a combination of Spanish and an indigenous language. Martín speaks standard Spanish well, but Jason wants to be sure that we don't miss anything when we interview him."

"What about Sergeant Nguyen?" I asked. "Won't he want to hear what Martín has to say?"

Stephen stroked his chin. "Absolutely, but *when* should we update Nguyen? That's up to Jason. The feds may want to talk to Martín too, because of his involvement with the cartel. I'm not getting involved in a huge cross-jurisdictional turf battle unless I have to."

I looked at Martín, who seemed oblivious to the mess he'd landed in. Perhaps he was so relieved to be out of the hands of the cartel that he didn't care about the logistical details that would ultimately decide his fate. I didn't know. But he had more of my sympathy now than he had a few minutes earlier. I felt my prickly exterior relax a little. He noticed, and smiled, revealing a missing front tooth.

I stood and walked to the other side of the room, then put down my coffee mug and stepped outside. I leaned against the cool tiles of the hallway wall, crossed my arms in front of me, and closed my eyes, fighting tears. About what, I wasn't sure. All of a sudden, everything that had happened to my kids, Teddy, Tess, and Patrick caught up with me. My knees shook, my teeth chattered, and I searched in vain for a chair or a bench. Instead, I slid to the floor, cringing at my increased proximity to the pathogens found on hospital floors. It didn't matter. I was unable to stand a second longer.

Chapter 28

Hiking safety in areas frequented by deer means protecting yourself and your pets from ticks, and checking carefully for the revolting arachnids when you return to an indoor environment.

From the Notebook of Maggie McDonald
Simplicity Itself Organizing Services

Wednesday, August 9, Late evening

Before I had a chance to pull myself together, Max slipped out of the waiting room and joined me on the floor, enveloping me in a hug.

I heard him talking about me to Dr. Poppy as though I wasn't in the room. "Overwhelmed, I think. The last few days have caught up with her."

The doctor crouched on the floor in front of me, putting her hands on my knees. That firm human touch, from both Max and the doctor, steadied me.

"Maggie," said Dr. Poppy. "What you're feeling is normal. You've been running on fumes for days, and it's caught up with you. You've been the duct tape that has kept your family and Tess's together, so everyone else is holding in there, but to carry my metaphor to a ridiculous extreme, you need to regain your stickiness if you're going to keep from falling apart yourself. Without you, where will everyone else be?"

"But..."

Dr. Poppy shook her head. "No buts. Maggie, I don't want to scare you, but I'm deadly serious. You need to take a few minutes for yourself.

If you don't, you'll find yourself in a hole so deep you won't be able to dig yourself out. Now, what'll it be? I can offer you a shower, clean scrubs, and a hairbrush. Or my on-call room for some quiet and rest. Or our chapel. Or a walk around the campus in your husband's company. Your choice."

I hesitated, and my brain scurried to find a way to get past Dr. Poppy and back into the waiting area to look after my family. But the doctor was on to me. And so was Max.

"Maggie, look at me," said Dr. Poppy. "If you don't do something for yourself, right now, I'll talk to your family about putting you on a psychiatric hold for seventy-two hours. You're not dangerous to yourself and others yet, but let's not go there."

Dr. Poppy's shocking words had the desired impact. I was terrified. I glanced at Max and saw worry and fatigue etched on his face too. "Don't look at him, Maggie. Decide what *you* need to do for yourself. If you can't decide, I'll decide for you. Is that what you want?"

Now I was angry. Dr. Poppy was speaking to me as if I were a toddler in the midst of a tantrum. I wasn't. I was just tired. I needed a break. I stepped back a moment and listened to what I was telling myself. Apparently, I agreed with Dr. Poppy.

"Code Blue in C 210. Code Blue in C 210," squawked the PA, making me flinch.

I stared down Dr. Poppy and said with a hint of toddler attitude, "If I wash my face, comb my hair, and get away from that loudspeaker for a walk, would that make you happy?"

Dr. Poppy's face was kind but held an expression I couldn't read. "You're angry. Pushing back. That's good. The question isn't whether it makes me happy," she said, standing and holding out her hand to help me up. "It's whether it makes you feel stronger. You're tough as nails, kiddo. You've raised great kids. You've got super friends. But you're still running on empty." She steadied me with one arm and peered up and down the hallway. "Let's do this. Max, why don't you tell the others that you and Maggie are taking a short walk? There's an ice cream place ten minutes from here that would make a perfect destination. Maggie, I'll show you where you can freshen up, and we'll meet Max in the lobby. How's that sound?"

I could tell from her voice that the only answer that would keep me on good terms with Dr. Poppy would be to admit that her idea sounded great. So I did. But I still couldn't get that hint of toddler attitude out of my voice. If I were a porcupine, she'd be pulling quills from her skin for the next month.

"If it makes you feel any better," Dr. Poppy said, "I'm going to be reading the riot act to everyone else in there next. You've been carrying the ball, and you need to be able to rely on the rest of your team. You can only do that if they're looking after themselves too."

It did make me feel better—like a toddler who was in trouble, but was happy that her siblings were also being scolded. I wasn't proud of myself, but I was in tune with myself. It would have to do.

By the time Max and I reached the ice cream shop, it was closed, but the neighborhood was quiet, and we sat on a bench outside for a few moments watching the stars that were bright enough to be seen through the still smoky sky. My skin felt caressed by the slightly misty air.

Back at the hospital, we reentered the conference room to find that no one seemed to have missed us. Stephen had found some oil and was desqueaking the door's annoying hinges. Brian handed me his discharge papers, which instructed us to make a follow-up appointment with his asthma specialist.

"David's back in with the orthopedist," Elaine said. "Bay eleven."

Max and I located David in an exam cubicle with a sliding glass door. A fluorescent light flickered and hummed, giving the whole area a timeless blue glow. "This is Dr. Paine," David said.

"Give me a sec to finish wrapping this splint," the doctor said. David's left leg appeared twice the size of the right and looked mummified, wrapped in beige Ace bandages from toe to mid-thigh.

The doctor fastened the edges of the last bandage, then tilted the foot, watching David's face to gauge his reactions. "No pain?" he asked. David shook his head.

"Great. I'll see you in a few days for a cast. When does school start?"

"Two weeks."

Dr. Paine turned so that he could address all three of us at once. "We'll get a cast on there later this week. The appointment will be on the discharge papers when they come, but you can call my office to change it if the time doesn't work. You've got a great kid here, and he should heal fast. From the looks of the break, he must have gotten his foot stuck and twisted his body as he fell." The doctor held out a tablet to show us the X-ray and pointed to faint fuzzy lines encircling David's bones. "He's got spiral fractures of the tibia and fibula. Typically we see these in kids who've been abused or who get their foot caught in something like a playground or bunk-bed ladder. We need to completely immobilize the bones. David won't be able to get away with a plastic boot, I'm afraid. We'll keep him in a splint for a few days until the swelling goes down, and then cast the leg from above the knee to below the ankle. We recast at three weeks with a shorter, lighter cast. After five weeks, he can put some weight on it and may be able to do without the crutches."

After providing more information about pain management and the logistics for taking a shower, Dr. Paine left to see another patient, and an orderly came to help David into a wheelchair. "We're giving you the VIP treatment," he told David. "I'm to return you to your family while you wait for your crutches and discharge paperwork. Ready?"

"I can't wait to get out of here."

When we reentered the waiting area, Elaine greeted us with her finger to her lips, pointing to Teddy, who, like me, had succumbed to his exhaustion and trauma, and was fast asleep on a sofa. Someone had removed his shoes, and the hospital appeared to have supplied a blanket and pillow that Brian eyed enviously. It was time to get this whole crew home and in bed. My recharge walk had been everything the doctor ordered, literally, but the benefits wouldn't last forever.

"Jason just left," Elaine whispered. "The vet called. Mozart is recovering, but they want to keep him sedated for several hours in case he has an adverse reaction to the antivenom or any of the other medications they've given him. Jason sent me a picture to show Teddy." She swiped through the pictures on her phone and held it out to us.

"He looks like he's having a funny dream," I told her. "Like he's laughing in his sleep." The tissue on Mozart's nose was badly swollen, exposing his teeth in an expression that resembled a snarl, except for the fact that the rest of him seemed calm and relaxed. "They're sure he'll be okay? Teddy and Tess need him."

Elaine paused before answering. "The biggest problem may be wound care. Venom can kill the tissue, particularly in that bony area of the snout where there's less circulation. He won't be winning any beauty contests for a good six months, with the skin sloughing off. Teddy will need to watch for infection, especially with Mozart's tendency to stick his nose everywhere. The doc says to keep him on a short leash outside, and restrict activity as much as possible while he heals."

She handed me an appointment card and a stapled sheaf of papers printed from the Internet. Between the ones I'd been given for Brian and David, I was amassing a small collection.

"Thanks so much for staying with us," I told her. "You've been such a help. But Mackie must be missing you. Do you want to head home?" Mackie, Elaine's West Highland terrier, was more high-strung than the larger dogs and apt to get himself into trouble if he was left alone and unexercised for too long.

Elaine glanced around. "If you don't need me for anything more. Do you want me to take Teddy home with me?"

I watched Teddy for a moment as he snored softly on the sofa. "Let him stay. He needs the sleep. Will you give me a call tomorrow? We need to take another look at everything we know about Patrick's death. Our suspects so far all have alibis. So, either we need to focus on someone else or recheck our timelines and the alibis. There has to be an answer somewhere."

"Fretting won't do anyone any good," said Elaine. "Can you set aside your worry overnight? I'll come up first thing, and bring breakfast. We'll tackle those timelines then and develop a new plan. I don't care how careful this killer was, we'll find him. I'm confident of that. But we all need a good night's sleep first."

Elaine gathered up her belongings and said good-bye to the rest of my family. "One of the food service people stuck their heads in about half an hour ago. They said not to worry about cleaning up. And to leave any food we don't want when we leave. They'll make sure the leftovers find a good home."

"Where are Steven and Munchkin?" I asked, suddenly becoming aware of their absence.

"Where do you think? They've headed to your house to organize extra security, just in case." The door swung shut behind her, but opened again immediately. "I forgot to tell you. Paolo will swing by your house in the morning to update us on some apparently significant progress. It has something to do with Martín."

It took us another hour to complete the paperwork for the boys. Max went to get the car while I collected our gear and reams of forms, instructions, and appointments. Teddy was awake but groggy, and said nothing as we climbed into the car. All three boys and Belle were fast asleep before we left the parking lot.

Earlier, I'd planned to talk tactics with Max on the drive home, but we were both too tired for clear thinking. My thoughts revolved around getting everyone safely into their beds as quickly as possible.

As we turned off the freeway and then up the hill toward the house, lights flashed against the low-hanging clouds and fog. I heard what I thought was a gunshot, but I told myself it must be someone tossing heavy items into a construction dumpster. I checked my watch. Two o'clock in the morning. Construction activity was unlikely at this hour. But gunshots? Again?

I glanced at Max, who'd scrunched down in an awkward position, trying to see more of the mountain ridge. "It looks like a war zone up there," he said. "What kind of fire crew needs a mobile weapon like that?"

I peered out the windshield, squinting in the direction Max had indicated. What looked like a Jeep with a roof-mounted gun was silhouetted against the flickering lights behind it. "Could it be a water cannon kind of thing?" Rapid-fire reports broke the silence that followed my statement. "Maybe not. Are we safe here?"

"Call Stephen," Max said. I tapped my phone to get Stephen on speed-dial and waited. As the car wound up the narrow roads, I began to feel sick, but I wasn't sure whether to blame my fear of impending doom or motion sickness.

Chapter 29

The best way to prepare your car for emergencies is to prepare the driver. Drivers should be rested, with eyewear that matches current prescriptions and protects against sun, glare, and reflections. Limit distractions. Older drivers may wish to take courses offered by the American Association of Retired Persons to refresh their skills.

From the Notebook of Maggie McDonald
Simplicity Itself Organizing Services

Thursday, August 10, Early morning

The boys stirred in the back seat of the car, and I felt Belle's cold nose snuffling the back of my neck. I willed them all back to sleep. The last thing I needed while we tried to figure this out was to field questions and suggestions from alarmed kids.

Stephen didn't answer his phone, and his voice mailbox was full. "No luck," I told Max.

"Let's keep going. The activity seems to be isolated beyond the ridge. We've got to be reasonably safe down here, right?"

I squinted up at the hillside again. Max was right. As far as I could tell, there were no flashlights, vehicle headlamps, flames, or muzzle flashes illuminating the darkness on the lower slopes of the foothills. That put at least a half a mile between us and the activity on the dirt and gravel ridge-crest road. Ranger Kon Sokolov had told Max that assault weapon shots could easily traverse that distance, but if we weren't in anyone's gun sights, we'd be safe.

That's what I told myself, but "relatively safe" wasn't secure enough when it came to protecting the health and welfare of three teenaged boys. I tried Stephen's phone again with no more luck than I'd had the first time.

Max slowed the car to a near-crawl. With no traffic at this hour, he could have stopped the car entirely. He glanced at me, his face full of questions.

"Keep going," I said. "I haven't heard any shots since that last batch. I'll call Paolo and see if he knows anything."

"At this hour?"

"Jason was just at the hospital with us. If he's awake, Paolo's got to be awake too, right? They're a team." Jason had been Paolo's mentor and partner when the younger man joined the Orchard View Police over a year ago. Now that Jason was chief, Paolo had been assigned a new partner we'd not yet met. But that early bond they'd formed hadn't diminished. Orchard View was also a small town, with few opportunities for the adrenaline-fueled escapades that most young law enforcement officers thrive on. If something was happening in Orchard View involving gunfire, flames, and Jeeps, Paolo would be close by.

But Paolo's phone sent me directly to voice mail.

Max pulled into our steep driveway. Our front yard resembled a military training camp. Several black SUVs were parked in front and at the side of the house.

A few more were in front of the barn. Some were equipped with emergency lights and sported law enforcement insignias I couldn't identify. Others were unmarked. A young woman dressed in black with SWAT insignia stooped to speak to us as Max rolled down his window.

"Mr. McDonald, I was asked to watch for you," the SWAT officer said from behind her clear face shield. "Please pull the vehicle close to the front porch. Sergeant Paolo Bianchi is inside and will brief you."

"What's going on?" Max asked.

"The sergeant will bring you up-to-date. For your safety, I need you to put the house between you and the law enforcement action as quickly as possible. Leave everything in the car, please. We'll bring it in later."

Max started to ask another question, and the boys woke up, wanting answers of their own. I put a finger to my lips to shush the boys and used my other hand to gain Max's attention. I shook my head and whispered, "Now's not the time for questions. Let's do as she says."

"Thank you, ma'am. If you'll pull up over there, sir."

Inside the house, static filled the air as Paolo, Stephen, and a friend of Stephen's I knew as Rocket spoke into cell phones and radios. A young woman in the uniform of the sheriff's department appeared at the top of the stairs and, moving silently, descended to join us.

She spoke first. "Mrs. McDonald, I'm sorry you've come home to all this. We tried to reach you at the hospital before you left. We want you to get down to the basement as quickly as possible."

I sighed, not realizing how much I'd hoped for a quick reunion with my pillow, and to regain the security that moms feel when their children are safely tucked in bed.

"You heard her, boys," I said. "Basement now. Questions later."

We trooped down the stairs, where I knew there was little to offer in the way of comfortable seating or the bedding we craved. My eyes teared up in frustration, and I felt my knees shake the way they had in the hospital before I'd collapsed. I gritted my teeth. Not now. Please, not now.

Several mismatched folding chairs leaned against the wall between the laundry area and the open part of the basement at the foot of the stairs. Max set up two dust-covered webbed aluminum lawn chairs that dated back to our university days, as David struggled with his crutches and Teddy unfolded chairs that matched a card table we no longer owned. Brian sneezed and disappeared into the laundry room, reappearing with a stack of beach towels he spread on the floor. Belle snuffled them, thinking it was a game.

Stephen descended behind the deputy, ducking his head to avoid knocking himself out on the stairwell's low ceiling. Munchkin followed, sniffed Belle, and curled up on the towels as if he'd slept there all his life.

The rest of us stared at Stephen, waiting. For what, I wasn't sure.

He rubbed his hand over the top of his bald head in a motion that would have brushed the hair from his eyes if he'd had hair. He sighed.

"I've got to get back upstairs. We're wrapping things up, and I'll be able to answer questions in about a half hour. Apologies for descending on you like this. I stopped by to make sure you all would be safe here tonight, and ran into the rest of this operation. It turns out your attic is the perfect vantage point from which to spot stragglers from the raid up on the hill. We've caught two already. Armed and dangerous."

"Two of what?"

"Members of a drug cartel. We found two of their pot gardens, with help from Martín. Both are massive illegal grow sites. We knew they'd be back to check, because the buds are almost ready to harvest. Twelve thousand plants worth nearly twenty million dollars. We picked up two big bosses in our first sweep, but some of the underlings—the guys who do the work or manage the supply chain—got away. We're picking them up now using dogs and infrared. We don't know if they're armed and might shoot back. That's why we've got you down here."

"Cool," said Teddy.

Stephen grinned. "You don't know the half of it, but I'll fill you in as soon as I can."

"I've got complete faith in you and Jason," I said. "Do what you need to do. We'll stay out of your way." After all they'd done to keep us safe, they were allowed considerable leeway as far as I was concerned.

Stephen and his guys were energized, pumped full of adrenaline from the hunt and endorphins from the win. "I got to get back." He started back up the stairs, but with one foot on the first tread, he turned and did a quick scan of the room. "You're dead on your feet. You got sleeping bags and air mattresses, Maggie?"

I nodded. "Attic? Barn?"

"Attic." I yawned, making the last word nearly unintelligible. In what seemed like seconds, young uniformed officers from a variety of law enforcement organizations, including what looked like California Fish and Wildlife, were shoving chairs aside, pumping up air mattresses, plumping pillows, and unzipping sleeping bags. I thought we'd all be too hyped up to sleep. Too alarmed by a house full of armed strangers. But then I was in my sleeping bag, feeling Max's hand patting my back and thinking that I should move Belle's tail off my pillow.

I woke in the morning to the realization that I'd slept in my shoes. That, and the fact that the other sleeping bags were empty. Taking advantage of the basement bathroom, I brushed my hair and washed my face.

When I trudged upstairs, my first thought was of the boys. I could pick their voices out of the cacophony. They both sounded strong and happy. But then I heard Belle and Munchkin snarl, snap, and scratch at the back door. Something was wrong. Again.

As I reached the top of the basement stairs, Paolo opened the back door, struggling to enter without letting three hundred pounds of dog get past him. He pushed the door shut behind him and leaned against it, breathing hard.

Max filled in the blanks. "They caught a straggler from the pot garden this morning. Either that or someone higher up who came to check on the crop and schedule the harvest. Didn't you hear the shots?"

I took the coffee cup Max handed me and inhaled the aroma. "Nothing. Not last night. Not this morning. I've gained a sudden urge to create a comfortable oasis down there, though, with pullout sofas, desks, and a boatload of emergency food and communications equipment."

"We'll add it to the list of essential home improvements. But I agree. If we're going to be running a hostel for exhausted young law enforcement teams, we're going to have to seriously up our game. Take a look on the front porch. SWAT team members are flopped around like throw pillows. "

"Poor kids."

Max handed Paolo the last cup of coffee from the pot and sent him through to the dining room. Max dumped the grounds into a nearly full plastic dish bucket. He refilled the coffeemaker, using a pitcher of water to fill the reservoir to the brim. "The kitchen was packed earlier," he said when he saw me eyeing the plastic bin. "I couldn't get from here to the sink and garbage without using my elbows. Not in less than five minutes. This was my solution."

"Good idea. Where are the kids? What about David? Is he in pain?"

"Kids are chowing down in the dining room. Stephen and Elaine laid out quite the spread. I'm not sure how Stephen ordered food at the same time he seemed to be coordinating the whole operation up here. Every time I think he's just a normal guy, he goes all Ninja Marine/Caped Crusader on me. I finally met Rocket, by the way. Got three whole words out of him."

"Awesome. A new record."

"Grab some food. There are croissants, bagels, doughnuts, Danish, cinnamon bread—Elaine has completely derailed the low-carb diet train this morning. She's touting quick energy and mood-enhancing B vitamins. Go get fed and catch up with the kids. I'll be in as soon as this pot finishes brewing."

I could tell at a glance the kids were on the mend. They had color in their cheeks and smiles on their faces. David looked comfortable tucked into an upholstered armchair with his feet resting on the window seat, where a pretty young lady with gray eyes and cinnamon-brown hair sat cross-legged with one hand resting on David's good foot.

He caught my eye and waved me over. "Mom, meet Emily."

Emily stood, and I greeted her, trying not to overreact to the introduction. It wasn't easy. Brian, out of view of either Emily or David, waggled his eyebrows and smirked.

Elaine held up a plate she'd filled for me and patted the seat next to hers. Belle barked, announcing the arrival of Jason and Mozart, who barreled through the front door and skidded to a stop in front of Teddy. His snout was still swollen, his grin lopsided, but he was clearly in exuberant health.

Laughing, I welcomed Jason. Martín stepped from behind the hulking police chief to shake my hand, but looked uncertain of his welcome or his place in our home.

"Most of you have met Martín," Jason said. "What you may not know is that last night and early this morning, we arrested four members of a deadly drug cartel. With Martín's testimony and insider information, we've got the evidence we need to go after dozens more."

The room erupted in applause, which embarrassed Martín. Max stood and offered his chair to our new guest. Elaine passed him a plate. He smiled with his endearing gap-toothed grin. Belle nudged her nose under his elbow, and he beamed, ruffling her ears and rubbing her chest.

As our new guests set to eating, the SWAT team gathered their gear. Conversation lagged. I collected my thoughts. With everyone safe and accounted for, including our canine crew, it was time to refocus on Tess, who continued to languish in jail. Despite my considerable efforts, I doubted we were any closer to freeing her today than we'd been when she'd been arrested. Teddy needed her. I needed her. And we still needed to identify the person who'd taken Patrick's life.

"I don't mean to diminish the achievements of your team, Jason," I said. "I lost count of the agencies deployed here last night, and I appreciate everything they did to keep us and our neighborhood safe, but does anyone have news about Tess? Are we any closer to nabbing Patrick's killer?" I glanced over my left shoulder and then my right, but none of the windows in the dining room gave me a view of the hills. I waved my hand in the direction of the kitchen and the ridge beyond. "With all that paramilitary equipment and personnel up there, is any of it designated to investigate Patrick's murder?"

Paolo winced, as though he'd heard judgment in my statement. I hadn't intended to scold him or anyone else, but I didn't want anyone to lose sight of Tess's plight, either.

Stephen jumped into the conversation. "Martín gave us some great leads on that score at the same time he provided the keys to breaking the cartel's hold on our public land." Martín ducked his head and gave Belle's soft ears the attention they were due.

Stephen continued, "The translator from the San Jose Gang Task Force has been working with Martín since he left the hospital. Martín's knowledge is invaluable. Despite being terrified that the cartel would kill him and his family if he revealed anything he knew, he's been open and helpful."

"But why? He doesn't owe us anything. Why would he risk his family like that?" David asked.

Chapter 30

Stow these emergency supplies in the trunk of your car:
Emergency LED flasher with extra batteries.
Tire sealant and inflator.
Tire pressure gauge.
Rain poncho (or other seasonally appropriate foul weather gear).
LED flashlight plus batteries.
Work gloves.
First aid kit.
Extra cash.
Commercially prepared kits are available and make great gifts for new car owners.

From the Notebook of Maggie McDonald
Simplicity Itself Organizing Services

Thursday, August 10, Morning

"It's the right thing to do," Steven said firmly. "Government troops and members of tribal factions have terrorized his people for years under the leadership of genocidal policymakers and the cartels. He was abducted and nearly killed in a raid four years ago. He fears that anyone he once knew from that village, including his parents, wife, and children, were killed."

Martín leaned forward and spoke softly in heavily accented and hesitant English, "Working here in field is not so bad, but I fear for my *niños*. I tell myself I stop these men. If I can. I stop them make *otros padres* hurt like me." Martín took a deep breath, leaned back in his chair, and turned his attention to Belle. At some point in the preceding evening, Jason had made sure Martín had a chance to shower and dress in clean clothing and new gym shoes.

Stephen continued, "Martín saved the labels from illegally imported pesticides and fertilizers—nasty stuff that's been outlawed in most Western nations for generations. He made sketches of cartel members and recorded their movements."

"Will he be deported? Can you protect him? Can you protect his family?"

Jason jumped in to answer that one. "Martín has requested asylum for himself and his family. We're trying to find out whether they're still alive and, if so, where they're living. That means we're working with Immigration, the State Department, numerous American intelligence agencies, South American and Latin American anti-drug councils, and the Nicaraguan embassy. We'll provide him with whatever protection he needs or wants. That's how valuable his intelligence is. But we're not sure how many of those agencies we can trust. Rumor has it that the cartel has infiltrated government investigative teams. They've got inside sources that have previously tipped off key people at all levels of the cartel's organization to avoid arrest and capture. Some of the Latin American law enforcement operations have sky-high mortality rates, thanks to information we believe has been supplied by moles disguised as good guys in the very agencies tasked with ending the drug trade."

"How do those law-enforcement agencies recruit people to work for them?" David asked. "I mean, I get that the cartels are awful, but signing up to help shut them down is like signing your own death warrant." David shook his head.

"I know right from wrong," said Martín. "I teach my *niños*. Good men fight bad men." He sighed again, looking dejected. "I lose family, home, everything. Fighting bad is only thing left."

"You're a good man," said Emily. I was pretty sure she meant David, although she was facing Martín when she said it. David's face flushed, and he looked down.

I was awestruck by Martín and yearned to learn more of his story—his background, his family, and what it was like to be forced to work for people who had conspired to deny him every freedom I took for granted. But it was time to renew our focus on Tess.

"Jason, did you say that Martín had information about Patrick?" I asked. "And that some of that activity up on the hill has to do with his death?"

Martín looked up. "I know Patrick. I follow him. He collects evidence. Like me."

My mouth dropped open. So did Teddy's. "My dad was fighting the cartels?"

Jason shifted in his chair to face Teddy. "Your dad was a hero. Among the evidence Sergeant Nguyen seized at your house were boxes full of material Patrick had saved. We can use it to nail these guys. Or at least to detain and question them. It may be difficult to convict them of their nastiest crimes. But there's plenty of evidence to show that they were poisoning public lands and wildlife and trafficking in illegal toxicants."

"Toxicants?" I asked.

"Man-made toxins with the power to destroy an entire ecosystem for generations. Their chemicals seep into the soil and groundwater. Every wild animal that the California Department of Fish and Wildlife has done a necropsy on in the past few years has shown deadly levels of toxic chemicals."

I wanted to know more. But Tess was still in jail.

"Right," said Stephen, in answer to the urging I hadn't realized I'd spoken out loud. "Martín and Patrick crossed paths for months. Last winter, when Martín had a bad case of bronchitis, Patrick brought him a coat, gloves, blankets, aspirin, and other medicines. Months later, Martín found Patrick and thanked him, but warned him that others were watching—people Martín didn't trust. Patrick was gathering evidence to nail the cartels. He didn't want them and their assault weapons and their chemicals anywhere near you kids or anyone else. He felt responsible because he was your cross-country coach and most of your training was out on those trails—trails that went right past the gardens Martín was tending."

"Who else was watching?" I asked Martín, who shook his head.

"Martín doesn't know," Stephen said. "They weren't part of the drug gang, as far as he knew. And they weren't law enforcement."

Martín nodded. Apparently, he knew enough English to follow along, or at least pick up the gist of the conversation. "Clumsy," he said, making motions like a lumbering bear. "Loud. I know where they are without following."

Jason frowned and picked up the story. "In the days leading up to Patrick's death, Martín saw a dark green SUV up there on several nights. Going slowly. Bumping over the ruts."

"What color are the rangers' vehicles? Or the ones the sheriff's office drives? How could he tell it was green? Wouldn't any dark color have appeared black? Was it an SUV or a van?"

Jason looked at Martín, who held his arms over his head in a circle, howled like a coyote, and then grinned. "*La luna. El todo terrano.*" He moved his fingers in the shape of a box, though, which made it seem as though the vehicle he'd spotted was more likely to have been a van or a panel truck than an SUV.

"Would he recognize it?" I asked. Martín nodded. David must have had the same idea I did, because his fingers moved in a blur above his keyboard.

"What kind, Mom?" David asked. "Did someone you talked to have a green truck or a van?"

"Yes," I said, leaning forward, biting my lip, and rubbing my face in my hands as if it would help me remember. "Your Mr. Santa Claus, Sean Philips, drives a forest-green van retrofitted for wheelchair accessibility."

Jason picked up his phone and tried to walk calmly into the kitchen, but I could hear the urgency in his voice as he barked out instructions to whoever answered. He wanted to know what vehicles were licensed to Sean Philips, Katherine McNamara, and Fiona Philips. And he wanted the information immediately, if not sooner.

David handed his laptop to Brian, who brought it to the table to show Martín. I leaned in to see the screen. "It was a big van," I said. "Not a minivan. More like a plumber's truck or something like that. A panel van."

"Sí, sí. Grande," Martín said.

"Is there a way to find out what companies make those wheelchair vans? Can you find pictures of them?" I sighed and buried my head in my hands. "I wish I could call Katherine and ask, but that would tip off her brother. I can't remember whether he had a wheelchair rack on the back or if there was anything else that was distinctive." I flapped my hand at Brian, searching for the words I needed and encouraging him at the same time. "What about handicapped parking signs? He must have a special license plate. Or one of those hanging things on his rearview mirror. Show Martín."

"But if he's handicapped and in a wheelchair, how could he have hurt my dad?" said Teddy, his voice slicing through the murmur of voices. "I mean, my dad was fast. And strong. Those dirt roads are super rutted. The mountain bikers even stay off them. I don't think you could maneuver a wheelchair up there. It would overbalance and fall." Teddy demonstrated by tilting his chair to the side until it balanced awkwardly on two legs. "And my dad could have easily run away. Down into the canyon. A wheelchair couldn't have followed him. No way." Teddy shook his head and righted the chair.

Paolo picked up his phone and, like Jason, moved into the kitchen to complete the call in privacy.

I turned to Stephen for an explanation. "We still haven't seen the report from the medical examiner," he said. "The sheriff may have it, but not Jason."

"Is Nguyen stalling?"

Stephen shook his head. "Maybe, but I don't think so. Between the fire, a murder-suicide in one of the homeless encampments on county land, the search for three missing teen boys, and rounding up Martín's cartel guys, he's been swamped. I suspect that's what Paolo's checking."

"If we can prove Sean was there..." But as soon as I said it, I realized the flaw in my reasoning. Just because Sean owned a green handicapped-accessible van, and we could place the van on the ridge the night Patrick was killed, we still couldn't prove Sean was driving it. Even if we could connect Sean and his wheelchair to the trail, and somehow verify that he was there when Patrick was killed, we still couldn't prove that Sean had killed Patrick. Not yet, anyway. And that must be what Paolo was trying to pin down. What was the definitive cause of Patrick's death? Could the medical examiner pinpoint the time of death? Had any more evidence turned up in the autopsy that could prove Sean was responsible?

Martín pulled a handful of papers from his pocket, sorted through them, and then smoothed a small piece of paper with both hands. He handed it to Brian, who squinted at it, and then waved it in the air. "A license plate. Martín got the license plate."

"Jason! Martín got the plate number." Brian thrust David's computer toward the center of the table and dashed through to the kitchen.

Paolo returned from the kitchen, followed closely by Brian, who smiled at Martín and gave a thumbs-up. Martín returned both the grin and the gesture. Paolo inched around the end of the table as Elaine scooted forward in her chair. I took a moment to study the health of my kids. They seemed much better than they had yesterday, but not as strong as they had earlier after a good night's sleep. David's lined face indicated he was due for another dose of pain medication, and I detected a slight wheeze in Brian's breathing as he eased past me. I glanced at the clock.

"Paolo," I said, "I hate to stop any momentum we've got going, but I wonder if now's a good time to take a brief break? It's coming up on lunch, believe it or not, and I'm out of dishes. I've got a few recuperating invalids here whose medication needs topping off. And some dogs who could use a run, now that you've cleared the bad guys from the neighborhood." I gasped then. "Unless...Stephen, you said that the groundwater and soil showed signs of these toxicants. Our back garden ends at the creek. It drains downhill from the ridge. Is it okay to let the dogs run in the grass? Drink the water?"

"I covered that subject with the emergency veterinarian last night," Jason explained. "Concerns about the groundwater and soil are greatest in the areas adjacent to the illegal grow sites. While, long term, your land could become contaminated, it's not a big worry for today."

Once he'd reassured Stephen and me, Jason turned to the rest of us and spoke in a slightly louder and more commanding tone. "Maggie's right. It's time to take a break here. We need folks to do dishes, and we need dog supervisors and ball throwers in the backyard. Paolo, can you check to see if the teams left any litter, clothing, or equipment? I want to leave the McDonalds' house looking as though nothing happened here. While Maggie acts as medic for these boys, Max and I can roll sleeping bags, let the air out of the mattresses downstairs, and start a load of wash." He put a hand on my shoulder, which effectively silenced any protests I might make. "And if anyone is worried that we're not paying enough attention to Tess's predicament or seeking justice for Patrick's killer, I assure you I've not lost sight of that. Officers are paying a visit to Sean's house right now with a warrant to search his van, the house, and the entire property. They'll bring him in for questioning and conduct a medical exam to verify how mobile he really is."

Chapter 31

Law enforcement officers contend that there are few callouts more dangerous than responding to reports of domestic violence. Professional organizers working in strangers' homes also need to be vigilant and protect themselves. Civilians witnessing or suspecting violence in a home environment should remove themselves from the situation as quickly as possible and call the police immediately.

From the Notebook of Maggie McDonald
Simplicity Itself Organizing Services

Thursday, August 10, Morning

Martín, David, Brian, and Teddy puffed up with pride as Jason recognized their contributions toward identifying a murderer. "The case isn't anywhere near closed, but the medical examiner has nearly completed his report. Many of his findings are still confidential, but he's confirmed that Patrick took a bullet to his scapula. It was a .22 round, which Orchard View officers and Santa Clara County Sheriff's deputies will be looking for at the Philips's home. We're questioning Sean's wife Katherine and his sister Fiona. Maggie, I want to talk to you about your interviews with these suspects. No one from the sheriff's department spoke to any of them earlier. Your information is the background they need to get the most out of their interviews."

Max passed me my laptop. "Show him your notes. I'll get the kids their meds. Jason, I'll handle the sleeping bags and air mattresses on my own."

Emily offered to help, but as soon as David had more pain medication, he'd be down for the count. I thanked her for coming and invited her to return soon.

I sent a copy of my notes to Jason's computer. He read them over quickly and then asked a few questions. I'd expected fact-checking follow-up queries from him, but he wanted more broad-strokes background. "If you had to describe Katherine to me, based only on the information from everyone you'd talked to, what would you say?"

I bit my lip and thought for a moment. I fought against my urge to answer immediately. Jason was asking me questions in his role as chief of police, not as my friend. It was important I get it right.

"There are no wrong answers, Maggie. No one is going to jail based on what you tell me."

"But what I say could help get Tess out of jail, right?"

"It could..." Jason was using that technique you hear about in police procedurals, where he let the silence linger as if hoping it would prompt me to talk, filling the empty spaces in the conversation. It worked.

"I liked Katherine. She was direct and no-nonsense. Funny. When I met her on Tuesday, it was a few days after she'd taken a fall and injured her leg. She was on crutches and moved gingerly, like she was in pain." I paused for a moment, remembering what Robert had said about the scars on her arms.

"What is it?"

"It's just... She said that she'd slipped or tripped at home on her hardwood floor and that's how she broke her ankle. That's where she said she was on Saturday, the night Patrick died—at the emergency room with her sister-in-law. But why wouldn't her husband go with her if she'd been hurt like that?"

Jason nodded. "You're right. If Stephen needed emergency medical care, I'd drop everything to take him."

"Robert—Robert Wu who worked with Tess—said that Katherine had designs on Patrick. I don't believe for a moment that Patrick was having an affair with her, though there may have been some flirtation and joking—they seemed like good pals. They worked together and ran together." I realized I was getting off track and forced myself to refocus. Jason scribbled with his stubby pencil in his notepad.

"Katherine's arms. Robert said she had scars and thought they could have been self-inflicted."

"What kinds of scars? Where?"

I shook my head. "I didn't see them. When I met her for lunch, she was wearing long sleeves and a jacket. It was chilly, and that was probably why, but what if she was concealing bruises? What if her husband was violent? What if that's what landed her in the hospital, not a fall, and Sean didn't go with her because she didn't want him there?"

Jason stopped scribbling and looked up. "I'll see if we can get a warrant for her hospital records—see if there is a pattern of suspicious injuries. We can also check to see if Sean has a history of violence or abuse."

"He's certainly got a bad temper. He was livid when I visited them asking questions."

"Did he hurt you? Were you afraid he might?"

I shook my head. "It never occurred to me that I was in danger. I don't like being barked at. Who does? But at the time I thought he was just having a bad day or in pain. In retrospect, the events look quite different."

"We'll see if the sister's alibi holds up and whether anyone else can confirm she was with Katherine the whole time she was in the ER. We'll make sure that Katherine's injury is real too." Jason tapped his pencil on the table. Paolo vowed that one day he'd get his boss to switch to a tablet for recording case notes, but I wasn't so sure. Jason's pencil and pad were an essential part of my portrait of the man.

"You met the brother and sister-in-law when you were with Katherine," Jason said. "What can you tell me about them?"

"Sean is disabled. He has a handicapped placard. But I don't know how mobile he is. Katherine didn't want to be late. She checked her watch with increasing frequency as the meeting time drew near. She could have been looking forward to seeing her husband, I guess. Maybe she was eager to get back to work or needed some more medication for her injuries. But she seemed anxious to me, edging toward fearful. Or maybe it was because she was in a work environment..."

"What?"

"Her body language was all wrong, now that I think about it. There was no warmth there. She stood back from the van. I think I was closer to it than she was. And she was slumped down, making herself small. But again, it could have been her injuries and the crutches that made her posture seem off. But she didn't kiss Sean or touch him or smile while they were talking. Not that I remember, anyway."

Jason nodded and made more notes. "What did you think of him?"

"The kids called him Mr. Claus. He's got the white hair and beard of a mall Santa. Rosy cheeks. A little plump. I liked Katherine, so I was predisposed to like him. But I didn't. And at his house, he put me off too."

"How so?"

I stared at the ceiling, struggling to remember the details. "He came into the living room from the back of the house, where he said he'd been working out. He was in a one of those racing wheelchairs made of titanium or carbon fiber for marathons. Super-light and high-tech. His gear looked brand new, like it was the latest, newest, trendiest model of whatever it was. And"—I stopped as I searched for the right words to explain my discomfort. I took a deep breath—"okay, I don't know if this makes sense. Let's say he strutted into the room on two legs, all sweaty with a towel around his shoulders, talking about his workout. The next thing I'd expect a guy like that to do would be to stand too close and *accidentally* bump into me."

Jason looked uncomfortable. Like Max and most other men, he respected women and had trouble stomaching the behavior of men who demeaned them.

I rattled off the rest of my words quickly, wanting to get it over with and stop reliving the experience. "He'd touch my butt or my breasts in a way that would make me feel super uncomfortable. But if I called him on it, he'd have laughed it off. Sean was in a wheelchair, but the whole time he was in the room, I felt like that. It was gross. As soon as I got home, I took a shower."

"Just because he's in a wheelchair doesn't mean he's not a jerk."

"Exactly. And it was almost like he played on that. Felt like he could get away with stuff and dared me to call him on it." I shuddered.

"What did his sister do?"

"She acted a little embarrassed. But it was weird. If that scene had played out in my house, and one of my brothers had made a guest that uncomfortable, I'd have apologized. But she made a point of *not* apologizing. The whole time I was there, I felt tension beneath the surface. A power struggle or a turf war in which I'd become an unwitting pawn."

I stopped and thought for a moment, trying to remember more about what had happened. "Oh, I asked them about alibis. Fiona said Sean's workout machines recorded his exercises, so they could prove when he'd been working out. But he's computer savvy and so is Katherine, so they could probably fiddle with that information. Do you have people who can detect that stuff?"

Jason scoffed. "People? We've got Paolo. There's no one better. Tell me more about the sister."

"Fiona? She really did look like Mrs. Claus. She was dressed in red and white stripes like an elf and was headed to a ballroom dancing class." I took a moment to reflect on my initial impression of Fiona. "I'd met her earlier when she and Sean came to Katherine's work. They were going to use Katherine's employee discount to get something from the company store—some kind of tech device. They didn't say what. Could that be a clue?" Jason made a note on his pad and underlined it. "I—" I stopped and felt my face grow warm. "Jason, everything I'm telling you sounds super-judgmental. Promise me that you won't repeat any of this unless it's unavoidable. I sound like a hypercritical gossip."

"That's exactly the type of split-second opinion I need," said Jason. He put down his pad and pencil. "The details of everyone's whereabouts are easy to nail down. We can record and transcribe their answers to our questions. But then there's this other aspect to investigations. And that's what experienced cops call a hunch."

"Seriously? But I don't have much experience and zero training. How is my information or intuition going to help?"

"It's more than intuition, and more analytical and scientific than it sounds. Our brains are amazing instruments. All the tech people in the world can't begin to duplicate what the human brain can do, nor the speed with which it analyzes certain kinds of information." Jason stopped for a minute, and his face reddened. "Sorry. I just took a class in this and the topic sucked me in."

He looked past my shoulder and I turned. Elaine stood in the doorway.

"I didn't mean to eavesdrop," she said. "We're done in the kitchen. I'm as fascinated by this information as you are. Teachers rely on hunches all the time. You say there's scientific evidence to support what we've known all along?"

Jason's face lit up with enthusiasm. "For years we've been teaching recruits not to make snap judgments based on appearances and to avoid stereotypes and prejudice. That's a good thing, don't get me wrong. But this new study is telling us that sometimes human instinct can work for us."

Elaine and Jason's enthusiasm was engaging me. "What do you mean?" I asked. "You can't be suggesting that racial profiling is a good idea." I rubbed the back of my neck, which was growing sore from peering up at Elaine standing behind me. "If you're going to listen in, come sit down. As it is, you're literally a pain in the neck."

Jason shook his head. It took me a minute to realize he wasn't refusing to let Elaine join us. He was responding to my question about racial profiling. "Absolutely not. And we're not sure yet how to incorporate this information into our training in a way that prevents some of the problems law enforcement gets into when it relies too much on preconceived opinions. I probably shouldn't have said anything about this at all."

Elaine pulled up a chair and sat down. "We're not going to repeat this or hold you to it, but it's fascinating. The value of experience has diminished in recent years. In lots of professions."

"But it's not all experience," Jason said. "Instinct plays into it too. It's what made David see a shape on the trail and jump out of the way before his conscious mind had time to identify it as a snake. His brain sent a 'danger' signal, and he moved."

"Cops must rely on those split-second warnings all the time," I said.

Jason leaned forward. "Everyone does. We're walking down a dark street at night, we get a prickle on the backs of our necks, and it makes us duck in somewhere and call for a cab. Someone invites us to a concert or a party, and we decline without a rational reason. Later it turns out that we were needed at home or violence erupted at the event. Some people call that instinct, fate, or divine intervention, but in my mind, it's our powerful brains making judgmental, prejudicial, critical, and sometimes lifesaving decisions based on experience."

Jason pushed his chair back and stretched. "I didn't mean to get all professorial on you. But that's why I wanted to hear more about your impressions of some of our suspects."

"But my impressions could be completely wrong," I protested.

"Absolutely. And none of your suspicions would hold up in court unless we found a boatload of additional evidence to back them up. But as an investigatory tool, they could be invaluable."

Elaine brushed some stray crumbs from the table. "Like any tool, instinct can be used for good or evil. Just because a piano wire is sometimes used to strangle people doesn't mean we should stop using it to make music, right? Or if Tess's garden tool was used to kill Patrick, should we stop breaking up dirt clods?"

I shuddered. "I'd forgotten about that pickax. What kinds of hardware do those cartel farmers use? Did you check it for fingerprints? Could Martín have used it?"

"We're still waiting for those results. But instinct tells me that Martín has had a terrible life, full of violence. And somehow, he's survived with his humanity intact. I don't think he'd kill anyone unless he had no other choice. I'm sure he's had many opportunities to kill those goons who held him captive. He had access to deadly poisons, fertilizers to make bombs, and an assault rifle. But his enemies are all still alive, and several of them are now in the Santa Clara County Jail."

I tried to relax and thought back to that first meeting with Sean and Fiona. "When I met the Philipses, I disliked them. I didn't care for the fact that Katherine had to limp to them on her crutches when she was hurting, and that she seemed so nervous. Then, when we reached the van, she used perfect manners in introducing me, but she slumped her shoulders and hung back, away from the vehicle. And Sean had this insincere nicey-nice behavior going on, like he was performing for my benefit and Katherine's."

"And Fiona?"

"She was in shadow, in the passenger seat. I didn't get much of an impression of her." I dropped my head, stretching my neck, trying to stave off an impending tension headache. "Except..."

The scratching sound of Jason's pencil on the cheap notepad stopped.

"Except that she seemed like a neutral party. There was a sub-current of tension between Sean and Katherine, as if he was testing her or taunting her and she feared she might fail the exam. Fiona seemed a step removed from that. Same thing at the house. She wasn't going to help me implicate her brother, but she wouldn't stop me, either. She didn't apologize for Sean's brutish behavior, but she rushed me out the door, getting me away from him. But then she didn't hurry me off or tell me to leave, either."

"I'll get your notes and your impressions to Sergeant Nguyen and the lead detectives in my department. It will help. And we'll get those alibis checked too." Jason opened a small tablet computer and typed furiously without looking up.

I'd been dismissed, but I took heart from the fact that he seemed eager, upbeat, and focused, as though the investigation into Patrick's death might finally be coming together.

Chapter 32

Instinct counts. So does experience. Trust the feelings that warn you about possible dangers. Get to safety. If you've overreacted, no problem. Regroup and make a new plan.

From the Notebook of Maggie McDonald
Simplicity Itself Organizing Services

Thursday, August 10, Near noon

In the kitchen, the dogs panted, sprawled on the cool tile floor next to their water dishes, their snouts dripping. They'd been run hard and were exhausted. Max crested the top of the stairs with a load of sleeping bags to cart back up to the attic. "Should we air these out before we put them away?" he asked.

"Let's wait a few days. There's still so much soot out there. Look at the dogs." The puddles Belle, Munchkin, and Mozart had made on the tiles sported a ring of black around the edges—particulates that still hung in the air from the fire. Our world no longer smelled of smoke, and my eyes no longer stung, but the remains of the burning vegetation persisted.

"After the smoke clears, we should be able to spread them out on the front porch. Leave the bags on one of the window seats near the door for now. The air mattresses can go up to the attic."

Earlier, Max had helped David upstairs and got him into bed moments before he fell asleep under the combined impact of the painkillers and exhaustion. Brian and Teddy were watching a movie in the upstairs den, lounging on the floor. Max reported he'd be willing to bet they were both asleep before he made it downstairs, yawning himself.

"Do we need to switch to decaf?" he asked upon his return, taking up his position at the coffeemaker. "Half caf it is," he said when no one answered him. "But we've got tea and soft drinks too. Water and lemon for the more health conscious."

Typically, a late August afternoon was a great time to settle into comfortable rockers on our back porch in the shade. But that side of the house faced the burned hillside, the prevailing winds, and the trail on which Patrick had died. Ash covered every surface, and none of us had the energy to hose it down. Not when we'd need to do the same thing again in a few days.

We regrouped to our trio of comfy denim sofas in the living room. Max opened the windows facing away from the ridge, and a gentle breeze wafted through. I yawned and sighed, and for the first time in a week realized I felt almost relaxed. Our diminished band—Max and me, Paolo, Martín, Elaine, Jason, and Stephen—seemed to have run out of both conversation and the energy to accomplish much of anything. And maybe that was okay. *But Tess.* Before I could say anything to move Tess's rescue forward, Paolo's phone rang.

"Hang on," he said, and moved into the dining room. The boy had manners, that was for sure. Perhaps deliberately, or possibly by accident, we were still able to hear everything he said. "Seriously? Exactly like the Olmos garage? Did you take photos? Secure the evidence? What about preliminary tests?"

Normally, manners would require that we pretend we weren't eavesdropping. None of us bothered. I strained to isolate words in the sounds coming through the phone from whoever had called Paolo, but I'd have to wait. I turned slightly so I could peer over the back of the sofa and watch the reactions on Paolo's face. He tapped his foot on the floor and his fingers on the side of his phone as he pulled his tablet out of his backpack. He then sat at the table with his back to us. Hunched over the phone, taking notes, his end of the conversation became muffled.

"Who's he talking to?" I whispered to Jason.

"The team searching Sean, Katherine, and Fiona's house, I suspect."

"Sounds like they found something. Something that might clear Tess." I raised my eyebrows in question, silently begging Jason to confirm my hope.

He patted my arm, took a sip of coffee, and whispered, "Wait. We'll hear soon enough."

Martín, who'd perched on one of the window seats, stood, walked to the archway separating the dining area from the living room, and stood with one hand on the wall, leaning forward until he was almost on tiptoes.

Paolo ended the call, typed silently on his tablet for a few seconds, then turned. "They found something in Sean's van." He stood and clapped Martín on the back. "A pickax, wrapped in an old towel under the back seat. Covered with blood. Human blood, if the prelims are accurate. Their garage has a pegboard tool wall identical to the one at the Olmos house, with an empty spot that matches the pickax. They found Patrick's wallet in the van, wrapped up in a bundle with the tool."

"Fingerprints?" asked Jason.

Paolo shook his head. "Nothing visible. Wiped clean. It's going to the lab. Their best guy will bring up latent prints if there are any. Rushed it."

Jason put down his coffee mug and leaned forward with his elbow on his knees. "Let's get back to the story I was telling before we took this break. Martín saw a muzzle flash and watched Patrick collapse. He was running toward him to help when the driver got out of the van and approached Patrick unsteadily, carrying something like a truncheon. He—"

Martín interrupted. "*O ella.*"

"—*or she* raised it overhead and slammed it down. The killer pulled back on the tool, and nudged Patrick with a foot. He or she opened the back door of the van, threw the tool inside, climbed into the driver's seat, and turned around at the next wide point in the road."

Martín made a noise that sounded like an engine laboring.

"For a moment, Martín thought the truck had become stuck in the soft shale at the side of the road, but that *todo terrano* option helped the murderer out. The driver switched into four-wheel drive and took off down the hill in a spray of pebbles. Martín just had time to jot down the license plate. He checked on Patrick, saw there was nothing he could do to help, and took off. He knew, with the fire coming, it was his best chance to escape the cartel. He also wasn't sure whether the murderer had spotted him, but he knew it wouldn't be safe to stay, either way."

Martín hung his head. Paolo patted his arm and whispered to him quietly in Spanish, then turned to translate for the rest of us. "Martín feels bad that he wasn't able to protect Patrick and stop his murder. I assured him that he did everything he could. And that Patrick would be glad to know Martín helped the boys and wants to stop the cartel from poisoning the land."

A murmur of agreement developed like a fresh breeze. Martín looked up, blinked, and nodded, but then moved into the kitchen. Paolo followed him.

"So, are we thinking it was the killer who put Patrick's gun on the workbench in Tess's garage? And who hid the pickax? Only the murderer could have known what type of weapon he used. And none of us knew about the tool. Not even the medical examiner, right? Last I heard, the report said he'd been hit with something that damaged his skull. Or was that left deliberately vague? Do the police hold back details the way you see on television?"

"We do," said Jason. "But I expect you're right on all counts."

"So, that narrows it down to Katherine, Fiona, and Sean? Is that enough to release Tess? Is there enough evidence to rule out the gun the sheriff found at her house and the pickax that hurt Teddy's foot? Do they need to know who did it before they'll give up on Tess? Should we call Forrest? How much time will they need? Can we pick her up today?"

Jason blinked under my barrage of questions. Paolo came through the dining room from the kitchen, walking while shifting his gaze between his phone and tablet, both of which were chiming continuously with dueling alert tones. Martín held out an arm to guide him away from a collision with the archway and the back of the sofa.

"Forrest is already on it," Paolo said. "He has spies everywhere, as far as I can tell."

Paolo's tablet blurted another signal, and Paolo scrolled through the screen. "Nguyen says he'll call when Tess can be picked up. He's not sure whether it will be today or first thing in the morning." He scrolled more and laughed. "Forrest says it will be today. He put 'WILL' in caps. He never uses all caps like that."

A cheer from the rest of us drowned out Paolo's words, and Elaine ran to the stairs to share the great news with Teddy.

Chapter 33

The National Park Service estimates that humans are responsible for 90 percent of wildfires, including those sparked by unattended campfires, burning debris, cigarettes, or arson. Increasingly, Cal Fire traces the source of devastating blazes to illegal marijuana growing areas. Whenever you are in an undeveloped area, follow fire safety guidelines. Remember that if a fire is too hot to touch, it is too hot to leave unattended.

From the Notebook of Maggie McDonald
Simplicity Itself Organizing Services

Friday, August 11, Early morning

Ultimately, Forrest was wrong. Santa Clara County released Tess at 12:15 a.m. Friday morning. Forty-five minutes later, Forrest's car pulled up to our front porch, and Tess was nearly bowled over by Teddy's enthusiastic hug and the attention of the three dogs. Mozart plopped his paws on Tess's chest and gave her an exuberant kiss. She tilted her head to examine his still swollen snout and asked if he'd been in a bar fight.

"We'll give you all the details later," I said, nudging the dogs aside so I could hug her. "When you've had a shower, put on real clothes, and polished off some fresh fruit, coffee, and croissants, we'll fill you in on everything."

As a group, we wanted to protect Tess from nosy neighbors and journalists as she adjusted to life without Patrick. For the first day at least, and then for as long as she and Teddy needed, they'd make their home with Mozart in our attic guest suite. Later, almost certainly before school started, I'd help her organize the piles of paperwork that follow any death. We'd sort out Patrick's belongings, hanging on to anything that warranted saving, and discarding or donating the rest. And I'd urge her to take her decisions one at a time.

Earlier, Elaine and I had taken Teddy back to his house to pick up a few things he needed, along with Tess's favorite clothes and toiletry items. We stopped at the store and bakery on the way home, while Teddy cleaned them out of his mom's favorite foods.

Keeping Teddy sane and busy while we'd waited for Tess's release had been a full-time job for all concerned. He'd played video games with David, walked the dogs with Brian and Max, patrolled the neighborhoods with Paolo, and had a not-strictly-legal driving lesson in Foothill College's parking lot with Jason.

Max and Brian had ordered pizzas and salads for dinner and downloaded a long series of cartoons the boys hadn't watched since their tween years. We wallowed in a love fest of calories, comedy, and nostalgia.

By unspoken agreement, we dropped our manic pursuit of the details of Patrick's murder. Tess was coming home, and that was enough for now. Later, we'd debrief everyone we needed to until we all understood exactly what had happened. Going over the facts of the case would be particularly important to Tess, who'd been almost entirely out of the loop while the rest of us had tracked down answers and hunted suspects.

Martín joined us for the cartoons and might have laughed louder than anyone else. In many ways, his situation was similar to Tess's. After the cartel had kidnapped and enslaved him, possibly murdering his family, he needed to rebuild his life on his own terms. Forrest and Jason were working with an alphabet soup of government agencies to get the answers Martín needed. For now, he was working with both national and international groups to take down the cartel.

Could he stay in Orchard View? We hoped so. But much depended upon how long he could be kept safe here, and how hard the cartel and their affiliated gangs were looking for him. U.S. marshals from the Witness Protection Program were in charge of those assessments, thank goodness. I was grateful for their expertise and for their willingness to shoulder the responsibility for his safety.

For now, he'd become one of us. The kids' Spanish, and even my rusty high school skills, were improving. So was Martín's English, which was far more extensive than I'd first thought. As long as we spoke slowly, and simply, without idioms, he understood most of what we had to say.

According to Jason, when they'd talked about where to house him, Martín asked if it would be possible to stay with us. With Tess and Teddy in the attic suite, my first thought was that there was no room for Martín. But he suggested taking possession of an air mattress and a sleeping bag, and helping us to remodel the basement, creating a bedroom for Martín, a small den, and offices for Max and me.

Housing strangers who'd become friends was becoming a habit with us. Max believed it was the influence of the house and the will of whatever remained of the spirit of his great-aunt, Kay, the previous owner of the home. Widowed at a young age, Kay was a Stanford professor who frequently took in students, visiting professors, those in town for a lecture series, and an ever-changing cast of interesting characters from around the world. We, and the house, were continuing her legacy.

While short-lived lightning storms developed later in August and threatened to revive the ridge blaze, Cal Fire maintained control. David had set up a motion-activated camera hoping to spot a mountain lion crossing our yard in an effort to find a safe haven, but he was ultimately disappointed. In the process, though, he realized that the nighttime wildlife in our backyard was far more diverse and active than he'd ever realized. He hoped to convert his impromptu study to a report and extra credit in his AP Biology class.

For right now, our primary concern was Tess. She showered for an hour, then dressed in her most comforting clothing: oversized sweats and worn sheepskin boots. She trudged down the stairs, toweling her hair dry, and occasionally sniffing the towel, her clothes, and her hair, to verify that a scent none of the rest of us could detect no longer clung to her skin, hair, or clothing. She called it *"Eau de l'incarcération,"* shuddering when she said it. She jumped at every loud noise and grew edgy and distracted when doors were closed. Upon entering any room, her first task was to locate the exits. A counselor Forrest had recommended later told us the bulk of those habits would fade away, while some might be with her for the rest of her life, or grow worse in times of stress. It didn't matter. She was home.

She plopped on the couch with a contented sigh. The boys bustled to bring her food and coffee, which she savored. Tess made eye contact with each of us, including Martín, whom she'd never met. "I'm assuming you had a key role," she told him. "Thank you. Now, who is going to tell me what's been going on while I've been locked up? That was the worst—knowing that I was missing out and that there was nothing I could do to help."

"Can we start with the parts that even we don't know, and then back up?" Teddy asked. "Like who killed my dad and why? How they did it and how they framed my mom? And how Jason and Forrest convinced Nguyen to let her go? Have they charged someone else? Will he get the death penalty? How long until the trial?"

I glanced at Tess. She winked and then laughed. "One question at a time, Teddy. You're already adopting Maggie's speech patterns."

Forrest, who was nearly as quiet as Martín, cleared his throat. "I like Teddy's idea," he said. "I know everyone here is starving for news, but I wasn't sure where to begin." He removed his glasses and cleaned them with a handkerchief he'd pulled from the pocket of his gray suit pants. He'd shed the jacket and loosened his tie, but he was still a dapper dude. "If we get the rest of you up to speed, you can fill Tess in on the other details she missed over the next few days...or months. This case was complicated, that's for sure." He sighed and I was glad he didn't have far to go to reach his own bed.

Forrest turned to Jason. "You want to do the honors? You know what evidence was most pertinent." Jason shook his head and sneezed. Stephen handed him a large mug of tea with lemon, honey, and the shot of brandy that he'd requested moments earlier. He cradled the mug. "I'm coming down with a cold, and my throat is killing me." His voice, rasping out the words, was barely recognizable. "Paolo?"

Paolo, who'd been hanging back, was seated on a window seat flanked by thick red drapes. He blinked, then pulled his tablet from his bag as the rest of us shifted to face him. He flushed and stammered out the next few words. "Ask questions as they occur to you, everyone. And if I get it wrong, jump in. I'm still organizing my notes and my thoughts. I'm meeting with Sergeant Nguyen and the district attorney tomorrow"—he checked his watch—"later today, to figure out what other information we need, if any, to prosecute the case."

"Who did it?" asked Elaine. "We'd narrowed it down to three: Katherine, Fiona and Sean."

"Right," Paolo drew the word out and paused, heightening the tension as we waited for him to finger the culprit who'd killed Patrick, destroyed Tess and Teddy's world, and frayed the fabric of our entire community.

Chapter 34

Professional organizers are all about, well, organization and efficiency. That process goes far beyond decluttering. Being prepared for a variety of emergency scenarios saves time and money. Our "What would you do?" approach to planning includes protecting yourself and your family when you're on the road. And that means protecting yourself from drunk drivers. According to the Centers for Disease Control, an average drunk driver has driven under the influence eighty times before his or her first arrest. You can help lower that number and decrease traffic fatalities by reporting suspected drunk drivers and stopping friends and family members from driving under the influence.

From the Notebook of Maggie McDonald
Simplicity Itself Organizing Services

Friday, August 11, Early morning

"Out with it," urged Elaine. Munchkin woofed softly, backing her up.

"Okay," Paolo took a deep breath, and the rest of us groaned in frustration, thinking he was stalling for time and dragging out the suspense. "Fine. Fine. We think it was Fiona."

"Fiona? *Fiona?*" said Tess. "Who's Fiona? And why?"

Everyone began talking at once, trying to explain Fiona's multiple connections to the case. After my initial shock, I began to replay Fiona's actions and comments in my head, and it all started to make sense.

"She took Katherine to the hospital," I said. "But then, if their experience was anything like ours, they spent lots of time waiting around for tests. Orderlies would have whisked Katherine off, giving Fiona the unsupervised freedom she needed to head up to the ridge and take out Patrick. But why?"

Paolo's head bobbed. "Exactly. One of our officers timed it. In the middle of the night, with no traffic, it takes fifteen minutes, considerably less if you're bent on murder and not too concerned with speed limits, to drive between El Camino Hospital and the ridge where Martín saw the green van."

"But what happened?" Tess asked. "Why did Fiona want Patrick dead? Did she know him?"

"Now *you're* doing it, Mom," Teddy said, nudging his mother with his elbow. "One question at a time."

"There's a fine line between a smart kid and a smart-ass," Tess responded. "Mind you're on the right side of that line."

Paolo smiled. "There was a whole lot of convoluted thinking involved, but it turns out that Fiona knew Patrick all too well." He cleared his throat. "Let me get this part out. It's complicated, and I don't want to lose my train of thought."

We sat up a little straighter, like schoolkids on our best behavior.

"So, Fiona is Katherine McNamara's sister-in-law. Fiona's brother, Sean Philips, is Katherine's husband. Sean's much older than Katherine, fifty-six to her thirty-two. He's a marketing engineer, the kind that travels to customer sites, customizes products, troubleshoots bugs, and tries to convince them to stay with his company's products instead of jumping ship and going with someone new. Katherine, Sean, and Patrick all worked for that same company. At one time, Sean had been successful. He was in charge of the largest accounts, and racked up a slew of industry awards and community recognition for his contributions to kids' sports. But he had his demons and they were getting the better of him. He'd lost a number of important clients in the past few years."

Paolo had been reading off of his tablet, but now looked up and blinked as if he was having trouble seeing. "Now, I need to back up a bit. Sean was a member of the 1980 Summer Olympics team. The one that didn't compete because Russia invaded Afghanistan. He ran the 5,000 meters. He qualified for the 1984 team, but an alternate took his spot after he got caught up in a tight grouping of runners and fell, messing up both knees. His rehab went well, but after that he avoided the inside track and suffered from panic attacks that kept him from perfecting his timing, breathing, and other technical racing details I'm not sure I completely understand. In short, he was no longer competitive. There were rumors that he'd actually caused the accident in an attempt to trip another runner and gain the lead, but no charges were filed."

"But what do the Olympics thirty-five years ago have to do with Patrick's death?" asked Tess, sounding impatient and exasperated.

"Sean went back to his engineering career full-time after that, but he missed sports. He was instrumental in helping Patrick launch the Orchard View Road Runners, and he did some coaching. He was good, and got a number of kids to the Olympics. He trained Katherine. That's how they met. But then, in a recreational race that Patrick took part in, Sean crashed again, doing even more damage to his knees. That led to a double knee replacement. During his stint in rehab, Katherine trained with Patrick." Paolo paused, took a sip from his water bottle, scrolled frantically, and then stopped. "Never mind. The timing doesn't really matter. At some point, he developed an infection. They had to remove the manufactured parts of the knee, along with a considerable amount of bone. Sean's been wheelchair-bound ever since."

"So he blamed Patrick?" Tess said. "But where does Fiona come in? It looks like Sean had more motive than she did."

"Right," Paolo said. "But there's more to the story. Sean became addicted to painkillers and was indulging in other self-medicating substances, none of which combines well with opiates. He'd always had an anger problem, but it grew worse until he was routinely beating Katherine. At some point, and I'm not sure of the exact order of events, Fiona came to live with them and help with Sean's care. He's pretty self-sufficient, and the couple uses caregivers for personal hygiene matters Sean can't handle on his own, but Katherine still had her hands full."

Paolo took another sip of water. "So, enter Fiona. She's the oldest of five, from a farming family in Kansas. She had four brothers who were into sports, and she was in charge of the laundry. She wanted nothing to do with athletics and stinky gym socks. But she was as coordinated and active as the rest of the family, so she poured that talent into dance. She didn't have the body type or the competitive drive required for ballet, but she taught ballroom dancing in Kansas before she moved here. She never married."

"Again, what's that got to do with Patrick?" Tess asked.

"She seemed so nice," I added.

"Maybe," Paolo said. "But she was tough too. She made Sean pay her, and she was well compensated, receiving more than any of the other caregivers they hired. Fiona defended Katherine from Sean and may have done a little Sean beating in retribution, but we can't prove that. Not yet."

"But why Patrick?"

"According to Fiona, Patrick's death was all Sean's fault. He blamed his disability on Patrick, and was growing increasingly jealous of the time Katherine spent with Patrick, the recognition he was getting from the community for helping with the sports teams, and his athletic ability. It made him furious that both Katherine and Patrick had been track stars in college, but were, in his words, squandering their athletic careers by pursuing the sport part-time while they focused instead on their professional careers, engineering, and in Patrick's case, family. In the high-tech arena, Patrick's career was going even better than Sean's. This guy who'd been top dog a few years back suddenly felt that Patrick was crushing him. And then Sean decided Patrick was after his wife."

"So again, wouldn't that be reason for *Sean* to kill Patrick?" Tess said. "What possible motive could his sister have had? Did she even know Patrick?" Her face flushed. She pushed her hair back and sighed. "You know it's ridiculous, right? Patrick would have welcomed Sean's help with the team, and my husband had neither the time nor the inclination to pursue another woman. He wouldn't."

I put my arm around Tess and hugged her. "We know," I told her. "We never thought that rumor was true."

"Never? I'll bet Pauline Windsor and Robert Wu relished it."

"Maybe, but none of your friends put any stock in it."

Paolo cleared his throat.

"Oops," I said. "Sorry for the interruption. Go on."

"To hear Fiona tell it, Sean was a complete mess professionally and personally, traumatizing Katherine with his violent outbursts. But then, a few weeks ago, he showed up at Fiona's Silver Steppers dance class at the retirement home, drunk out of his mind. Someone from the class called the police. Sean had driven to the class, but how he managed it without killing someone is anyone's guess. We tested him when we brought him in, and his blood alcohol level was more than twice the legal limit, without taking into account all the painkillers he had on board. And he wasn't showing symptoms."

Jason coughed. I couldn't tell whether it was due to his oncoming cold or whether he was sending a message to Paolo. The younger man flushed and turned his attention back to his tablet. "Please don't repeat any of that," he told us. "It's confidential, at least for now."

Elaine spoke up then. "Let me get this straight. It seems Katherine might have had a motive for killing Sean, since he was probably racking up bills from the drug use and he was knocking her around. Sean might have had a motive for killing Patrick, since he was jealous and off his head on booze and pills. So, where does Fiona come into it? Was she unhappy living in that house? If she was, why didn't she just head back to Kansas and leave her brother and sister-in-law to their miserable fates?"

Paolo shook his head. "She probably should have left. But she's the sort of person who likes to resolve problems. She's fiercely protective. When Sean became so disagreeable and refused to go to rehab or do any of the other things a responsible person does when they realize the kind of damage their lifestyle is inflicting on them and their family, she shifted her allegiance to Katherine. And at some point after the Silver Steppers incident, when she realized Sean was routinely driving drunk and imperiling the whole community, she decided to protect everyone else in Orchard View by killing her own brother."

I gasped. Everything else Paolo had told us led to this revelation. Paolo held up his hand to forestall any questions and added, "The death of one of her students last month in a hit-and-run accident may have pushed her over the edge. She believes Sean was the driver and has asked us to investigate it."

"So, then, why Patrick?" Tess asked, her voice catching. "What did Patrick have to do with any of this?"

Chapter 35

It's never too late to rethink your career plan. Many professional organizers are pursuing second careers. If you sense that you are wasting your talent and energy in your current occupation, take the time to rethink your options, gain additional training, or consult a career planning professional.

From the Notebook of Maggie McDonald
Simplicity Itself Organizing Services

Friday, August 11, Morning

Paolo swallowed and cleared his throat.

"Do you need a break?" I asked him. "Does anyone? It's getting late. Or early, I guess. It's time to think about breakfast."

Paolo shook his head. "No, I want to finish this. Tess and Teddy need to know where we are." Tess and Teddy nodded their agreement, and no one else seemed interested in stopping. So on we went.

"Katherine said that Fiona had become increasingly impatient with Sean's reckless driving, with his treatment of Katherine, and with his endless tirades about Patrick," Paolo said. "It was getting so that any mention of work or Patrick put Fiona into a temper nearly as black as those from which Sean suffered. Katherine thought that Fiona might have been dipping into Sean's pill stash. She was certainly drinking more. When we picked her up she had— Well, the amount doesn't matter, but she was legally over the limit."

Jason jumped in, giving Paolo a break. "Katherine thought Fiona had tried to kill Sean. There was one morning a few weekends ago when he fell asleep at the table. Katherine and Fiona moved him to the sofa, and Sean slept for nearly thirty-six hours straight. He claimed to have been fighting off the flu and catching up on his sleep, but in retrospect, Katherine wasn't sure. She suspected Fiona gave him what, for anyone else, would have been an overdose of pills. Sean had been dosing himself at such a high level that what could have killed someone else may have just knocked him out for a bit. No matter how angry or disgusted by him she became, Fiona couldn't bring herself to try again. Sean was her little brother. She loved him. But Patrick. *His* name began to send Fiona into homicidal rage, the same way it had Sean. She seemed to join Sean in blaming Patrick for Sean's situation, but compounded Patrick's supposed crimes by giving him responsibility for her near-murder of her brother, for her anger, and for Sean's treatment of Katherine. Fiona convinced herself that, without Patrick, normalcy would be restored to her family, and life would go back to the calm, predictable life she craved."

"But it sounds like that ship had sailed," I said. "Nothing about their household had been normal for a long time."

Jason leaned forward. "You're right, Maggie. But that didn't matter. If we've got this right, Fiona convinced herself that everyone's problems would be solved, her friend's death would be avenged, and order would be restored—as long as she killed Patrick. Fiona did a ton of research. She knew what kinds of guns Patrick had. She knew how his garage was organized, since Patrick had helped Katherine set theirs up the same way. With Sean wheelchair-bound, she'd taken on all of the household maintenance and repairs. While Sean had been stalking Patrick, Fiona had been following Sean and Tess. She even knew about Teddy's accident with the garden tool."

Jason took a long gulp of tea. "We've got a record of her buying the same model of antique Olympic target shooting pistol that Patrick had. She'd begun target shooting with it."

Tess leaned forward. "I remember. Patrick mentioned he was meeting someone at the range. This had to have been months ago. Back in January when it was raining so hard—I remember because they had trouble finding a dry weekend. Could that target-shooting buddy have been Fiona? Had she been planning Patrick's death that long?"

"She bought the gun last November," Jason said. He paused, and expressions of shock appeared on the faces of everyone around me. I felt the muscles in my own face move to mirror theirs.

"That's cold," I said. "Asking the person she plans to murder to help her become adept enough with a gun to pull it off? Who does that?"

Jason shook his head. "I want to talk to a psychologist about that myself. My guess is that each step of this plan, initially at least, didn't necessarily lead to Patrick's death. Fiona may have legitimately wanted to learn to target shoot, and the choice of an Olympic pistol grew naturally from Sean's connections to the Olympics. Somehow, maybe through Katherine, Fiona learned about Patrick's granddad and that's how they eventually ended up shooting together at the range. Then, as her rage grew, it overpowered whatever budding friendship she had with Patrick."

"The target pistol was all she needed to disable Patrick," Stephen said. "Although she was much smaller than he was, once he was injured, he would have struggled to get up. It didn't matter where she hit him. Any injury would have made regaining his footing very difficult on that steep hill. The target bullet wouldn't kill him, but it would slow him down enough so that she could finish him off without endangering herself."

Tess broke in then. "And because Fiona had been stalking Patrick, she knew she'd find him up on the ridge. Did she set the fire to cover her tracks?"

Paolo shook his head. "We don't think so. The fire started much farther down on the other side of the ridge. She probably wishes that she did start it, though. That fire consumed a lot of the evidence, and the firefighters trampled other evidence into the ground. The fire danger itself delayed Sergeant Nguyen's investigation."

Teddy broke in, "So, is Fiona the one who left Dad's gun out on the workbench? Did she plant the pickax? And did she set up that awful website to implicate my mom?"

Paolo's head bobbed. "Good thinking, Teddy. That's the scenario we're working on, but she hasn't confessed to it. We're also not sure which tool is yours and which is hers. We'll need you or your mom to help us with that. It doesn't matter, though. The lab is still working on the DNA evidence, but we've got your dad's blood and a woman's blood on one of the garden tools, and we're nearly certain that female DNA will match up to Fiona."

"And one of them has *my* blood on it," Teddy said, waving his foot in the air. "But Fiona could have used either our pickax or her own. We never lock the garage, so she could have taken the tool and the pistol at any time, then just as easily returned them without anyone knowing."

"Right," said Paolo. "Does anyone remember seeing Fiona at Tess and Teddy's house the night after Patrick died, when everyone else was there?"

After a brief silence, David spoke up. "I did. I went into the garage to get a soda for Emily, and Fiona was in there. She was fussing with a towel on the workbench as if she was drying off a bottle of seltzer that had been in the ice bucket. I didn't think anything more about it. There were so many people there, and I couldn't have known who had an attachment of some kind to Patrick or Tess or Teddy, and who didn't."

"We've got a lot more work to do before we can bring charges against Fiona, but we'll get there," said Paolo. "Despite his misstep in arresting Tess, Nguyen's team knows what they're doing, and the Orchard View Police Department will help out as much as we can."

"And the website?" asked David. "Will they charge her with a crime for that?"

Paolo shook his head. "We're looking at someone else for that. The site is down, and we're cleaning up all traces of it. The culprit has taken responsibility. Other than that, I can't talk about it." He looked at me and nodded. No one else noticed, but I took that to mean that Rebecca had kept her promise and Paolo was helping her.

"So, what happens now, Mom?" Teddy asked.

"We go on the best we can, Teddy. And we help each other to do that." Tess said.

"We'll help too," I said.

"I've had a lot of time to think in jail," Tess added. "And I'm sure Stephen will agree with me that this business of sitting in a cell when you've done nothing wrong is terrible. I don't want anyone I know, or even a stranger, having to do that again, ever. I know you're not supposed to make any big changes after someone dies, but I'm thinking of selling the real estate business to my partner, Robert—he's been trying to maneuver me into it for years."

"But what will you do?" I asked.

"While Teddy finishes high school, I'm going to take every law enforcement or legal studies class offered at Foothill College," Tess said, lifting her chin as if daring us to try to change her mind. "When he's finished, I'll transfer to San Jose State or Santa Clara University and specialize. I don't know whether I want to become a criminalist and work in the lab, if I want to be a lawyer and work with the Innocence Project, or if I want to do something else. But I've got a plan that's good enough to start with, and I can fine-tune it as I go."

"Whatever organization gets you in the end," said Jason with the authority of his vast experience in a wide range of military and law enforcement fields, "they'll be lucky to have you."

Forrest agreed. "If you need any help exploring legal careers, let me know," he said. "Or if you need a recommendation for those college applications or even an internship, I'd be happy to tell them that you were the most organized, determined, and honest client I've ever worked with."

"I'm not sure being the most honest of the people you've defended from murder convictions is much to be proud of," Tess said. "But thanks."

Then she gave me a nudge. "And this is getting to be a habit for you. This *'oh dear, my friend's in jail, I'd better investigate a murder'* stuff. Don't let it happen again. Ever."

She took bite of a crunchy croissant and moaned with pleasure. "But if I'm ever in jail again, bring me a dozen of these, every day. I can exchange them for privileges. And you could also smuggle in tools that I could use to break out."

"What tools?"

Tess shrugged. "How would I know? This is only the first time I've been charged with murder." She took another bite. "But you? What is this, your fourth murder case? By now you should have a pretty good idea what tools are required. And if you don't, you'd better figure it out soon. Unless you think you've single-handedly cleared out every murderer in the greater Bay Area. Murder has a way of finding you, doesn't it, Maggie?"

I shrugged and grabbed another croissant for myself. What could I say to defend myself? Nothing. As usual, there was no arguing with Tess.

Epilogue

One Year Later

The following August, Orchard View celebrated the first annual Patrick Olmos Memorial Marathon and Fun Run. As often happens in Silicon Valley, the race title was shortened to its initials: POM. Race planners, with permission from the Olmos family, promoted the event as the great Silicon Valley POM-POM run. Pom-pom trimmed jerseys, sneakers, and tufted hats completed the race-day outfits of even the most serious runners. Charities and schools sold cheerleading accessories to spectators who encouraged runners with pom-poms representing the colors of their school, company, or favored cause. Race proceeds benefitted youth athletics, and would help maintain the running trails Patrick loved at Rancho San Antonio County Park. Patrick Olmos's memory and his sense of community, sport, and fun were honored, celebrated, and remembered in one fell swoop.

Page eight of the local paper reported the final disposition of a legal case in which an appellate court affirmed an earlier Santa Clara County Superior Court ruling. According to the article, both courts ruled that land purchased or donated for public use must remain available to the general public in perpetuity. The verdict ended Pauline Windsor's quest to rezone the land for luxury apartments and upscale homes.

If the McDonald family's story has inspired you to kick your emergency preparations up a notch, Maggie offers these sources of information and materials:

Road ID
Simple identification and emergency information you can wear all day.
800-345-6336
www.roadid.com

Citizen Corps/Ready.gov
Uniting Communities, Preparing the Nation.
Includes lists of strategies and materials that will help you and your family become disaster ready. Content is focused on reaching both kids and adults.
www.ready.gov

CDC: Preparing for the Zombie Apocalypse
The Centers for Disease Control and Prevention (CDC) takes its role in protecting Americans seriously. But when their Office of Public Health Preparedness and Response was looking for a way to reach more people, particularly young adults, they latched on to the popularity of zombies and other dystopian fiction. People prepared for a fictional zombie apocalypse, they figured, would be darn near ready for anything. And their most popular series of preparedness pamphlets and videos was born. (The site also offers more mundane and direct preparedness information.)
https://www.cdc.gov/phpr/zombie

Red Cross
Be Prepared and Ready to Respond at Home and Your Workplace
The Red Cross offers training in many of the health and safety skills helpful in emergencies. Call or check their website for programs in your area.
http://www.redcross.org/get-help/how-to-prepare-for-emergencies

National Fire Protection Association
The leading information and knowledge resource on fire, electrical, and related hazards.

NFPA offers educational pamphlets and other communications materials for a variety of at-risk groups. They offer ways to prevent and prepare for fires within your home, school or workplace and outdoors.
www.nfpa.org/public-education

National Association of Productivity and Organizing Professionals
NAPO professionals are equipped to help you with your emergency preparedness plans. They charge for their services but can speed the process and help you update and fine-tune your plans as your life changes.
www.napo.net

This list is only a start. Your local fire department, Red Cross, police department, or city planning office may also be of assistance, particularly in tailoring your plans to the risks most prevalent in your geographic area.

Meet the Author

Mary Feliz writes the Maggie McDonald Mysteries featuring a Silicon Valley professional organizer and her sidekick golden retriever. She's worked for Fortune 500 firms and mom and pop enterprises, competed in whale boat races and done synchronized swimming. She attends organizing conferences in her character's stead, by Maggie's skills leave her in the dust. Visit Mary online at MaryFeliz.com, find her on Facebook at Mary Feliz Books, or follow her on Twitter at @MaryFelizAuthor.

Scheduled to Death

If you enjoyed Dead Storage, be sure not to miss this thrilling installment in Mary Feliz's Maggie McDonald Mystery series

Professional organizer Maggie McDonald has a knack for cleaning up other people's messes. So when the fiancée of her latest client turns up dead, it's up to her to sort through the untidy list of suspects and identify the real killer.

"Fans of Feliz's first book as well as newcomers to the series won't be disappointed... Moves forward quickly with freshness, a few surprises and a couple of real scares."
—*Kirkus Reviews* on *Scheduled to Death*

Keep reading for a special look!

Chapter 1

We don't use the word *hoarder* in my business. It holds negative connotations, few of which are true of the chronically disorganized.

From the Notebook of Maggie McDonald
Simplicity Itself Organizing Services

Monday, November 3, 9:00 a.m.

I couldn't be sure where the line was between a mansion and a really big house, but I knew that I was straddling it, standing on the front porch of the gracious Victorian home of Stanford Professor Lincoln "Linc" Sinclair. The future of my career here in Orchard View straddled a similar line—the one between success and failure.

I rang the doorbell a second time and glanced at my best friend, Tess Olmos. She was dressed in what I called her dominatrix outfit— red and black designer business clothes and expensive black stilettos with red soles. I wore jeans, sneakers, and a long-sleeved white T-shirt, over which I wore a canvas fisherman's vest filled with the tools of my trade. I'm a Certified Professional Organizer and my job today was to finish helping the professor sort through three generations of furniture and a lifetime's collection of "stuff" he was emotionally attached to.

The professor was a brilliant man on the short list for the Nobel Prize in a field I didn't understand, but his brain wasn't programmed for organization and never would be.

And that's where I came in. Organization is my superpower.

I glanced at my watch. It was 9:10 a.m. We had arrived promptly for our appointment at nine. Tess had arranged to use the house for her annual holiday showcase to thank her clients and promote her business, but she wanted to double-check our progress on clearing things out before she finalized her own schedule. All but one of the rooms was empty, but Tess had a sharp eye and might well spot something I'd missed. If she had questions about anything Linc and I had done, I wanted to be on hand to answer them immediately.

Participating in Tess's holiday event would give my fledgling business a huge boost. Endorsements from Tess Olmos and Linc Sinclair were likely to bring me as much—if not more—business than I could handle.

"We did say nine o'clock, didn't we?" I asked Tess. "I wonder if he overslept after that storm last night?" A rare electrical storm had coursed across the San Francisco Bay Area the previous evening, bringing buckets of much-needed rain. With it came winds that downed trees and power lines. Thunder shook my house to its foundation.

"What did the weather folks predict? Isolated storm cells with a chance of lightning. The morning news was showing footage of funnel clouds in Palo Alto. My dog whined all night." Tess bent to peek through one of the front windows. "Wow, you've really made a lot of progress in there," she said. "I can see clear through to the dining room."

I smiled as I stepped off the porch and onto the fieldstone path running across the grass and past the chrysanthemums and snapdragons that edged the front garden.

"Linc's been working hard," I said. "All that's left, beyond a few boxes, is his upstairs workroom with all that electronic equipment and research papers. I'm hoping to organize most of that today and take it to his freshly cleaned and cataloged storage unit. If it goes well, we'll tackle his office at Stanford."

I looked up and down the street. No professor.

"Where is he?" asked Tess, echoing the question I'd already asked myself.

"I'll take a look 'round back," I said. "He may be working in the garden or kitchen with his headphones on and can't hear the bell."

I followed the flagstone walk around to the side of the house and let out a yelp. My hand flew to my throat and my heart rate soared.

"Oh my! Sorry—I'm so sorry," I said to the woman blocking my way. I fought to regain my balance after my abrupt stop. "You startled me. Can I help you?"

"Humph!" said the woman, straightening as if to maximize her height. "I could ask you the same question. Does Professor Sinclair know you're here? He appreciates neither visitors nor interruptions." Her face was overshadowed by a gardening hat the size of a small umbrella. Green rubber boots with white polka dots swallowed her feet and lower legs, which vanished beneath a voluminous fuchsia skirt splattered with potting soil. A purple flannel shirt completed her outfit.

Tess's stilettos clicked on the path behind me. With one hand on my shoulder, she reached in front of me, holding out her hand to greet the woman.

"Tess Olmos," she said. "I'm Linc's Realtor and this is Maggie McDonald, his professional organizer. We're here for an appointment." I scrambled in my cargo vest for a business card as the woman picked up the business end of a coiled garden hose. I had the distinct impression she was waiting for an excuse to turn the nozzle on us. I found a card, plucked it from my pocket, and handed it to her.

"I was checking the professor's house for damage after that storm last night," the woman said as she took my card and put it in her pocket without looking at it. "My nana would have called it a gullywomper. Nice to meet you ladies, but I need to get to work. For twenty years, the Sinclairs have allowed me to use their water in my community garden." She waved her arm toward an overgrown hedge at the back of the half-acre property. "In exchange, I provide them with fresh vegetables."

"Of course," Tess said as if she knew all about the arrangement.

"And you are?"

"Oh, sorry." The woman wiped her grubby hands on her pink skirt before shaking Tess's outstretched hand. "I'm Claire Domingo, but I go by Boots. I'm the president of the Orchard View Plotters Garden Club. We run the community garden in back of the house."

Before any of us could say anything more, I heard the screeching of bicycle brakes. Linc careened around the corner with his legs outstretched and his jacket flapping behind him. His Irish wolfhound, Newton, loped beside him and made the turn easily.

Out of breath, the professor jumped from the bike and let it fall to the ground beside him as if he were an eight-year-old who was late for lunch.

"Sorry. Sorry. Sorry," he said, scurrying toward us. "I had an idea for a new project in the middle of the night and I rode over to the university. Time got away from me. Sorry to keep you waiting."

Newton barked in greeting and lunged toward me.

Linc unhooked the dog from the bicycle leash he'd invented ten years earlier but had never sought a patent for. Once he'd created it and proved it worked, he'd lost interest.

Newton barreled in my direction. I stepped back and knelt to give him more room to slow down before he plowed into me. Linc had trained him well, but his exuberance sometimes got the better of him. I scratched him behind the ears in a proper doggy greeting before turning my attention to Linc, who picked up the bicycle and leaned it against the fence.

"No problem, Linc," I said. "You're here now. Shall we get started?"

Linc patted the pockets of his jacket, his jeans, and his sweatshirt and looked up, chagrined. "I'm afraid I've forgotten my key again."

Tess, Boots, and I each reached into our own pockets and plucked out keys labeled with varying shades of fluorescent tags. I laughed awkwardly and headed toward the back porch, knowing that the lock on the kitchen door was less fussy than some of the other old locks on the house.

"Let's add installing new locks to the list of jobs," I told Tess.

Boots followed us. We stepped carefully around some of the boxes of discarded clothing and housewares that awaited pickup by a local charity resale shop. I unlocked the door and we trooped in.

Linc shifted from one foot to another, took off his glasses, and cleaned them with his shirttail. He looked around the room, blinking as if surprised to find he was no longer in his Stanford University lab. I flicked the light switch, but the room remained dim. Last week I'd brought over a supply of bulbs to replace several that I'd found burned out. I must have missed this one.

"Did you lose power in the storm?" I asked Linc.

He answered with a shrug. "I'm not sure. Maybe? I was at my lab working on my project."

Boots pulled open the refrigerator door and plucked a bag of lettuce from the darkness within. It had turned soggy in the bag.

"I'll take this for compost and bring you back some fresh spinach this afternoon," she said. "The kale's coming along nicely too."

"Can I get you all a cup of tea?" Linc asked. It was a delaying tactic I recognized from experience. Sorting and organizing were nearly painful for this man, who was said to have several ideas that could reverse the effects of climate change.

"Let's get started upstairs," I said. "I want to show Tess how much progress you've made."

Boots rummaged in the refrigerator. "I'll see what else needs to be tossed, Linc. Go on. I'll let myself out."

"I can't withstand pressure from all three of you." Linc shrugged and turned toward the staircase that divided the kitchen and living room. I started up the steps behind him, then stopped and called over my shoulder. "Tess, I'm going to show you Linc's workroom first. He's been working in there while I've been tackling the other rooms." I mouthed the words *praise him* to her. Linc hadn't, actually, made all that much progress, but he had agreed on broad-based guidelines for culling the equipment and organizing some of his papers.

Newton nudged past us to lead the way up the stairs. When I reached the hall landing, it was dark. *Right*, I thought. *The storm. No electricity.*

Newton growled, low in his throat, then whimpered. Linc moved down the hall toward his office and workroom. In the doorway, he gasped and froze. His mouth dropped open. His eyes grew wide. He stepped back, but leaned forward with his arm outstretched.

"Whatever it is, we can fix it," I said, rushing toward him, terrified I'd tossed out something of great value. "Everything we moved out of here is still in the garage."

Peering over Linc's shaking shoulders, I bit my lip, swallowed hard, and grasped his arm as he tried to move forward into the room. We couldn't fix it. Not this.

"No, don't," I said, pulling him back. "Tess, get the police. An ambulance."

Tess moved forward in the narrow hall, apparently trying to get a look at whatever had shocked Linc and me. I shook my head and whispered, "It's Sarah. Just dial. Quickly."

I hoped my voice would carry to the kitchen. "Boots, do you know where there's a fuse box or electrical panel? Can you make triple sure the power is out all through the house?"

"What's going on?" shouted Boots.

I couldn't think of an appropriate answer, but I gave it a shot. "We've got a problem up here, Boots. Can you make sure the power is off, now? Please? Right now?"

"Kay," said Boots, though I could hear her grumbling that she wasn't our servant to command. Her voice was followed by the creak of old door hinges and the sound of her rubber boots galumphing down the basement stairs.

I forced myself to look at Linc's workroom again. Nothing had changed. Sarah Palmer, Linc's fiancée, lay sprawled on the floor in a puddle of water. Sarah, one of my dearest friends, whose caramel-colored skin normally shone with warmth and health, lay facedown with her hand outstretched, clutching a frayed electrical cord.

Worst of all, the body that had once been Sarah's looked very, very dead.

Address to Die For

For professional organizer Maggie McDonald, moving her family into a new home should be the perfect organizational challenge. But murder was definitely not on the to-do list . . .

Maggie McDonald has a penchant for order that isn't confined to her clients' closets, kitchens, and sock drawers. As she lays out her plan to transfer her family to the hundred-year-old house her husband, Max, has inherited in the hills above Silicon Valley, she has every expectation for their new life to fall neatly into place. But as the family bounces up the driveway of their new home, she's shocked to discover the house's dilapidated condition. When her husband finds the caretaker face-down in their new basement, it's the detectives who end up moving in. What a mess! While the investigation unravels and the family camps out in a barn, a killer remains at large—exactly the sort of loose end Maggie can't help but clean up . . .

Dead Storage

As a professional organizer, Maggie McDonald brings order to messy situations. But when a good friend becomes a murder suspect, surviving the chaos is one tall task . . .

Despite a looming deadline, Maggie thinks she has what it takes to help friends Jason and Stephen unclutter their large Victorian in time for its scheduled renovation. But before she can fill a single bin with unused junk, Jason leaves for Texas on an emergency business trip, Stephen's injured mastiff limps home—and Stephen himself lands in jail for murder. Someone killed the owner of a local Chinese restaurant and stuffed him in the freezer. Stephen, caught at the crime scene covered in blood, is the number one suspect. Now Maggie must devise a strategy to sort through secrets and set him free—before she's tossed into permanent storage next . . .

CPSIA information can be obtained
at www.ICGtesting.com
Printed in the USA
LVHW09s2140150918
590261LV00001B/113/P